was born in 1907 in Dublin, where her father was minister in one of the city's Presbyterian churches. In 1913, he took up a new post at Birkenhead; the family moved and Janet was sent to the town High School. She went on to St. Andrews University, from which she graduated with an M.A. in Classics. As a student she was closely involved in the University's dramatic life—she acted as well as writing one-act plays. Her father's ill-health and consequent retirement forced the family to return to Ireland. Here, Janet completed a secretarial course with the intention of becoming a journalist. She worked for two years on *The Belfast Telegraph*, but in 1933 she married and her career was halted for eleven years. She and her husband, Robert P. Alexander, a civil engineer, moved to Lisburn in Northern Ireland, where they brought up their four children.

In 1946, Janet McNeill won a prize for a radio play in a competition organised by the Northern Ireland BBC, and with this encouragement, she resumed serious writing. Over the next twenty-five years she wrote extensively and for a varied audience. In 1955, *My Friend Specs McCann,* was published, the first of twenty-four extremely popular books for children. Her first adult novel *A Child In The House* appeared in the same year, followed by *Tea at Four O'Clock* (1956). Janet McNeill has written ten other adult novels, including *A Furnished Room* (1958), *Search Party* (1959), *The Maiden Dinosaur* (1964, reissued 1984), and *The Small Widow* (1967). She has also published articles and three collections of short stories for children: *A Light Dozen: Eleven More Stories* (1957), *Special Occasions: Eleven More Stories* (1960), and *Dragons Come Home and Other Stories* (1969). Theatre has remained an interest throughout her writing career, and in 1968 a collection of plays, *Switch On Switch Off and Other Plays* was published, together with two short opera libretti for children.

In 1964, Janet McNeill and her husband moved to England to be nearer their scattered family. Now a widow, she lives in Bristol.

JANET McNEILL

TEA AT
FOUR O'CLOCK

WITH A NEW INTRODUCTION BY
JANET MADDEN-SIMPSON

PENGUIN BOOKS — VIRAGO PRESS

PENGUIN BOOKS
Published by the Penguin Group
Viking Penguin, a division of Penguin Books USA Inc.,
375 Hudson Street, New York, New York 10014, U.S.A.
Penguin Books Ltd, 27 Wrights Lane,
London W8 5TZ, England
Penguin Books Australia Ltd, Ringwood,
Victoria, Australia
Penguin Books Canada Ltd, 2801 John Street,
Markham, Ontario, Canada L3R 1B4
Penguin Books (N.Z.) Ltd, 182–190 Wairau Road,
Auckland 10, New Zealand

Penguin Books Ltd, Registered Offices:
Harmondsworth, Middlesex, England

First published in Great Britain by
Hodder & Stoughton Ltd. 1956
Published in Great Britain by
Virago Press Limited 1988
Published in Penguin Books 1991

1 3 5 7 9 10 8 6 4 2

LIBRARY OF CONGRESS CATALOGING IN PUBLICATION DATA
McNeill, Janet.
Tea at four o'clock/Janet McNeill; with a new introduction by
Janet Madden-Simpson.
p. cm.
Originally published: London: Hodder and Stoughton, 1956.
ISBN 0 14 016.221 6
I. Title.
PR6063.A26T4   1991
823'.914—dc20   90–45418

Printed in the United States of America

Introduction

Introduction

If there can be a novel which is typical of its author's canon, then Janet McNeill's *Tea At Four O'Clock* (1956) stands as a paradigmatic work: it affords the reader immediate entry to the mixture of tough-mindedness and subtlety which characterises the emotional and psychological territory which she, of all Anglo-Irish novelists, has marked out as her own. A novelist who has written both juvenile and adult fiction, McNeill as adult novelist is just that—a writer who concerns herself with the middle-aged, the disillusioned, those who are haunted by pasts with which they have not come to terms.

McNeill is also a Belfast novelist, and it is tempting to speculate on the importance both of her adoption of Northern Ireland as her home (although born in Dublin in 1907, she spent much of her adult life in the Lisburn area) and her professional life as a writer and journalist there. The middle-class Protestant sector of that troubled and divided city, moreover, provides McNeill with the ideal material for her novelistic scalpel. Because her intent is not to merely explore, but also to trace connections which will illuminate the world of which she writes, McNeill focuses on a diminished population. This Belfast is no longer the terrain of the confident and prosperous merchant and manufacturing class. Instead, as Seamus Deane points out, McNeill's vision is directed towards the recording of the "plight of a lost Protestant gentility which looks back".

"Looking back", in fact, is a condition of many of McNeill's characters. In *Tea At Four O'Clock*, as in her other Belfast novel, *The Maiden Dinosaur* (1964), the backward gaze neither shelters nor sustains: McNeill views the past not as a distant country but as a factor which elementally and inextricably—and terrifyingly—shapes the present. And McNeill is utterly cognisant of the psychic minefield which the past represents. As an Anglo-Irish writer who chooses to probe the Belfast psyche, she could not be otherwise. But the politics which

McNeill recognises are not those of the state. Her concentration is focused on the internal dynamics of the family, replete as that microcosm is with issues of dominance and power.

The genteel title of *Tea At Four O'Clock* provides a sly clue to McNeill's methodology as well as to her subject matter, for the reassuring familiarity, almost triteness, conceals the sinister element of crushing repetition beneath the ritual of ceremony. The title's hint of the archaic and symbolic, however, does alert the reader to McNeill's interest in the subcutaneous, in the inevitable unpleasant results of the dissection of the ordinary and the obvious. It is only when the reader becomes absorbed in the work that McNeill, whose elegant prose can mislead as easily as it points up and reflects the interiority of her world, reveals her true purpose. For characters who inhabit McNeill territory, such seemingly innocuous ritualism as afternoon tea conveys not security but suffocation: through such conventions of polite formalism is the individual first subordinated, then quashed.

Perhaps the most startling aspect of *Tea At Four O'Clock* comes in the intensity of McNeill's questioning of order and structure, for she reveals herself to be something very like an anarchist, at least where family is concerned. Pointing out the predicament—or even the pathos—of her heroine/victim does not satisfy McNeill, who raises some unpleasant questions about Laura Percival's psychological inertia, and her own complicity in her bondage. She therefore aims to do more than dramatically reveal the damage which Laura has suffered as the oppressed and repressed younger daughter: the essence of McNeill's enquiry deals with the very nature of power and status, and how, in the metaphoric form of the family, attempts at control damage both those who exert and those who experience them.

In its investigation of the theme of children's—and, particularly, daughters'—lives which have been blighted by parental pressure, *Tea At Four O'Clock* closely parallels the Katherine Mansfield story, "The Late Colonel's Daughters". McNeill's novel, however, moves beyond Mansfield's almost stereotypical depiction of patriarchal oppression, for although McNeill, too, points to an overbearing paterfamilias as the chief culprit in the miserable lives which all his offspring experience, she proves herself to possess a far more radical vision than the reader expects. In McNeill's severe judgement, not simply the biological father, but the entire structure of patriarchal society is implicated in the withering of young lives and the ineffectual gestures of the unhappy middle-aged.

One of McNeill's most dynamic methods of conducting her argument about the destructive nature of this structure comes in her use of the house as dramatic symbol. Emblematic of selfhood, the visible representation of status and taste, the house in *Tea At Four O'Clock* has been built as a monument to the Percival progenitor. Its continuing function as a symbol of the values of the solid, bourgeois linen industry, rather than as a home, is crucial to the shaping of the Percival children. And, as McNeill shows throughout the story, the house is itself a collaborator with the patriarchal order. Indeed, it haunts because it has become a living entity, an extension of the patriarchal impulse which has built it and the patriarchal allegiance which has maintained it. Like the Big Houses of which Elizabeth Bowen writes, Marathon makes a statement, for its naming is itself an indication of its builder's cast of mind. The analogous naming of the house—the nexus of Byron's Greece to the Percival claim to Castlereagh and Belfast Lough—eventually proves to be ironic in two important and interrelated ways. In looking at the sea and being watched by the mountains, the house acts out the watcher/watching relationship which, from the house's inception, characterises the Percivals in relation to each other. The motif is continuously re-enacted. When George watches the bay windows of the drawing room to see if he is observed by his father, at the same time that his father, positioned at this vantage point, watches him, McNeill sums up not only the antagonistic nature of their relationship, but expresses the diligent scrutiny which the imposition of any system requires. Later, when Mildred, the agent of patriarchal values and order, takes her father's place, she uses these same windows to watch Laura. And when, after Mildred's death, Laura comes up the drive and encounters the predacious Miss Parks watching from that same observation post, she realises, at last, that, like her father and her sister, Miss Parks is another representative of the domineering and polarised mentality which has dominated her all her life.

Although McNeill's primary interest in the novel is Laura,

she is almost equally fascinated with George, the only son and therefore the putative heir of Marathon, the family business, and all the values and responsibilities which those twin foundations of Percival life represent. For George, the pressure occasioned by the ever-present watching is particularly acute, and especially damaging. In revealing himself as "a playboy come to make sport with a hard-won inheritance", George proves that he is unable and unwilling to measure up to patriarchal expectations while still desiring to benefit from them. As he recognises, his betrayal is not only of the order, but also of himself. The irony of his defection is that he never escapes: even in middle age, free at last from both his father's and Mildred's diapproval, George still has

> the odd feeling that even behind those blinds he was still observed. The blinds were like the heavy lids lying over his father's eyes, so that the glance beneath them appeared not to be direct, but a kind of spying. Marathon was still watching him.

Marathon's uncanny quality for observation is almost precisely the "faded, dark-windowed and somehow hypnotic stare" which Elizabeth Bowen describes in "The Big House", her 1942 essay which deals with the identification of the inhabitants of such houses with their buildings. This nearly Frankensteinian vision of creation underlies *Tea At Four O'Clock* and is repeatedly expressed through the imposing presence of Marathon. All three Percival children ultimately define themselves in relation to the house. Mildred, the dutiful daughter gives her life to its upkeep and its ceremony, meanwhile enacting its tyranny on her siblings. George, the prodigal son, lives a bitter exile, yearns to possess the house, and understands that it is only in this house that he will be able to "establish" himself, to exorcise his past, to "be rid of the last tatters of his unhappy immaturity". Laura, who submits to the repression of Marathon, comes finally to need it. For Laura, escape is almost, but, finally, not possible; when she receives the telegram which appraises her of her father's illness and urges her to "come home", her response is not simply reflexive. Laura is aware of the implications of her decision, and her return signals her choice to be entombed within Marathon's walls.

The dark vision of *Tea At Four O'Clock* is not unrelieved—

McNeill proves herself capable of deliciously sharp flashes of
humour, as when, after the disposal of Mildred's clothing,
Laura is aware that she must "arm herself against meeting a
distressed gentlewoman coming along the street disguised as
Mildred". But, as both her subject and her approach are based
on serious psychological investigations, McNeill's tone tends
to the sombre and the pessimistic. It is never more so than in
relation to Laura, for, of all the Percivals, Laura is the most
poignant; she, at least, has had the possibility of shaking off
Marathon's malign influence in order to make a life for herself.
The "secret" of what McNeill calls Laura's "long captivity"
has its origins in both heredity and environment. When the
mother of the family dies in supplying the house of Percival
with its heir, their father's delight in having a son is equal to
his guilt at his wife's death in the realisation of this ambition.
Unable to show affection to his children but determined to act
out the role of head of the family with them, his grim regime
involves reading about the needs of children and then strictly
ordering their lives according to his interpretation of what is
best for them. The failure of his method is due in no small
measure to his rigidity of purpose, motivated as he is not by
love, but by patriarchial notions of duty and curatorship.

To a father obsessed with such matters, a man whose
bifurcated vision focuses on his house and business on the one
hand, and on his continuously disappointing son on the other,
Laura, the quintessential middle child, nervous and insecure,
is an "irritating conundrum". Percival family life, "under
cover of conventional behaviour", consists primarily of non-
communication; Laura, so little valued that she is effaced
almost completely, nevertheless manages to find an avenue of
self-expression. Her technique for survival, George recalls, is
doing "what they wanted her to do, and in some strange way of
her own [she] had thereby preserved her dignity and her
individuality". In developing "as much as any flower could
blossom in the stifling air of Marathon", Laura exhibits the
marks of creative individualism, and McNeill's analogy is both
appropriate and carefully established. In the midst of the
"self-isolation" which characterises life at Marathon, in an
ambience which is both secretive and mistrustful, Laura's art
literally and symbolically expresses the human urges which
will not be denied. "Moved" and "excited" by the "the shapes

of flowers and leaves, of any green thing", Laura's art comes
from the most elemental biological need, inimical as it is to life
at Marathon. Her fascination—it might almost be called an
obsession—with emblems of fertility indicates her capacity for
life and love. Ironically, her father dimly realises that self-
expression lies beneath the lady-like pursuit; his decision to
send her to study art at the technical college is a further irony,
freeing her as it does from the scrutiny of Marathon and
enabling her for the first time to experience the world outside.

Because Laura's experiences at the college are directly
related to her attraction to symbols of life and nurturance, her
romance with Tom Richardson, like its outcome, is inevitable.
Like any fairy-tale heroine, Laura is awaiting an awakening,
and, good novelist that she is, Janet McNeill provides the
necessary combination to ensure that the awakening will take
place. What happens after that, however, as McNeill makes
clear, is the business of life, and, psychologically plausible as
always, McNeill keeps her reader, like her heroine, to the side
of reality. Plagued by what she herself regards as "personal
treachery", Laura's real crime is the inability to believe in
either herself or Tom; unable to imagine an alternative, she is
unable to actualise one. Her return home, her breakdown at
Marathon, her eschewal of painting and drawing, all form a
single response to life: in turning away from her chance to be
free, she truly does choose bondage.

Guilt, as McNeill demonstrates, underlies Laura's motiva-
tions. A lesson learned well and learned early, guilt is the basis
for her relations with her father, her sister, her lover, herself.
Guilt, McNeill suggests, is the legacy of the patriarchal order.
Like the charge laid on the seven-year-old Mildred to look
after the family, the weight of responsibility is a force which
twists in unforeseen ways. The guilty secret which Laura
harbours, and which McNeill unravels throughout the course
of the novel is, finally, traceable to the betrayal of the self.
From all the perspectives which McNeill provides—Hannah,
George, Mr McAllister, Tom's son, Laura's own—the message
is the same. The sins of the fathers at some point become those
of the children: those who refuse to see, and who are not brave
enough to forge new lives deserve the tyranny which they
thereby validate.

Replete as *Tea At Four O'Clock* is with images of death, its images of the daily routine are far more chilling. Like the ceremony which gives the novel its name, punctuations in the meaningless round of days are meaningful in themselves in such lives as Laura's and Mildred's. The petty becomes momentous; the ordinary is elevated to the status of the sublime; the habitual comes to serve as the portentous. For all its initial consequence, life at Marathon has dwindled into a depressingly pathetic round of pointless gestures. Its sterility is Laura's legacy as surely as it is her condition. The paralysis of her life is reflected on all sides: in her father's stroke, her sister's cancerous illness, her brother's moral debility. Taken together, the decline of the Percival family serves as an index to the fortunes of the world which they represent. Like the encroaching suburbs which render Marathon an anachronism, the people outside the house are more vital than those within it. If the outlook for the houses and their people is bleak, so too, McNeill argues, is the present condition. And it is difficult to argue with her logic, for what reader would choose Laura's lot? The passing of time—or, more precisely, the question of how to pass the time—has vexed her since girlhood; revelation is unlikely to come now.

In her use of such devices as flashback and repetition of theme, Janet McNeill does more than convince through reiteration. Her deft meshing of past and present provides the reader with an irrefutable illustration of thwarted life and certain failure. The connections between Laura's art and her life, the patriarchy and its consequences, the Protestant place in Irish life and its inexorable waning, are all subjects which McNeill takes up with a delicacy akin to Laura's brushwork. In conveying a story which is a microcosmic end of a way of life, McNeill's triumph as novelist is that she allows us to simultaneously grieve for Laura and breathe a sigh of relief at escaping her: adult novelist that she is, McNeill does not allow us the luxury of false pity. But she does allow us the opportunity to observe, and to make our own judgments from the rivetingly human material from which she shapes her moral tale.

Janet Madden-Simpson, Torrance, California, 1987

TEA AT
FOUR O'CLOCK

Chapter One

THE double hall door of Marathon had lain open since noon while those attending Mildred Percival's funeral were admitted, and the April day had blown in with them scattered petals from the apple trees. A few of these now rested on the coffin which took the central position in the square tiled hall, and Laura deplored them almost as much as she knew Mildred would have done and had been greatly tempted, during the short service of prayer and Bible reading, to step forward and brush them onto the floor. But the service was nearly over now. The words for which Laura had been waiting for six years were spoken, as the minister prayed for the spirit of consolation to visit " the sister who with exemplary devotion did not spare herself in the long months of nursing." Remembering these words, writing them indelibly on her memory, distracted Laura's attention from the vagrant apple blossom. Her mouth moved a little as she repeated the words to herself, shutting out the concluding sentences of the minister's prayer. " The sister who with exemplary devotion did not spare herself in the long months of nursing." He had said it. The words had been spoken. They could not now be discounted or taken back.

The prayer was over. The minister was offering her his hand. Other gentlemen followed him, and her passive palm was passed from one sympathetic clasp to another. Were they sympathising with her loss, or congratulating her on the medal which the Rev. Mr. McClintock had just pinned on her breast ? She was a little confused, but afforded each comer a grave smile, all except the two cousins from Armagh whom she never saw except at a funeral, and whose facial resemblance to herself always seemed a faint impertinence. The gentlemen now were collecting their hats—tall hats for Mr. McClintock and Mr. McAlister, the solicitor, soft black hats for the two gentlemen who were now the directors of the family business in Belfast, and bowlers for the cousins from Armagh. It seemed as if some action were called for

5

on her part. Miss Parks stepped discreetly forward and opened the drawing-room door, and Laura passed into the darkened room, followed by Miss Parks, with Hannah, trying hard to mute her creaking stays, in the rear.

Laura sat down beside the empty hearth, with Miss Parks opposite her. Hannah edged past the sofa that stood in the bay window, and took up her post beside the drawn blinds. Because of the dimness of the room it seemed that the hearing of the three women was sharpened to an unnatural pitch to recompense for their partial blindness. They were each acutely aware of what was going on in the hall outside. The four bearers had stepped to their appointed positions—the efficient undertaker would see to it that each man knew his post—then it was as if the tightened muscles and the effort of lifting became actual sound. Then a muffled command —the undertaker again—and finally the slow tread of footsteps across the hall. One bearer out of step—it would be one of the cousins from Armagh—quickly stepped twice to conform with his fellows. The hall mat was crossed, the threshold negotiated, the crunch of gravel told that the party had reached the drive. With a couple of deft clicks the undertakers' men had collected the trestles on which the coffin had been resting and were bringing up the rear. The feet of the funeral party passed out of hearing.

Hannah poked her finger between the blind and the window, and a shaft of April sunlight spread across the room.

"They're down to the foot of the drive now," she said.

Laura drew a long breath, and expelled it slowly. The fingers on her lap loosened. "Come away from the window, Hannah," she said.

Hannah stood her ground. "I can see down the side of the blind. Now they're turning out through the gate. Are you not coming to see the last of her, Miss Laura?"

"No." Laura's fingers tightened again. She knew Miss Parks was longing to join Hannah at the window, but that she would not go unless Laura went.

Hannah sighed massively and her aproned bosom slid up and down the window blind. "It's a thin enough crowd," she regretted.

Miss Parks waited for Laura to speak, but as Laura remained silent she took the initiative herself. "It's no occasion for a crowd, Hannah."

"Hannah, come away. People will see you," Laura said, but without urgency; only because it was what Mildred would have expected her to say. Hannah knew this as well as she did.

"Only the two gentlemen from the business and Mr. McAlister and them two Mr. Percivals from Armagh. It seems odd, doesn't it, Miss Laura, not one of her own to be there?"

Laura was ready for this one. "Not really, Hannah. After all, who is there that could be there, when the funeral was private?" Then quickly, in case Hannah would supply the answer to that question, she went on, "And you know Miss Mildred didn't approve of women going to the cemetery."

"So wise of her," Miss Parks put in; "typical of dear Mildred."

Hannah let loose a respectful snort. "It's one way of thinking, anyway. And if she wouldn't have him in the house she wouldn't want him at her grave."

"Hannah, please!" Laura spoke sharply.

"And twenty years is a long time," Hannah said, greatly daring.

Long, but not endless, Laura said to herself. Even twenty years must end. Either time finishes with it, or one finishes with time, which comes to much the same in the end. But there *is* an end. That is what is important. There must be an end.

"The cars are moving off now," Hannah reported; "it'll be a better-looking funeral when they're in their cars. And it's a good day for her, anyway. I thought this morning we would have had rain."

Laura did not reply. She was listening to the sound of the funeral cortège passing the gateway of the house. The hearse, power cut down to a minimum of noise through professional tact, the minister's car, antique, fussy, busy about the Lord's business, the cars of the two gentlemen from the office, a little racy for the occasion, but doing their best to behave soberly, and then the cousin from Armagh, missing his gear change at the rear. Through the long slow minutes the sounds rose, swelled, were gone. Nothing of them now remained. Mildred had made her last exit through the gates of Marathon. There would be nothing heard of her again—no voice, no footstep, nor the insistent invalid bell. People would speak of her, of course, as they spoke of her father and mother; letters might still come addressed to her name; the house was full of her clothes and all the evidences of the fifty years she had lived there. Miss Parks, Laura knew, would be a tower of strength. Her distressed gentlewomen's guild would gladly take over what lay in Mildred's wardrobe and chest of drawers. Laura must arm herself against meeting a distressed gentlewoman coming along the street disguised as Mildred. But Mildred herself had gone.

Into the silence which succeeded the sound of the last of the cars the everyday noises crowded again, as if they had held their peace long enough out of respect for the dead, but could hold it no longer. A couple of aeroplanes rose briskly from Sydenham Airport behind the house; children from the tiny gardens of the housing estate which had crept to the high garden walls of Marathon called and cried, as they threw balls to each other; from the Queen's Island across the river came the noisy fever of the shipyards. Time was moving again. The twenty years were indeed over, but there might still be twenty more. Tiredness came on Laura like a blow.

"Aye, it was well she got a good day," Hannah repeated, and edged her way past the empty sofa that lay there in the bay, the rug still folded over the foot of it. "It's a shame to shut that sun out. We'll get the blinds up in the evening."

Miss Parks waited for a moment for Laura to speak, but Laura said nothing. She is missing her cues, Miss Parks thought, not without a little satisfaction, it is the shock. Then she said, on Laura's behalf, "Not till tomorrow, Hannah. Miss Mildred always said the blinds should not be drawn up in a house of mourning until the day after the funeral."

Hannah looked at Miss Parks as boldly as she dared. "What difference can it make to Miss Mildred now?" she asked; "and wouldn't it be more heartsome for Miss Laura here to see the light of day?"

Laura roused herself sufficiently to say, "We'll get the sun tomorrow, Hannah. Don't touch the blinds."

Hannah bore her no ill-will. She had been long enough in service to know that Laura would have to support Miss Parks. But she peered at Laura in the half-light. "Miss Laura," she declared, purposely excluding Miss Parks from the conversation, "you're tired out. Will I bring you in a cup of tea? It'll be a while till they're back. Dear knows what we're thinking of, standing here and you that tired."

It will be a while before they are back, Laura thought, and they won't all be coming back. Tea, hot, sweet and strong, seemed an immediate necessity. She knew that by the suggestion Hannah was also implying Miss Parks' neglect in not thinking of it first, but she could not resist the thought.

"Will you take a cup, Miss Laura?"

Laura carefully concealed her sudden craving. "That would be rather nice, Hannah," she said. Then, "Would you like a cup of tea, Miss Parks?"

"Tea?" Miss Parks appeared outraged. But, making a charitable allowance for physical weakness she said, "Well just as you like, dear. It just seems—a little unusual."

"It's what you need, Miss Laura," Hannah persisted, "a good strong cup. It'll not take me two minutes, the kettle's on the boil."

"Not for me, thank you, Hannah," said Miss Parks decisively. She hunted a little distractedly in her black dress and found her handkerchief. She blew her nose. "Don't bring me any tea; I couldn't drink it. One forms habits, you know. She never took tea till four o'clock."

Instinctively the three women looked towards the empty sofa, with the folded rug across the foot.

"I don't think I'll have any tea either, Hannah," Laura said. "I should like a cup afterwards, but not just yet."

"Don't let me stop you, please," Miss Parks implored, through the tears that now poured uncontrolled down her cheeks, "it's just that—I couldn't think of drinking tea, not at a—a moment like this." Then she finished firmly with crying, dried her face and returned the handkerchief again to her pocket. "I think, Laura," she said, "I think I shall go and lie down for a while on my bed."

"Yes, Miss Parks, of course."

Miss Parks moved towards the door. "But if you want me you'll be sure to call me, won't you?"

"Oh yes, I will."

"You promise me now that you won't hesitate? I shouldn't like Mildred to think that I'd failed you in any way."

"Certainly I'll call you. And you've been wonderful."

"Thank you, my dear. I've been only too glad to do what I could." Miss Parks directed a wan smile at Laura, ignored Hannah altogether, and picked her way a little uncertainly across the large dim drawing-room. They heard her feet tapping across the tiles in the hall, then falling softly on the cushioned treads of the wide stairs, then at last her door was closed.

"How long will she be staying here, Miss Laura?" Hannah asked bluntly.

"I don't know." Tired as she was Laura clutched at the conventions. Hannah was taking liberties. It was wrong that she should enquire into the length of stay of a guest. The sooner Miss Parks goes the better Hannah will be pleased. I will not be sorry either, Laura thought. Hannah knew that too, it was no good pretending to Hannah. Hannah knew everything. For a moment Laura was tempted to throw herself on Hannah's ample bosom, where so many secrets of the household were safely locked away. But the very idea recalled Mildred, Mildred to whom the feminine form was endowed by nature, sometimes over-liberally, with an elevation between the neck and the waist known as the bosom, or, more delicately, the chest. This was overlooked, if possible, was ignored sartorially, and was never thought of any biological importance, either for the nourishment of the child or the consolation of his father. If one must use the word breast one used it in the singular, and with an emotional, not a physical connection. It had no plural form.

"She has no call for that carry-on," said Hannah, referring to Miss Parks' weeping, "and it's you should be resting. Would you not take a lay-down, Miss Laura? You could lie here on the sofa?"

She moved towards the sofa, fussing with the cushions at the head of it, the large down cushion with the embroidered cover, the little firm bolster that lay beneath it, and supported the small of the back. For one dreadful moment Laura thought she was going to lift the folded rug and shake it out, ready to swaddle her in it.

"Come on now, Miss Laura," Hannah coaxed.

"No," said Laura, and hoped her voice did not betray her revulsion, "no, Hannah. I don't think I will."

"But you must rest."

"If I want to lie down, Hannah, I'll go upstairs to my room." There was no need to say it so fiercely, and Hannah would think it odd of her. But it was suddenly very important that the rug should not be unfolded. Hannah gave in. "Very well, Miss Laura." Then, taking courage, she began, "Miss Laura——"

"Yes ? " said Laura. She knew what was coming. Hannah would ask it sooner or later. She might as well ask now.

"Did you write to him ? "

"No."

Hannah sighed. "I thought maybe you would have written. He would see it in the paper, well."

Of course he would see it in the paper. Both of them had realised that. He had seen it in the paper, and had given no sign. But he must have seen it.

"Ah well," Hannah sighed, "what's done is done." Her large lined face was sad. She waited for Laura to speak again, but Laura gave no sign, and Hannah reluctantly turned to another topic. "The Reverend McClintock spoke lovely, didn't he now ? "

"Yes," said Laura, "he spoke very well."

"The length of that prayer ! But then that's the way she would have liked it. And that was a good piece he said about you, Miss Laura. It's just a pity she couldn't have heard it. ' The sister who——' What was it again, Miss Laura ? "

"' Who with exemplary devotion did not spare herself in the long months of nursing.' " I should pretend that I cannot remember the words, thought Laura, but later on I can do that. Now they are too new. I must say them aloud to someone.

"Aye, them were the very words. And the dear knows,

Miss Laura, if ever a body deserved them, you did. You could take that cup of tea rightly now, couldn't you?"

The craving for tea returned, and made bold by Hannah's endorsement of the minister's testimonial, Laura agreed, and Hannah took herself off to the kitchen.

Laura hoped she would not be long. It was odd for her to sit in the drawing-room by herself. She could not remember ever having sat there alone before. She remembered it first as her mother's room, a room into which she was propelled by an anxious nurse, after a final wipe to her nose, and there passed from one guest to another, until the circle had been completed, and with a kiss from her mother's soft lips on her cheek she was again on the other side of the door, and the attendant nurse ready to remove the laces and frills which had decked her for the occasion. Then, quite suddenly, her mother was dead, and for a long time it seemed that the room was not used at all. Later there came memories of the first command appearances of Mildred and herself as young ladies, entertaining at their father's wish such company as he selected for his daughters to know. Mildred had been equal to it from the first. Laura, intimidated by her self-possession, was glad to take second place. Then there were the years she still could not think about—two years when she was happy—then her father's death, her own long illness and the creeping, reluctant recovery. And finally the long reign of Mildred as the invalid, throned first on the sofa in the window, later, when the pain had beaten her, on her bed in the room above. Once Mildred had taken to her bed the drawing-room was rarely used. Occasionally Laura had received callers there, to assure them that Mildred was not well enough for visitors ; sometimes the family doctor had stepped in there to instruct her in the use of a new drug before each in turn proved useless, sometimes Mr. McAlister, the family lawyer, had waited there until Mildred was ready to see him. But the room had lost its social uses, though the furnishings remained the same : even the cushions on the sofa, even the folded rug.

At last Hannah came back with the tea-tray. It made Laura self-conscious to have someone fuss about the room, serving her with tea. Automatically her own hand groped for the little table and settled it carefully into the thick pile of the carpet. She knew, from her own long experience, how easily the little table could capsize. But Hannah had seen to it that the tea was hot and strong. Laura drank it gratefully. Hannah lingered to watch her.

" Didn't I know that was what you were needing," she said ; " that'll put heart into you, Miss Laura. And she " —with a jerk of the head to indicate the prostrate Miss Parks —" she'll never be a bit the wiser."

Hannah had left the door open as she came in with the tray. Suddenly there were footsteps on the gravel : they halted on the doorstep and the bell-wire creaked as it was pulled. Away in the distant kitchen the bell jangled. The two women looked at each other.

" Who in all the world could that be ? " asked Hannah. The death in the house had cut them off from the normal going and coming of life, and it seemed an affront that any-one should be on their doorstep at three o'clock on this impossible afternoon. Laura emptied her cup guiltily and set it down on the tray. The bell rang again, this time impatiently. " Go and see who it is, Hannah," Laura said, " but if it's flowers, they're too late."

She sat listening as Hannah left the room. She knew who it was before she heard his voice, but still didn't believe it. She had known so often during the long years that it would be George, had been as sure as she was now, and it never was. Even when she heard his voice, and Hannah's voice answering, she couldn't believe it.

Hannah came wide-eyed into the room again. She closed the door carefully before she spoke. " Miss Laura——" she began, and excitement and emotion choked her.

" Was it flowers ? " asked Laura, keeping up the pretence while there was still any doubt.

" Miss Laura—it's him ! It's Master George ! "

Laura could say nothing. She stared at Hannah. Now that it was true it seemed quite incredible.

" As true as fate—Master George himself. And her only just down the street."

Panic seized Laura. " Tell him to go away. Tell him I won't see him. Tell him I'm ill—anything you like, Hannah, only send him away."

Hannah gaped at her. " Is that—what you want me to say ? "

Hannah was turning to the door. " No, wait a minute. I don't know. Oh, wait a minute, Hannah. How does he look ? "

" Older, miss. Shabby—not like we remember him." Then she smiled. " But the same way with him—he hasn't altered in his way of going. He put his arm round me out there on the doorstep, and ' Hannah,' says he, ' I'm home.' " She savoured her pleasure at George's embrace.

" I'll see him, Hannah," Laura said, trying to conquer the breathlessness that grew on her, " I'll see him. Will you please ask him to come in."

It was all she could do to keep on her chair. She wanted to rise and run out onto the doorstep and herself be caught up in George's clutch. Oh, Hannah, be quick, tell him to come. " Right away, Hannah, I'll see him right away."

" Indeed you will, Miss Laura," said Hannah in satisfaction, and took herself off to summon George Percival into the room.

Chapter Two

IT had been two days earlier that George had finished his evening meal and unfolded his evening paper over the wreck of it. He handed the fashion page across to his wife. Kathie, his schoolgirl daughter, had propped a bottle of nail varnish up against the butter dish and was busy painting her nails.

" Do they let you wear that stuff on your hands at school ? " George asked her.

Kathie made a face at him, and said " No " good-naturedly.

" Money down the sink," said George. He thought it his duty to discourage every echo of his own extravagant nature that he heard in Kathie.

" It's only Woolworth's," she said ; " of course there is much better stuff that I could buy, if I had the money." She got up to turn on the wireless, using the pads of her fingers, to keep the stuff from getting on the knobs and making them sticky. They weren't schoolgirl nails, and her figure in that gym tunic was another anachronism. It was a good thing, George reflected, that she had only one more year at school. She'd be earning her own money then, anyway. He finished with his paper and wished Amy had done with her page, because he had still the reverse side of it to read. But there was no good hurrying Amy where clothes were concerned. Though, bless her, she could spend hours studying Paris models, and then be perfectly happy in a smart little number bought from one of the Jew shops for a couple of quid. Amy read thoroughly, following the print with her finger, spelling out the longer words silently with her lips. George turned the paper over again, and for lack of something better to do scanned the Births, Marriages and Deaths.

" Good God ! " he said suddenly, " Mildred's dead ! "

Amy blinked at him for a moment, and then came out of a dream of swathed organza with a chinchilla wrap. Kathie caught at her bottle of nail varnish just in time. They gaped at him.

" Mildred," said George again, as if the repetition would make it sound more credible. " Mildred—she's dead."

Amy turned on Kathie. " Kathie, put off that wireless right away. I don't know what you're thinking of. Don't you hear what your father says ? Your Aunt Mildred's dead."

" Oh all right," said Kathie, rising to obey, but George said, " No, don't bother. It's a good tune, I like it. Let's have it a bit louder." So Kathie turned the tune up louder and hotter, and collecting her nail varnish retired to sit in the full blare of it while her father and mother shouted at each other across the litter of newspapers and teacups.

" George dear—what a shock !—well, I am sorry," Amy said. George thought, good old Amy. Trust Amy to have all the stock reactions of her class to death and the dead. She will sympathise with me in a moment, he thought, she will think of something nice to say about Mildred whom she never met. But she will have to think hard, for she knows quite well that I hated Mildred like hell. It would be interesting to find out what form her condolences would take, and it would give him time to get the thing sorted out in his own head.

"What does it say?" Amy asked.

He read it out. "'At her residence, Marathon, Holywood Road, Belfast, Mildred, elder daughter of the late James and Eleanor Percival. Funeral private.'"

"No 'Deeply Regretted'?" Amy was shocked.

"No."

"Well!" Amy knew better than to question the strange omission. "I wonder was she ill long. Of course you wouldn't know. It doesn't say 'after a long illness'?"

"No."

Amy was rather at a loss. "Well—she's gone anyway. But of course she would have the best of everything, and all attention."

She would, George knew that.

"Have another cup of tea, George, there's still some in the pot. It will help you. Poor George, I know just how you must feel."

No, you don't, George thought, but he didn't contradict her. That was one of the joys of being married to Amy. In her eyes, what appeared to be obvious was true. She credited him with the stock reactions to each situation. She gave him all the intimacy he asked of her in one direction, but never interfered with the privacy of his mind. It had always been like this. Amy was a chemist's assistant in a shop where he called in for a pick-me-up after a blind, and she had ministered to him faithfully and effectually. Soon the range of her ministrations was enlarged, and he married her. Because he had married her she was satisfied that he loved her. There had been no tortured attempts at self-analysis, no necessity to explain the pleasure they found in each other, or its depth or its degree. She was dumb, anyway, and that was the way he liked her. She thought he was perfect, and he let her go on thinking it. And because he knew he was the full stature of a man to Amy he probably came nearer to it in any case—felt nearer to it, which was all that mattered to George. When you had long ago stopped believing in yourself it was comfortable to have someone who unfailingly did the believing for you. Of course her voice was common, but it was kind. Kindness, though he would not himself have admitted it, mattered a great deal to George.

" You'll have to take a day off for the funeral," Amy was saying.

" Who's going to the funeral ? " George said. " Anyway, it says ' Funeral Private '." He passed the paper across for her to see.

" ' Private ' to all except the family, or by invitation, that's what it means," Amy said, " but that doesn't mean private to you." She had funeral etiquette at her finger-tips, her class were great sticklers for propriety.

" It doesn't even say when the funeral is," George argued.

" It'll be the day after tomorrow, in the afternoon, at two o'clock, that's when it'll be, and of course you must go."

" I don't see why," he grumbled. He had every intention of going, but he wished to be persuaded into it.

" Your other sister—Laura—she'll expect you," Amy pursued. She had always been a little diffident about speaking of Mildred and Laura by their christian names. She had never met them, and it seemed presumptuous. He liked that about her.

" You would only need the half-day off," said Amy, " but you must wear your good suit to the office in the morning."

" I'm not wearing my good suit," he said flatly. His ' good suit ' was one of which he was privately ashamed. Amy had bullied him into buying it ready-made from a cheap tailor. Its pseudo-gentility affronted him as much as it delighted her. He wore it to attend the marriages and funerals of her many relatives, but he had no intention of wearing it to Mildred's funeral. Mildred could have told the quality of the cloth from across the room without laying a finger on it. Not of course that she could stir to lay a finger on it, in any case. All the same he would not wear it.

" If I go—if I go—I will wear my ordinary clothes."

" A black tie, of course."

" I'll take a black tie in my pocket and change at the office." And with that Amy had to be content.

All the same when he caught the bus to take him out the Holywood Road to attend Mildred's funeral the black tie was still in his pocket. He and Mildred had made no attempt to meet for seventeen years, and it was hypocrisy for him to wear it. That was why he had told Kathie to turn the dance music on louder, that was why he had refused to appear shocked at the news. It was a matter of pride with him that the dislike he had for his home and his sister Mildred would not be lessened by the fact that she had died. Dead or alive, he felt the same way about her. It was, in any case, cheating on her part to die. But then Mildred had always cheated, and he would not take a leaf from her book. Her death shocked him. No matter how often death occurred it was still, in each individual case, a surprise. But he felt absolutely no sorrow at the news.

He had not been out along the Holywood Road for years. His own home was one of many hundreds at Ballydrum, along the Shore Road, at the other side of Belfast, half of a small rectangle, standing in a row of rectangles, each enclosed in so many inches of garden. When he'd married Amy first they'd lived in a couple of rooms over a shop. George had been content enough there. There was to his mind something picturesque in poverty, but little in the respectability of a home among these spawning maisonettes. To Amy it represented the height of her ambition, and she'd had a tough fight to get him there, give her her due. She'd done a lot for George. It was because of her that he'd stuck to the one job now for five years. She'd been clever, of course, Amy was clever, in her own dumb way. Though the little house pleased and satisfied her, she never forgot that to her husband it must seem a sad decline from the way of life he had been born into, and she let him know that she appreciated this. So George could enjoy his bourgeois comfort without offending his conscience. It made him feel good and generous to have elevated Amy to suburbia.

Sometimes in the summer the three of them took a day's trip to Bangor, and as the train passed by Amy always craned out of the window to see the roof of Marathon, and pointed it out to Kathie. " Look, Kathie, there's your father's old home. That's where your father was born. Your aunties live there." And her undisguised admiration of its solid grandeur and the child's wide-eyed interest—it ranked in her young imagination as an enchanted castle—never failed to warm George, and reconcile him to the humbler respectability Amy had so happily established him in.

Marathon had been built in the spacious days half-way through the last century. It had been George's great-grandfather who had built it, for one of his sons. This gentleman was a wealthy farmer from County Armagh, whose worldly prosperity had kept pace with his wife's intrepid production of sons, and who had seen each of the sons well established on the way to like prosperity. Three he kept on the land; two he despatched to America. The sixth son was a problem. This boy hadn't either the physique of a farmer or the pioneering spirit to make good on the other side of the Atlantic. But the booming linen trade in Belfast seemed a fool-proof investment, and the sixth son, Lawrence, was duly financed in a business there. Lawrence was by way of being a dreamer and a poet, and once released from the parental roof he had built for himself this large square handsome house on the road leading out of Belfast to Holywood, between the Castlereagh hills and the Belfast Lough, and called it Marathon. " The mountains look at Marathon, and Marathon looks at the sea," was the only explanation he offered to his visiting relatives. His Aunt Augusta, who knew her Byron, was able to complete the quotation, "And musing there an hour alone, I dreamed that Greece might still be free "—and she kept a careful eye on her nephew for any deplorable symptoms of Home Rule tendencies, and was relieved when she was able to detect none. Marathon lay overlooking green fields, which sloped gently down to the Lough shore. Lawrence Percival's brothers came to inspect the house—" Marathon looks to the sea," they said, and smiled. The tide was out, and there was no water visible beyond the thread of a channel in a waste of grey mud. They sniffed at the smell that came up off the mud, cast an eye at the Antrim hills beyond, lying half-obscured in rain, and took themselves back to Armagh, prophesying that Lawrence's Marathon would be too much for him, even with his father's lavish financial backing, and that he would have been safer on a less extended course. They might have been right, too, had not Lawrence's business interests taken him over to Courtrai in Belgium, where he had met and married a Flemish girl and brought her back to Marathon. This girl's ready appreciation of wealth and her brisk management of it had pulled Lawrence through a bad patch, and not content with this she had given him a son with all her business acumen, George Percival's father. So that by the time George was born the linen firm of Percival was well established, and Marathon was still the family home, though time had brought changes to the surrounding country. The 'expanse of foreshore had been reclaimed and was to become Sydenham airport. The green fields around the house were quickly built up with other large houses, and then the infiltration of the little houses through the old mansions had begun. So that now, though Marathon itself was surrounded by an ample garden and high stone wall, the other side of the wall formed the boundary for a dozen small gardens, and if the wall had not been higher clothes from a dozen clothes-lines would have flapped up at the big house. There was even a row of shops beside the bus stop.

It was twenty years since George had left his father's house, but he had been back once, three years later. It was during the war. He was in the Navy and home on leave. Amy was living in a room at the back of Shaftesbury Square ; she had had to give up her job because of the baby who was coming. The evening before he was due to go away he sat with Amy in the dark little room and then helped her to bed. Amy was tearful and frightened, her eyes huge in her face. He had never seen her like this before, bereft of that provocative challenge that was as good as a tonic to him. She lay in the bed looking at him, and he fidgeted about the room ; though this was his last night in Ireland there was nothing left for them to do or say. In spite of the child she was carrying Amy seemed small, lost in the big ugly bed. She was due to go into one of the big city Hospitals to have her baby. She'd been there for a pre-natal examination the day before, and had come away crying from weariness and fright, and fear of the shining antiseptic efficiency of the place. They hadn't had any air raids yet in Belfast, but it looked as if they were coming. There was talk of evacuation. People who could afford to were moving their wives and families out into the country on their own. There were Cottage Hospitals, smaller, homelier places, where she could have had her baby. But of course that took money.

He sat on the bed beside her, and they looked at each other, and still there was nothing to say. He held her hand, small and soft, in his own. Her relatives in the city had enough

to do with their money to be able to spare any, and George
had cut himself off from any friends who might have helped.
Suddenly he decided to go out to Marathon and visit Mildred
and Laura, and tell them about the coming child.   If he was
on the other side of the world there must be someone who
would give it a welcome when it was born, poor little devil.
His sisters knew he had married ; Amy, with her delight
in the respectably conventional, had put the notice in the
paper.

It was dark when he got off the bus on the Holywood
Road, inky-dark in the black-out.   He felt his way to a little
shop on the corner, to get some cigarettes.   There used to
be a pretty girl in the shop, he remembered.   Her father
was behind the counter.   He looked at George from under
heavy brows.

"You're not often out this length these days, Mr. Percival," he remarked, and sucked his teeth.

George said no, and wished he would hurry up with the
cigarettes.   He felt uncomfortable.   It hadn't occurred to
him he would be remembered.

"Time sees changes," the man went on, deliberately
loitering at the back of the shop where his hoard of cigarettes
was kept, "your father now—he didn't last long."

George said no once more.   He had known nothing of his
father's death except the bleak notice in the paper two years
earlier.   And he paid no attention to the notice.   He didn't
come up to the house.   He wrote a brief letter to Mildred,
but she didn't answer.   He had not expected that she would.
This fellow knew more of his home affairs than he did.

"And your sister now—it's a pity of her," the man said.
What sister, George wondered.   It must be Laura.   Mildred would never require pity from anyone.   He nodded,
non-committally.

"You're in the Navy, eh ? " the man enquired.   He
slapped down a packet of cigarettes on the counter.   "King
and Country ? "

George said yes, and gathered the cigarettes up.   He laid
down the money.

The man gave a short laugh.   "A good steady job," he
commented, handing over the change with a smile that was
half a sneer.   George was glad to get out of the shop.   He

wasn't forgotten as the scapegrace son of the house of Percival. These outskirts of the city still retained the characteristics of villages. Interest in the private affairs of the gentry had not died. This old man knew him, knew his father, knew what his father had hoped for him, and how those hopes had been disappointed, and his sympathies were with the father. "A good steady job," he had said. It had amused him to think of George Percival in a good steady job.

It was a bad start to George's visit. He felt his way through the gates of Marathon—the black-out was very efficient, Mildred would have seen to that—and came a little uncertainly up the drive to the dark house. He went over the verge in one place, and landed in a flower-bed. This shook him considerably. Surely he should have remembered the curve of the drive, and he was stone sober this time. He had to feel for the bell, too. At first no one answered. Then at last the door was cautiously opened. It was Mildred. She stood peering out, unable to open the door wider for fear of throwing light onto the wide steps.

"Who is it?" she asked.

"George," he said, wishing again that he had not come.

Mildred was quite unstartled. "Come in, George," she said, and he followed her into the hall. His wide trouser-legs swung about his ankles. He saw Mildred glancing back at them, and fancied that she smiled. Able Seaman Percival! Of course the cousins from Armagh would have commissions. It was the first time a serviceman of his rank had walked in through the hall door at Marathon.

Mildred led the way into the small room at the back of the hall that they called the morning-room. There was a little fire burning on the grate, her knitting lay beside a chair. A dog got up from the hearth and growled at him.

"You look very well," Mildred said. She implied that he had found his level, and that he flourished in it.

"I am well, thank you," he answered. "Where is Laura?"

"Laura has been ill. She only comes downstairs for a couple of hours in the afternoon. She is not strong. Of course you wouldn't know that."

"I'm sorry."

Like a cold tide he felt the old dumbness creep over him.

It was so long now since he had felt it. Never with Amy, never once. To Amy he was eloquence, or if he chose not to talk his silence was godlike. There was no need for talking when they were together. The nature of their attachment required no explanation. She took him at his face value, and the mask he wore was handsome. The heroic quality she attributed to him made him a hero to himself, which was warming and comfortable for a man who needed admiration as another man might need strong drink. But inside this house he had never come near to being a hero. Since his time in the Navy he had acquired a kind of swagger which afforded him a great deal of satisfaction. The other men knew that he came from a shelf above them, they admired his smoother tongue, his repertoire of sophisticated stories, his finicky ways. But now this too seeped out of him. His face was no more a mask that he could wear with confidence, but a naked reflection of the soul behind it. His clothes were not naval uniform, but a child's sailor suit. He was stripped of the assurance he had so carefully gathered round him.

"I'm sorry Laura has been ill," he said.

"Why have you come, George?" Mildred asked. In spite of the three years' absence she still claimed the privilege of the close relation to dispense with the ordinary preliminaries of polite conversation.

"I'm going off again tomorrow; I may be away some time."

"I see."

Mildred sat still, waiting. George, on the edge of his chair, watched her. Out in the hall the clock struck nine. The familiar sound brought hot tears to George's eyes, and he cursed himself for a fool. Sentiment—in this house! There was nothing he could remember about his childhood to bring this kind of tears. He hoped to God Mildred had not seen, and got down awkwardly on his knees to settle a log that was threatening to fall. The dog chewed at his heels. Mildred did not trouble to call the dog to order. She sat and waited. She is waiting, George thought, for me to ask her for money. Now that I have the excuse of going out on the dangerous seas, she thinks I am going to try again. And suddenly he couldn't do it. Not even for

Amy, lying in the big bed in the shabby digs, with his child stirring in her, and the antiseptic labour ward waiting for her to come when the pains started.

" We read of your marriage in the paper," Mildred said at last. She is handing me out my cues, thought George, she is inviting me to ask for the money she has no intention of giving me. He couldn't do it. The child would have a mother. He did not remember his own mother. He had had Mildred, the elder sister. Amy would do better for his child than that. And the child would be born in six weeks. They had only been married four months. Mildred would have more to smile at. He couldn't do it.

" I came to say good-bye," he said, getting up stiffly, reaching for his cap. " Will you please say good-bye to Laura for me, and tell her I am sorry she is ill."

Mildred followed him out into the dim hall and opened the door for him. He clattered over the steps. By common consent they had not shaken hands. She did not close the door immediately and he knew that she was standing watching him through the narrow crack. He spat loudly into the flower-beds and banged the gate, and felt suddenly childish and lost.

Amy was awake when he got back, awake and waiting for him. He told her the house was empty, that he had seen no one. Then he had wept and she comforted him. She thought he was grieving for the coming separation. This helped him to reassert himself, and to forget his chagrin at giving Mildred another chance to let him remember he was a fool.

That was the last time he had been at the house. It was broad daylight now, and seventeen years later. He knew it was close on two o'clock, but as he came near the house he felt the same constraint dropping on him. It was ridiculous, of course, Mildred would not open the door to him this time. But he loitered at the corner, watching the steady stream of traffic coming and going to and from the city, and smoking one more cigarette. There was still the same shop at the corner, but he didn't call in there this time. He pretended to be interested in all the new little houses that had been built since he knew the place. At last he stubbed out his cigarette on the pavement and turned towards the house, but as he did so, the hearse emerged from the gates, paused a moment to give a grave elegiac warning on the horn, and then joined the traffic. Passers-by paused a moment, a dustman set his bin on the pavement to take off his cap, George removed his hat. Other cars followed the hearse. In the first George recognised a minister's collar, and the gaunt profile of Mr. McAlister. The next two cars carried men whom he remembered during his own brief disastrous spell of work in the family business house. The bowler-hatted cousins from Armagh came last. That was all. Traffic on the thoroughfare resumed its normal course. The dustman heaved his load of less venerable dust into the cart; George put his hat on, and walked in through the big gates.

The blinds in the house, of course, were all pulled down. The hall door lay open. It seemed stupid to ring the bell at the door of his own home. There was no sound from within, no evidence of the funeral except the tyre-marks on the gravel. He pulled the bell and waited.

Hannah came. Her gasp and the look of pleasure in her eyes set him on his feet again. "Master George," she said, her hands clasped on her ample bosom. "Master George —you've come."

It was easy now. He put an arm round her. "Hannah," he said, "I'm home."

Hannah withdrew in a flutter of excitement. He heard the drawing-room door close quietly behind her. After a few moments she came to beckon him in. "Miss Laura's in here, Master George," she said, standing aside while he went into the drawing-room. And George went through the door into the darkened room, where a middle-aged woman was rising unsteadily from her chair to greet him—his sister, Laura.

Chapter Three

GEORGE'S memories of his home had been dominated so strongly, and for so long, first by his father and then by Mildred, that he had thought little of Laura during his years

of absence.   Any picture he had of her was of a quiet child
who in her obedience to her father's or Mildred's bidding had
seemed to accomplish much more than George ever had by
his flouting of it.   She had done what they wanted her to do,
and in some strange way of her own had thereby preserved
her dignity and her individuality.   He had gone all out for
rebellion, and had lost both.   And yet he always knew that
her sympathies were with him.   Her cowardice in declaring
them stood between them, so that he had never drawn any
strength from her.   There was a while when he thought she
might have come out on his side : this was before the final
break, while he was still living at home, and his father's failing
health made a certain amount of liberty possible in the house.

He remembered one year in particular.   His time was
divided between the business and classes at the Technical.
He'd gone around with Tom Richardson and that crowd from
the Art School.   Tom had even been out at the house a few
times.   He had envied Tom his ability to ignore the sourest
of Mildred's remarks.   Tom didn't seem to hear them, while
every syllable of them was written deep in his own memory.
All the small sly remarks, the quiet cut and thrust of her clever
tongue, they went off Tom like water off a duck's back,
whereas George had an anthology of such remarks, polished
by recurrent bitter consideration.   Was Tom clever to dis-
count Mildred so easily, he had often wondered, or was he
merely stupid, and did the shafts not pierce his thick hide ?
Mildred didn't like Tom, that was obvious, and she liked him
no less because her dislike made no difference in the world to
Tom.   Tom got on better with Laura.   He had admired the
delicate paintings she did of flowers, though whether he
admired them for their own sake or for Laura's, George was
never quite sure.   For Laura had blossomed that year, as
much as any flower could blossom in the stifling air of Marathon.   She had been attractive, George had thought, though
not in any conventional way—certainly not in *his* way.   She
seemed to George always a little Edwardian—not unlike the
photographs of his mother that hung in the drawing-room.
But that year, as her womanhood flowered, her timidity had
become a quiet elegance, she had claimed her right to her
own small personality, though she did not wish to advertise
or enlarge it.   Here again George envied her—he who was

unable to pass by any opportunity for self-display, and was always out to prove himself a finer fellow than he knew himself to be.

So he did not know, as he came into the drawing-room at Marathon, what he expected Laura to be like, or how he expected her to greet him, but he was certainly not prepared either for her physical appearance or her manner. He wished for a moment that he had not come, because he saw, as we all see in any close blood relation, a variant version of himself, and it vexed him to recognise that in spite of the deliberate build-up of his way of life, in spite of Amy's devotion, he was not altogether unique. It was evident that she was moved by his coming. He had not wished to be moved. God, how she had changed ! A small hesitant inelegant figure, as sexless as it was possible for a woman to be. She used to have such a pretty bearing. Poor Laura ! The years had not been kind to her. He pulled in his own stomach and pushed back his shoulders.

" Well, Laura," he said, unwilling to be the first to establish the relationship after so many years.

Laura just took his hand in both of hers and held it, and kept saying, " Oh, George. Oh, George." She said it again and again, and still held his fingers.

" I saw Mildred's death in the paper," he said. It sounded lame and stupid, but he felt a traitor tide of emotion rising in him and could find no other words.

" But you're too late, George. The funeral's just gone."

This gave him his cue. He was once more the large bold brother who didn't care, and to whom death made no difference in the world. It was an easier role than it used to be, now that Mildred was dead.

" I know the funeral's gone," he said. " I stood at the corner and watched it go."

She said, " You shouldn't have come," but she held on to his fingers more tightly than ever.

" If you tell me to go away I will," he said. He was sure of his ground now, he was in the right key.

" Oh no," she said, as he had known she would, " but George—why did you come ? "

He said, " I came to see you. I thought you might be glad to see me." That was as near the truth as he could get.

He was sorry he had said that, because Laura began to cry. The tears ran unheeded over her tired little face, flattened by the long years, and still she didn't let go of his hand to dry them.

"Oh I am glad, George," was all she said, "very very glad."

He wished she would dry her face. "Don't cry, Laura." This made her aware that she was crying, and she let go his hand and made busy with her handkerchief. Her own hand was unsteady, she dabbed ineffectually, he was irritated and tempted to take the handkerchief from her and make a job of it.

"I should have written or something," he said. "I only decided to come suddenly."

"I thought of writing to you," Laura said, "but I didn't. In any case I hadn't an address. Where are you living now, George?"

"At Ballydrum," he said, with a little grimace, admitting and condemning the locality at once. "We've been there five years."

"I wondered where you were. I—I used to look up your name in the telephone directory, but you weren't in it."

"A telephone!" he said, laughing. How he loathed the small economies, but the best way was to make a joke of them. "We can't afford such a luxury as that."

Laura looked worried and enquired after Amy and Kathie. "I suppose Kathie's getting quite a young lady."

"She is indeed, only another year at school. Time soon goes in."

"Not soon," said Laura, "but it does go in."

They were both silent, thinking what time had done to them since they had been in this room together.

"The room hasn't changed much," George said, looking round. "All the old pictures—and the sofa in the window. Father used to lie on that sofa—remember?"

Laura remembered. It could hardly be called lying. The body was erect from the waist, the only concession to his growing weakness was that the feet were off the ground. And the brain never rested. The heavily lidded eyes moved from door to window and from window to door, nothing escaped them.

"He didn't miss much," George chuckled. It made him feel grand and fine and easy to be laughing.

"Mildred lay there too," said Laura. She wasn't looking at the sofa, her eyes avoided it.

"How long was she ill, Laura?"

"About six years. Not really ill all that time. At—at the end she was only ill for about a month."

"Father—he died suddenly too, didn't he?"

"Yes, very suddenly."

"It was another stroke, wasn't it?"

He fancied that Laura answered him oddly, almost gratefully, "yes, it was another stroke—that was it, a stroke."

"I knew he wasn't well, of course. But the first I knew of his death was seeing it in the papers. I wrote to Mildred then, but she didn't answer it. Did she tell you I had written?"

Words came from Laura in a sudden nervous rush. "No, she didn't tell me. You see, George, I was away at the actual time—I mean at the time he died—of course I came straight home at once as soon as I heard—I was staying with Hetty Carmichael—you remember Hetty, don't you, George?"

George couldn't be sure that he did, but Laura seemed so anxious that he should remember her that he nodded, and Laura babbled on, "Of course she is Hetty Ferguson now. She lives in Wales and has three lovely children, George, two girls and a boy—oh, beautiful children they are. I don't know when I saw such lovely children."

Laura is overwrought, George was thinking. I wish I hadn't come. She is explaining all this to me as if it mattered vitally to her that I listened and understood. What do I care about Hetty Carmichael and whether she has three or thirty children? Poor Laura, she is talking as if she had wanted to talk to someone for years and years, and found no one to listen to her. It will do her good to talk, let her babble away about the infant prodigies of Hetty Ferguson, née Carmichael.

"The youngest of them, the little boy, was just a baby when I went to stay with her—oh, George, such a beautiful house he built for her—and then of course when I heard from Mildred—about father, I mean—when I heard I came straight back."

She stopped speaking as suddenly as she had begun. The sudden gush of unimportant details was spent.

" And you've been looking after Mildred ever since ? " he asked her, encouragingly.

" Not all the time," she said. " I was ill for a long time myself, after father died."

He said, " I heard about that," and told her about the visit he had paid to Marathon during the war. She flushed. " Oh, George, you were in the house and I never knew."

" It's odd I never saw you in Belfast," George said, but he thought to himself that if he had seen her in Donegall Place as she appeared today he might have passed without recognising her.

" I don't often go about," was all she said. And then she asked suddenly, " Have you been happy ? "

George didn't like this sudden poke into his private life. He would have expected it of Mildred, not of Laura.

" As happy as anybody else, I suppose," he said, and countered, " What about you ? "

Laura didn't like it either. " I—I've had Mildred," was all she said.

" And your painting of course," George said.

" I haven't done any painting."

She said it so lightly, as if it were a matter of small consequence.

" You haven't done any painting at all ? "

" There were always other things to be done. Anyhow my painting was never very important."

" Tom always said it was."

Ah, that got home. He heard her indrawn breath, saw her small teeth settle down hard on her lower lip.

" And talking about Tom," he said carefully, " funny thing, I had a letter just the other day."

" You mean you kept in touch with him ? "

Dear foolish Laura, George thought. How much better I would have done it. She is transparent, poor soul. She hasn't the artifice of a flea. And how undignified that after twenty years his name can make her heart flutter and bring that unbecoming flush to her tired cheek.

" Did you keep in touch with Tom, George ? "

" Not for long. He went to America—just about the time

father died, it was. A crazy business, if you ask me, Tom going out there by himself. He hadn't any friends to go to. He thought he'd get rich quick and then be able to come back and go ahead with his painting."

"But the letter, George?"

"Oh, the letter—it was from Tom's son."

Poor Laura. Of course she wouldn't have known. Anyway, she had to have it some time, and there it was now.

She said, "I didn't know Tom had married."

"I don't suppose you did. That was a sudden business too, as far as I could gather. He married an American girl, a week after he'd landed."

"I see."

Better leave it at that. It couldn't really matter so much to her now. "But this boy of his," George went on, "Terence he's called—he's by way of being a painter too. I'd a letter from him a couple of months ago to say he was coming over here on a visit. He'd found an old letter of mine among his father's papers, he said. It chased me round half a dozen addresses before I got it."

"Tom didn't write himself?"

George cursed himself for a fool. Why had he started to tell Laura about Tom? Now he'd begun it he'd have to go on. Somehow he'd thought she would at least have known that Tom was dead.

"Tom died, ten years ago." He stood looking out of the window, and then said gently, "Poor Tom, he was a decent soul and a good friend, wasn't he, Laura?"

She didn't answer. Then she said, "Have you seen the boy, Tom's son?"

Safer ground now. He hurried across on to it. "Not yet, but he's here, in Belfast. I saw a notice of his exhibition in that Art Gallery in Donegall Place. You should go in and have a look at them, Laura. You know something about painting. Come along with me some time." It would do her good, he thought, give her a thrill. It was all so long ago, it can't have meant so very much to her, she will see it through the golden mists of recollection when we select what we wish to remember and what we would like to forget. Tom must have given her something to remember.

Laura hesitated. "I don't know, George."

" Oh yes," he said, " you'll have to come. You must get about more now, Laura. And you'll be able to, you know. I expect you've got yourself into a rut."

" I've been looking after Mildred."

He was annoyed at her placid acceptance of this duty.

" Couldn't she have paid someone to help you ? The money wouldn't have hurt her."

" Oh we had nurses, two of them, of course, while she was very ill. And Miss Parks has been staying in the house with me for the last fortnight."

He remembered Miss Parks, the sister of a nonconformist minister in the district. Her brother was unmarried, and she kept house for him, and held—and enjoyed—the rank his wife would have held on Church committees and platforms.

" How did the Reverend Cuthbert get along without her ? " he asked.

" Oh he married, you know, just a couple of years ago, so of course Miss Parks has had a lot more time on her hands."

She would have. Good for the Reverend Cuthbert. He hoped the wife was worth it. He had never liked Miss Parks.

" Miss Parks has been very kind to Mildred," Laura was telling him, a trifle reprovingly.

" I'll bet she was. Mildred would see to that."

Laura frowned, but didn't contradict him.

" You know, you'll have to think now, Laura, what you'll do when you leave this house."

Laura turned startled eyes on him. " Leave ? Leave Marathon ? But, George—why should I leave ? "

" Well, you'd hardly want to stay on alone, would you ? It's such a ridiculous barn of a house for you to go on living in all by yourself."

Laura seemed upset. " I hadn't thought of it that way. In any case, George, I don't know what Mildred would——"

" Mildred ! " he burst out, " always Mildred ! Damn it, Laura, Mildred's dead. It doesn't matter now to you or to anybody else what she liked or what she didn't like. It's yourself you have to think about. I suppose "—he said it as casually as he could—" I suppose all the money does come to you ? "

Laura started again. Dear fool, he thought, it hasn't even

occurred to her. Something akin to pity for her warmed his heart.

" You'll be quite a wealthy woman now, won't you, Laura ? "

" Wealthy ? I don't know. I don't know at all. Mildred always looked after things like that."

" And how," he thought. Mildred knew how to look after the money.

" But I'm sure she will have—seen to all that. In any case Mr. McAlister will explain it all to me and keep me right."

He didn't like that so much. " You must let me help you if I can. I—well, I may know about these things, more than you do. And don't you worry ; if there's been any funny business with the money you just come and live with us. Amy will be glad to see you."

He hadn't meant to say that at all. And he wasn't prepared for the effect the words had on Laura. Her eyes brightened with pleasure, her tired face softened and relaxed, and for a moment he saw in her a glimpse of the girl she had been. She took his hand again, and would have held it, but he pressed hers gently and let it go.

" Thank you, George, oh thank you so much," she said.

He was embarrassed at her show of affection, and more embarrassed at the response he felt rising to meet it in himself. He had disengaged himself from the ties of family as early as he could—and at some considerable material loss to himself—and he did not now wish to become involved with a sister to whom, even as a little girl, he had not been deeply attached. He felt the whole family set-up closing in on him again, and rose and went to the window, where he stood fumbling for the blind cord.

" I can't see properly ; it's so dark in here. These damn blinds, how do they operate ? Let's have some light in."

" Oh no, George, no ! " He turned to look at her, she had almost shouted at him.

" Why not, when the funeral's over ? It's a lot of nonsense keeping them down any longer."

" Please, George, let the blinds stay the way they are." She was pleading with him now. She came across the room to stop him, and in her haste upset the little table that stood beside the sofa, and it crashed with its load to the floor. A couple of books, a jangling brass bell, other articles were scattered.

"Now what have we gone and done between us ? " he said, and left the window to help her gather up the debris. His foot trod on something that cracked and crunched into the carpet. Laura gave a little cry and knelt down. "Oh! Oh, George ! "

"Well, what have we broken ? " he said roughly. It was ridiculous that after so many years he, a middle-aged man, could feel the cold guilt creeping up the back of his neck, just because he had trodden on something and it was broken. Good God, were our childish fears sunk as deep as that ? Was there no escaping them ?

Laura was on her knees, groping ineffectually. "Well, Laura, what's the damage ? "

Still crouching on the floor she looked up at him. There was real horror in her voice. "It's Mildred's glasses, George, they must have fallen out of their case. Her new case, the new glasses. The ones she got for reading. She only got them a couple of months ago. She couldn't do without them."

Get up off the floor, he wanted to shout at her. Get up off the floor and behave like an adult. Anybody can break any-thing in this ridiculous twilight. What does it matter any-way ? We've as much right to break things as anybody else. Yet all the while he knew he was angry because he too had, for a moment, been appalled at what they had done.

"Her new ones, George," Laura lamented ; "just new they were. She couldn't do without them."

"She can now," he said.

For a moment Laura didn't understand what he meant. She sat back on her ankles, a ridiculous attitude for a middle-aged woman, and looked at him. Then she said, "Oh, George, how silly of me ! " and began to laugh. "How silly, how terribly silly ! "

He laughed too, partly at her, partly in his relief because the hoodoo was broken, and put out his hands to pull her up off the floor. But she was unsteady with laughter, so he held on to her, and they were still both laughing and clutching each other when the door opened and Miss Parks came in.

"You—have a visitor, Laura," she said, standing stock still

just inside the door. Laura stopped laughing at once and pulled herself together. " Oh, Miss Parks, this is my brother George. You remember Miss Parks, don't you, George ? "

" I do," said George, wishing he could say just what and how he remembered. " How are you, Miss Parks ? " He held out his hand. She touched it as briefly as she could.

" We're bearing up as best we can, thank you, Mr. Percival," Miss Parks said. We—Laura and herself—Laura, who had been a moment before giggling like a schoolgirl on the floor— " We " are bearing up as best we can.

" I'm sure you are," George said. He hated this sharp-faced weak-eyed wisp of a woman, who in using the plural pronoun had counted herself in, and him out, of the circle of those directly and most intimately affected by Mildred's death.

" Of course it has been a very sad time for us all," she was saying.

Blast her, thought George, she's been having the time of her life. Assistant chief mourner, there's nothing she would relish more. Tear for tactful tear, she would deliver the goods. And with Mildred safely in her coffin it was all hers— there was no risk of any backchat from the corpse. But if she'd settled herself in here—and it certainly looked as if she had—he would need to be careful to keep on the right side of her. So he said, " Laura tells me you've been very kind to her."

If Miss Parks was surprised by this bouquet she showed no sign of it.

" I've been glad to do anything I could for Laura," she said, " especially when she has had none of her own family to turn to."

All right, George thought, I know what you mean by that. Now we know how the land lies between us ; no more flowers from me, Miss Parks.

Laura sensed the declaration of war. " It won't be long now till they come back from the funeral," she put in, a little diffidently. " George—are you going to stay ? "

Five minutes ago George would have said no, but Miss Parks had made him angry. " Yes," he said decisively, " I'm going to stay."

Laura looked worried. " They'll think it—odd that you

weren't here before, George. And—you're not wearing a black tie."

" I don't see the necessity of a black tie when I didn't come to the funeral," he said, " or maybe you're ashamed of me in this suit—it is a bit shabby, isn't it ? "

" George, you know I didn't mean anything like that," Laura protested, " and of course you must stay. You and I are all the family that are left now, aren't we ? "

George smiled at her and patted her hand. It was Miss Parks' turn to be uneasy. She knew she was on difficult ground herself.

" I don't know whether you care for *me* to stay, Laura dear," she said. " Of course I'm not one of the family, and when Mr. McAlister comes to—talk business over with you, as he will, of course—well, as you say, it *is* a family affair."

Laura looked at George as if she expected guidance from him, but he gave no sign. No use hurrying things, he thought. She hesitated a moment and then said, politely but without enthusiasm, " Stay of course, if you care to, Miss Parks."

Miss Parks was still uneasy. " Just as you wish, dear, but you wouldn't hesitate to tell me if you'd rather I didn't, would you ? Of course I know Mildred really looked on me as one of the family, but if you want me to go away——"

" No, no, of course not."

In her relief Miss Parks babbled on. " It was such a privilege to be here for the little service in the house. The minister spoke so sympathetically of Mildred and her long illness—and of you too, Laura dear. I'm only sorry you weren't here to hear him, Mr. Percival."

" Are you ? " said George, and smiled. " What did he say ? "

" What was it now ? He expressed himself so well. Let me see, how did he put it ? Oh yes, he spoke about your sister's ' exemplary devotion ' to dear Mildred, and how she had never spared herself in the long months of nursing."

More reflections on me, George thought. I should have been here to help, that's what she means, only she hasn't the nerve to tell me outright. Laura only did it because she got caught in the net that I was clever enough to escape from.

She was weak where I was strong. He was sick of hearing
how well Laura had behaved.

" ' Exemplary devotion,' " Miss Parks repeated, " that was
how he put it."

" Did he now? Good for him." George laughed.
" Top marks for you, Laura."

To his surprise Laura turned on him, her eyes angry, her
voice ugly. " What are you laughing at, George? It isn't
funny. It was true, can't you see. Six years she was ill.
Six years. Can't you see, it was true!"

He did not know what to say to her. She began to sob
harshly, putting her hands, with spread fingers, in front of her
distorted face. He took a step towards her, but she thrust
him off and made for the door, and they heard her troubled
breathing until the door closed behind her.

The room was very quiet after she had gone. Laura's
distress had spoiled the game he was having with Miss Parks.
" I'm sorry I upset her," George said at last.

Miss Parks was quick to seize the advantage that this gave
her. " It's no wonder she's overwrought, Mr. Percival.
Perhaps you don't know it, I don't suppose you do, but for
many years Laura has been—far from strong. And after all,
she had had the strain of Mildred's illness entirely on her
shoulders."

George hit back. " All right, Miss Parks, I know what you
imply by that. Laura had it all, I wasn't here to help when I
was needed. But let's get this straight ; my father turned me
out of this house twenty years ago. When he died I wrote
to my sister Mildred, asking her if I could help her in any
way, or if she'd be glad to see me again. She didn't answer
my letter, and I wasn't invited back. Laura chose to stay
here. I thought I made less trouble for her by my absence."

The direct attack flummoxed Miss Parks. " Oh quite.
Quite. It has all been most unfortunate, I'm sure. I'm only
saying, Mr. Percival, that your sister Laura has had a trying
time, very trying. Laura is so conscientious. Mildred's
slightest wish was law to her. I sometimes thought Mildred
was—well, just a tiny bit outspoken, but we have to make
allowances for invalids, don't we ? "

Before George could answer the clock in the hall struck
four, the slow unhurried notes that George knew so well.

The clock again! Unwillingly he was moved and cursed himself for a fool. Why should a boy whose home life had been consistently unhappy have any sentimental reaction at all to the sights or sounds of his childhood? He had never been happy till he had cut himself off from home, and then—well, of course he had been happy. But he knew that the clock in the hall striking four touched him more deeply than anything that Amy had ever said to him, than any baby memory of Kathie. And yet he had been happy with Amy and Kathie, never happy in this house. He resented its unreasonable hold on him.

"It's a good many years," he said, a little uncertainly, "since I heard that clock."

Miss Parks was quick to emphasise her more intimate acquaintance with it. "Four o'clock! That's always been a very special time with us. Mildred rested in the afternoon, you see, and Laura brought her tea-tray in at four o'clock. Mildred did like regular habits, you know. It's a great help to an invalid, and Laura understood that so well. Do you know, Mr. Percival, I've seen Laura waiting outside the door in the hall, with the tray in her hand, and the minute the clock had finished striking she would knock and come in. 'Mildred,' she would say, 'Mildred dear, it's four o'clock.'"

George could suddenly bear no more of it. He could see Laura standing there waiting, the tea-tray with all its appointments of lace and china and silver correctly placed for the personal satisfaction of one querulous invalid. He could imagine Laura's hand, a small hand, never very clever at anything except the delicate brushwork of her paintings, poised ready to knock when the sound of the clock had sunk to silence. Then the hesitant rap and the opening door, and Mildred on the sofa turning her ailing body to feed on Laura's apparent health. He felt sick and turned to the sofa to reassure himself that it was indeed empty. "I'm going out into the garden," he said, "for a smoke," and fumbling his way through the blinds he opened the french windows and went out onto the lawn.

The garden was smaller, more crowded than he remembered it. The memory of children uses a generous scale. The trees and bushes, of course, had grown, and closed in on the place, indeed they were overgrown and needed drastic pruning. That could all be attended to in due course, George thought, and then realised he was a couple of months ahead of himself. There was a long way to go before that stage was reached, and things would need careful handling.

Perhaps he had been wrong to suggest to Laura that she might leave the house. What he should have done was to impress her with the inadvisability of living there alone. And yet did he really want to install himself and his family here in Marathon? The house was large and comfortable, elegant in its solid way, but old-fashioned. The neighbourhood had gone down considerably since he had lived here. It had now little to commend it. Why not urge Laura to sell out, and settle, along with himself and his family, in a modern villa up the Malone Road? But no—that wouldn't accomplish what he had set himself to do. It was here, in this house, that George knew he had to establish himself; it was only here that he could really hope to be rid of the last tatters of his unhappy immaturity. He needed to clatter across the wide hall, shout up the stairs, pass certain doors without lightening his footstep, sprawl in front of the fire, or whack it to a flaming furnace. At one time his whole idea had been to get out of the place. Well, he had got out, and built up a very creditable act of self-assurance. But the proof of it, the transmuting of that act into reality, must take place here, in Marathon.

Amy wouldn't like it, of course. The idea would tickle her no end, and Kathie would be thrilled, but once inside the hall door and Amy would put on that show of careful gentility that amused or exasperated him. She would affect all the little airs and graces that she thought suited the house, and she'd do it damn well, bless her. But he liked her common. God, how comfortable it had been, being common with Amy —and realising at the same time, that she regarded it as an act of godlike condescension on his part! But her clothes would look suddenly cheap, hanging in the vast wardrobes at Marathon. Mirrors that had reflected Mildred's expensive but unremarkable garments would show up Amy's little numbers for the flashy bits they were. Her small broad feet in high-heeled snub-nosed shoes would not be at home on these wide floors. Kathie would learn, she was young enough to learn. There was more than a trace of her father in Kathie. She would pick up the natural elegances which the house called for. By the time she was grown-up she would have forgotten all the humiliating economies, the second-rate treats—holidays in boarding houses, conferences before chartering a taxi, seats in the Upper Circle, sale bargains that were never quite the bargains they had appeared. She would be ready to enter into her inheritance.

George did not deceive himself. He had no scruples about what he intended to do. When he had given up his birthright because home life stifled him he hadn't contemplated the possibility of a come-back. But he was ready to seize the opportunity now that it so clearly presented itself. After all, it wasn't his fault that he hadn't been able to get on with his father.

Possibly it wasn't his father's fault either. After Mildred and Laura were born, their mother's health had never fully recovered, and the birth of the longed-for son and heir had cost Mr. Percival his wife's life. Perhaps it was remorse that made Mr. Percival so dutiful and demanding a father. He had robbed the children of a mother's love and care, and he took it on himself to make amends. Governesses and nurses were selected personally by him, after very thorough enquiries into their antecedents. He refused the offers of help from sisters and sisters-in-law alike. The children were his ; he wouldn't in any way shirk his full responsibility towards them. Studies and holidays, friendships and enthusiasms were supervised and directed by the lonely father. He was determined not to be found lacking in any way in his duty.

In Mildred, as soon as she was old enough, Mr. Percival found an ally. She accepted her father's standards of what was and was not fitting, and from early years learned the joy of feeling righteous. It was, perhaps, the only joy she felt secure about. Duty was a glory, and her father's approval almost recompensed for the affection he had forgotten how to display. So from the first Mildred had come out on her father's side. George and Laura were different propositions.

Laura didn't remember her mother clearly—only the sudden want of her that brought with it a lasting insecurity. She was a nervous little girl, given to storms of weeping. Her mother would have rocked her till the storms were spent, her father read books about the subject and dealt with her psychologically and ineffectually. Her lack of control distressed and then irritated him. It seemed a reflection on his careful up-bringing. The books had been wrong somewhere, or did the fault lie with the children ? Why should she so often blink dumbly at him when he asked her the simplest question ? As she grew older she attained a certain composure, but she never gave him her confidence. It dawned on Mr. Percival that in spite of his careful study of his children and their characters, in spite of his devotion to their interests, there was something about them that escaped him, something he did not understand. This vexed him, it seemed an admission of failure. He would have liked to be able to say, " I can read my children like a book." But he could never read Laura.

When it came to George Mr. Percival felt that here was a book he could indeed read, but he didn't like what he found there. His joy in having at last a son born to him was always overcast with guilt that his wife died in giving birth to the boy. It was necessary that George should fulfil all his father's ambitions ; that was the only way he could forget the sense of guilt. He wanted to be able to say, " My wife died, but my son was worth it." So that the hopes had been higher, the scrutiny more minute—and the disappointment more catastrophic. George was a declared rebel where Laura was an irritating conundrum. The psychological approach was useless. It had done no good with Laura, how much less with George ? He was a stubborn thrusting child, and a sullen unresponsive little boy. Every advantage that money could buy was bought for him, and he took them all with both hands and showed no gratitude or appreciation. He was sent to Campbell College, but his school reports spoke consistently of ability misapplied, of lack of concentration, and of careless-ness. The friends he made there were the children of families with only one generation of wealth to their credit, while the house of Percival boasted three. Every school holiday com-menced with a storm over the report on the previous term's work. All the patience which Mr. Percival had vowed he would exert was exhausted by the end of the first week. But he could not leave the boy alone, or keep his tongue off him. He knew each twist of George's character, and had fortified himself against continued disappointment by anticipating each successive failure. Knowing himself to be the constant subject of his father's impassioned concern George made a deliberate business of rebellion in his bid for privacy. His father thought he was a failure. Rather than prove him right George set himself to be a bigger failure than his father had imagined. They could not be together in a room without that hypersensitive awareness of each other which stifled all spontaneity at its source.

George threw away his cigarette and lit another one. He had already smoked the ration he allowed himself each day, but at Marathon it seemed laughable that George Percival should ever practise any of the domestic economies which in the little house at Ballydrum were part of the routine self-imposed for Amy's sake and Kathie's. It would have amused Mildred to see him take out his case and put it away again because five cigarettes in the day were all his wife told him he could afford.

He had reached the end of the garden, the high wall beside the rustic summer-house, where the laburnum tree gave convenient footing over the top when entry up the front drive would have been too conspicuous. It was from here that, as a boy returning on some private errand, he would first be able to see the house and find if his coming was observed. Instinctively now he eyed the house, the window of his father's study, the bay windows of the drawing-room. Habit that had been broken for twenty years re-established itself, and he cursed himself and laughed. The row of large blinded windows confronted him blankly. But he had the odd feeling that even behind those blinds he was still observed. The blinds were like the heavy lids lying over his father's eyes, so that the glance beneath them appeared not to be direct, but a kind of spying. Marathon was still watching him.

George thumbed his nose at the house, and then laughed at himself for the foolish gesture. The middle-aged man playing schoolboy! He recovered his composure just in time to see a car come up the drive and stop at the hall door. Thank God he hadn't been overlooked in his capers. Two men got out of the car, Mr. McClintock and Mr. McAlister. George went over to greet them, thinking that the prodigal son's respectful welcome might give him a temporary advantage. He composed his features to play the part. He was going to get a kick out of watching the surprise on Mr. McAlister's face.

Chapter Four

UP in her bedroom Laura sat fighting for her self-control. That George should have come after twenty years of absence was the fulfilment of twenty years' hoping. That he could have laughed at the minister's words of praise was a sore blow. Memory is always selective, and she had remembered what she admired in George and had chosen to forget much that had always hurt her. He had seemed so like the George of twenty years ago as he came into the drawing-room. The darkened room, of course, hid the traffic of the years on his face. But he still retained the easy manner, the slight cultivated swagger that she always envied him. The boy playing the man—that was what it really amounted to, but Laura had never realised this. George had been her hero during their difficult childhood and the aching years of adolescence. Where she had been too timid and nervous to rebel against their father's strict supervision of their daily living and Mildred's endorsement of it, George had always rebelled. She hated herself for the courage she lacked, and George's flouting of rules and regulations had often served as a safety valve for her own emotions. Their father visited on George the iniquity which she knew she shared with him. This guilty knowledge added to the admiration she felt for George's rebellion. The fact that George could oppose such parental omnipotence made it just endurable.

While things had been at their worst with Mildred the knowledge that George was somewhere in Belfast was an inexplicable comfort to Laura. She hoped that perhaps Mildred would send for him when she finally became desperately ill. She had even wondered vaguely whether she should try to find him herself. But Mildred did not send for George, or speak of him. Pain and bodily weakness brought no softening of her character. It almost seemed that they sharpened her faculties for criticism and disparagement. As her sphere of influence shrank first to purely domestic affairs, then to the four walls of the sick-room, then to the ordering and control of her own sick body she never sought comfort or asked for sympathy. The sisters were as far apart on the day she died as they had ever been. Even the manner of her dying was typical of Mildred.

It was only three days ago, but to Laura it already seemed much longer. Mildred had been very ill now for a full week. For long periods she was semi-conscious. But even at this stage there was no relaxation, no gesture, or look, or half-caught phrase for which one could pity her. Either she was alert, in full possession of her faculties, or else she was silent. Laura was tired, had become so used to being tired that it was difficult to remember she had ever been anything else. She spent most of her time in the sick-room. Although there were two nurses in the house she had not had her clothes off for two nights. Mildred was dying. It appeared impossible that, though they had never been close to each other, she would not turn to Laura before she died, so that the constraints and bitternesses of her long servitude might be washed away in a tide of compassion. Laura had always hoped for this, had left the door open. It seemed, however, as if a kind of paralysis had come over the two sisters, to prevent them from drawing together. But still Laura hoped. Death was so big a thing, Mildred couldn't go out like that.

It became doubtful whether Mildred would live until the morning, but Laura was persuaded, against her will, to go to bed, with the promise that the night-nurse would call her at once, if there was any change. She did as she was told and went to bed, but with no expectation of sleep. It was, indeed, with a conscious effort that she persuaded her stiff eyelids to close. But she had slept, the long deep sleep of exhaustion that lasted through the night, and had woken with a start of guilt as the night nurse came into her room with a cup of tea. No, the nurse assured her, the patient had had quite a restful night, there was no worsening of her condition. She was still in a light sleep.

Laura drank her tea gratefully. The night nurse was a young thing, a girl with a broad brow and a pleasant face that warmed Laura's heart. She stood, comely in her uniform, fingering the tasselled blind cord, looking out into the early spring morning on the garden. A blackbird was busy on the lawn, prospecting for worms. " I'd like fine to know where he has his nest hidden," the girl declared. She started to tell Laura about her own home in the country.

Propped on her elbow, Laura drank her tea and listened, and watched the nurse. She had a strong plump neck and rounded arms. How pleasant a thing the human body was while it was still young and healthy! It seemed amazing that so young a girl could have come from a night spent with Mildred in the shadow of death, alone in a sleeping house, and emerge to smile at the sun and watch a blackbird, and yawn healthily and happily in secure anticipation of a sound day's sleep! Laura felt restored and reassured. Nurse said something that made her laugh. It was a long while since she had laughed. She stifled the sound quickly, finished the last of her tea and put on her dressing-gown to go with the nurse to Mildred's room before she bathed and dressed.

Mildred wasn't there. Her body was, the features as withdrawn in death as they had been in life. Her mouth seemed almost to smile. After exacting six years of unremitting service it looked as if Mildred had amused herself in choosing to die while Laura, after a good night's rest, was lying in bed drinking a cup of tea and gossiping with a talkative nurse.

The iniquity of her neglect settled on Laura like a dumb horror that passed for grief. To have done so much, and then, by so small a thing, to have failed in the completion. If she had been there would Mildred have given her the sign she had looked for? Had Mildred known that she was alone? Seeing her condition, but not knowing its real cause, the solicitude of the household now switched directly to Laura. Miss Parks fussed over her, Hannah wept over her, the doctor prescribed pills which made her sleep, a few friends and neighbours sent messages of condolence. The nurses packed their cases and expressed their concern for her well-being and their satisfaction that Mildred had gone so easily at the end. All this helped Laura to see things in a truer perspective. Mr. McClintock's words at the service in the house had completed her confidence in a sense of achievement. The long task was ended. She had done what she had set herself to do. It was over. And then George's flippant words—" Top marks for you, Laura "—had shaken her again. To George it seemed a little thing, a light thing, what she had done. But then she reminded herself that no one but herself and Mildred knew why she had done it—and Mildred was dead. No one knew now but herself. And, in any case, the debt was paid.

But it was true that she remembered what she chose to remember about George and had forgotten what she chose to forget. It had always been like this, she told herself. As a girl she anticipated George's school holidays with pleasure and excitement. He came home, a little larger, a little more glorious, and for half a day the world was made new for her. Then the trouble started—the long envelope containing the school report lying on her father's plate at breakfast—endless interviews between George and her father behind the closed doors of the study, punctuated now and then by a voice raised in anger. Mildred went about her daily procedure with her usual composure, but Laura's brain and fingers could accomplish nothing. There were long difficult evenings spent with the four of them round the drawing-room fire—Mr. Percival considered it one of his duties to spare as much time as he could for his children—hours of uneasy leisure which Laura spent with a book on her knee, but rarely turning a page, waiting for the cold politeness between George and her father to flare into some fresh trouble.

" What are you reading, George ? "

" A book."

" I hope it is an interesting one."

" It is, thank you." And George would go on reading, until Mr. Percival demanded the title of the book and he handed it over for his father's scrutiny, and usually for his condemnation.

" You were late last night, George."

" Yes."

" Where were you ? "

" Out with friends."

Then Mr. Percival would christen his curiosity parental duty, and enquire the names of the friends and how they had employed themselves. Sometimes Laura, tense in her anxiety that a clash should be avoided, would wish that George could just once in a while co-operate with the ageing man, and make him a gift of the information that must always be wrung out. She saw the relationship was inevitable but could never accept it.

When George left school, with a dismal record of ability misapplied and opportunities wasted, he had joined his father in the business for a few years, and the relationship between them became even more acutely strained. Mr. Percival had, in his dreams, looked forward to the day when he could introduce his son to the work, and to his staff. They knew in the office how seriously he took his responsibilities as a father. He had a reputation for success among his business acquaintances. And this was what he had produced ! This smooth youth with the flippant tongue, and no knowledge of the business or interest in it. A playboy come to make sport with a hard-won inheritance. Mr. Percival was not loved by his staff, but he was respected. In any case, if the control of the firm were to pass into the hands of this incapable youngster, they would all stand to lose by it. The sympathies in the office were with the father.

George was acutely aware of this hostility. At school he had always had an audience of friends who admired his escapades and grand manner. George needed an audience. At home Laura's unspoken sympathy sometimes supplied the need. But now, in the big linen house, it seemed that his father sat at every desk, condemning him. Any effort he might have put into the work was stifled. He knew he didn't earn the small salary his father paid him, so he made no effort to live within its bounds. Laura had helped him sometimes from her own small allowance. He found other ways of helping himself. Some of the junior members in the firm were flattered to be touched by the boss's son for a small loan. Attending classes at the Technical College he made friends outside his father's circle. They were a mixed lot, given to extravagant behaviour not in itself vicious but a gesture of independence. George drank too much, not consistently, because that was beyond his means. Anyhow, he didn't really enjoy it. But if there was a party, and he found himself the centre of other young people whose tongues weren't as clever or their wits as sharp as his, whisky fired his brain and prolonged the exaltation.

Laura found it hard to forgive him for this. Drunkenness was only a word in her sheltered life—or at the worst a man who lurched and leered at her across a crowded tramcar, a horror and a disgust on which one turned one's back. She had nearly always been in bed when George came home drunk —in bed, but not asleep, lying tense, listening for the shambling step on the gravel, the foolish voice seeking for the lost merriment, the stumble on the stairs.   One night he stumbled and did not get up again, and she wrapped her dressing-gown round her and went out onto the landing.   Her father was standing there already.   George was crawling up the stairs on his hands and knees.   This manœuvre apparently called for immense concentration.   Then he looked up and saw them watching and laughed, and stood up with difficulty and was sick over the banisters.

Remembering all these things about George—things she had deliberately put out of her mind—Laura was not surprised that he had spoken those mocking words about the service she had done for Mildred.   Now that George had come home again his true colours were immediately more apparent.

In recalling all this she was amazed that she had forgotten the news of Tom.   Tom was dead.   It was the first, the only news she had had of him for twenty years.   Tom was dead, and Tom's son here, in Belfast.

It had always seemed to Laura as part of her personal treachery that she referred to Tom as " One of George's friends," for it was not through George that she had first met Tom.   After she had left the private school which their father had selected for his daughters' education, Laura's duties at home were inconsiderable, and her days hung heavily on her. Mildred already had the household organised down to the last polish on the last teaspoon.   She did it all with an impeccable efficiency, was jealous of interference, wanted no help.   The servants worked well for Mildred, her father was proud of her prowess, there was nothing left for Laura to do.

There were concerts to be attended.   They went in a body —Mr. Percival's books on family life informed him that the corporate enjoyment of the arts contributed much to the deepening of understanding between parent and child.   Laura enjoyed the concerts—would have enjoyed them more had she not been aware of George and her father sitting beside her ; George shuffling as much as he dared, heaving great sighs that made the party conspicuous, while Mr. Percival tried but did not succeed in concealing his annoyance.   Laura was invited to the houses of her school friends, to large casual parties where young people, left to their own devices, amused themselves, talked their fill of light-hearted chatter, and experimented with flirtation.   Parents were rarely seen at these functions—one shook hands with them on arrival and departure, and presumably they supplied the food, but apart from that the houses belonged, for that evening, to the younger generation. The house of Percival issued invitations to return this hospitality, but the evenings were dismal failures, with Mr. Percival doggedly trying to unbend to the frivolity of the youngsters, and George giving him no help. Small wonder that Laura's circle of friends did not increase. Several girls she knew were married, and Laura was a nervous and bewildered bridesmaid. Mr. Percival had always avoided the chapters in his books which informed the parents of the importance of early and correct sex instruction. The Bible and a few schoolgirl vulgarities were her only sources of information.

Much of her tedious leisure Laura employed at her drawing. This was the only subject in which she had shone at school, and she had been encouraged by a teacher who appreciated her delicate skill. The shapes of flowers and leaves, of any green thing that grew, had always moved and excited her. The ordering of a bud's unfolding, the pattern of the veins in the leaves, the frilling at a petal's edge, none of this escaped her. From the natural symmetry of plants and flowers she drew and painted delicate studies and designs. She studied a little botany. Familiarity with growing things pleased her and their constancy of form gave her assurance. Plants were predictable where human beings were not.

A business acquaintance of Mr. Percival, visiting the house, remarked on her skill. He suggested that she might make use of it in linen designing. Mr. Percival thought it unbecoming to commercialise his daughter's aptitude, but he knew from his reading that any form of self-expression should be fostered, and he sent her to the Art School at the Technical College.

Laura was frankly terrified. She was quite happy sketching and painting in the garden, visiting the Botanical Gardens, or collecting wild flowers on the annual family holiday to staid seaside hotels. But to the Technical she was duly despatched. It was a large many-windowed building, clamorous, when Laura presented herself, with young men and girls. On the entrance steps, in the hall, up the wide staircases they tramped and laughed, and called to each other. It took five minutes' timid query before Laura found her class. The room was crowded. She found a place at the back behind a large untidy young man who worked with a concentration which alarmed her. It was the back of Tom's head and his hands with which she became familiar long before she saw his face. He had a high untidy crown, from which the hair grew haphazard. His hands were large, pale-skinned, every bone visible. Dark hairs grew along them. The wrist bones were prominent, the nails long and oval, almost like a woman's, the ends of the fingers flattened.

For some weeks this was all that Laura knew about Tom, and more than she knew of any of her other fellow students. Her nervousness in the large high-ceilinged room, filled with light and so many moving and talking creatures, had not lessened. She worked with an exaggerated concentration, to hide her lack of ease. The teacher spent little time with her, praising her deftness, but remarking her lack of personal initiative. With the young man in front he lingered much longer. Words passed between them, long vehement arguments. Tom had evidently no fear of authority, but unlike George he argued from conviction, not from sheer cussedness or self-display. Laura, her head bent over her own unprovocative work, listened shamelessly. One day the argument became louder, more vigorous. Tom spread his arms to illustrate his point, tipped Laura's desk, sent her work onto the floor. He knelt beside her to retrieve her scattered belongings, and picked up the sketch—it was a study of aquilegias, frills, horns and leaves in significant convolution. He glanced at it and handed it back. " No damage done to your pretty flowers," he said, and went back to his impassioned study of perspectives.

But he paused to watch the progress of the ' pretty flowers ' on other days, as if her preoccupation with growing things was a rest from his study of masses and surfaces and the light that fell on them. He asked her opinion on his work as if he assumed that it might be worth hearing. She was surprised into giving it without embarrassment. An acquaintance that never ventured any further than their knowledge of each other's work ripened between them. Mr. Percival reflected with satisfaction that he had been right to insist that Laura attended the Art Classes. It was obvious that they were of benefit to her. She seemed more alert, happier in every way.

The books had been right. No effort at self-expression must be ignored.

But for George, who was also a student at the Technical at this time, learning the intricacies of the linen business, Laura and Tom might never have known more of each other than this. One Saturday afternoon coming in through the gates of Marathon, Laura heard George's voice coming across the lawn, and another voice answering it. She was not surprised. Mr. Percival was away for a week on business. George had taken the opportunity to invite a friend. She looked across the lawn. It was one of those golden days that October steals from summer. There was George, perched precariously in the low-spreading apple tree, delivering a harangue for the benefit of a friend who lay in the long grass of the orchard which had not yet been cut. Of the stranger only one bent knee lying across the other was visible. George's peroration was apparently amusing—his gift of mimicry was as unerring as it was uncharitable—and the unseen listener laughed in appreciation. The laugh seemed familiar. Laura wondered which of his friends it was, but did not pause to find out. She sped on towards the house. If Mildred were about trouble might brew up, and her instinct warned her that she were better out of it. But George had seen her. Inflated by his success and wanting to enlarge his audience he called to her and beckoned, " Come on, Laura. Come and join the party." Unwillingly she crossed the lawn and came into the orchard and looked down at the still-prostrate visitor, sprawled in the shade with a half-eaten apple in each hand. It was Tom.

Sitting in her bedroom now on the day of Mildred's funeral, Laura remembered these forbidden days. Suddenly the big clock in the hall struck four. Four o'clock! Four o'clock and she was late. Panic gripped her, and she started to the door. How could she be here idling in her room while the tea-tray was waiting in the pantry, and in the drawing-room— then a tide of recollection poured hotly over her. No, no one was waiting for the tea-tray today. While shocks were still fresh in the experience one could deal with them. It was when the tension had begun to ease and for a moment one forgot the thing that had happened and was then jerked back to remembrance that the worst of it lay. Her hands were shaking, and she felt sick.

A car drew up at the hall door and the need for action helped her to pull herself together. That would be Mr. McClintock come to pay a final condolence. Mr. McAlister would be with him. Mildred's soul had been safely committed to eternity, Mr. McAlister would want to explain to Laura how she had disposed of her temporal possessions. Laura bathed her face and smoothed her hair. George was here. He used to say she had pretty hair. He would not think so now, but she spent longer in front of her mirror than she had done for a number of years, and then went downstairs to the drawing-room to hear what Mr. McAlister had to say.

Chapter Five

MR. McALISTER, when he came back to Marathon after Mildred's funeral, was not altogether so surprised to see George as George had expected. Both he—and Mildred— had realised the probability of his return, though he had not expected it quite so punctually. He might have had the decency to let a week or so elapse. And yet, perhaps it was as well he had come now, while he, Mr. McAlister, was explaining the contents and terms of the will. He could take every opportunity to point out the intention behind it. Rather he should come now than that he should sneak in on Laura when she had acquired a cheque-book and Mr. McAlister were not about.

The Rev. Mr. McClintock spoke a few words to Laura, a few less to George, and took his departure. Mr. McAlister sorted the papers in his case and snapped impatiently at rubber bands while the remaining people settled themselves for what he had to tell them. He noted with annoyance that Miss Parks had not left the room. It was not his business to ask her to go, and Laura made no move to do so, and so he discharged his duty and read the will.

" You see, Miss Laura," he said, at its conclusion, " everything is quite straightforward. I only wish every will I handled were half so simple, or, if I may say so, half so wise

—especially those that involve as large a sum of money as this one does."

He addressed himself directly to Laura, obliquely to George, and ignored Miss Parks, as was her due.

Laura expressed her thanks for his good offices. "Mr. McAlister," she ventured. "Mildred didn't say—she didn't mention any wish as to how the money should be used, did she?" She bore herself, he was glad to observe, with commendable calm, seeming neither pleased nor flustered at the news of comparative wealth.

"The money comes to you in its entirety," he said. "Your sister said nothing as to what use you should make of it."

"Oh." Laura sounded a little upset at this.

"Your sister showed her trust in your good sense, Miss Laura, when she worded the bequest," he went on quickly. "I remember she phrased it herself."

"So like Mildred," purred Miss Parks, between thin lips. "What were the words again, Mr. McAlister?"

With a little more emphasis than was necessary he read them out—"All I possess to my sister Laura Evelyn, in the confident trust that she knows how I should wish her to use it."

George gave a short laugh. "That *was* like Mildred."

Mr. McAlister ignored the interruption. Laura shot George a puzzled glance.

"So you see, Miss Laura," the old man went on, "you are not tied in any way whatever. The money is yours and yours alone. And I think that, as an old friend of the family, I may be allowed to say that I wish you joy of it."

Miss Parks murmured agreement. George said, "Hear hear!" under his breath.

"You've had a sad time recently, my dear," Mr. McAlister continued, "and you have shown great fortitude in circumstances which have been far from happy. You owe it to yourself to—to expand your life a little, take up new interests—in short, Miss Laura, to learn to enjoy yourself."

Laura gave him a timid smile of thanks, and he found himself remembering what a pretty girl she had been. It gave him quite a shock to remember it. Before her father's death he had been a frequent visitor at Marathon, and he remembered her then; a graceful young thing she was, shy, with a downbent head and eyes that looking up suddenly had that startling quality of limpid depth, mermaid's eyes. And here was a tired woman in her forties, the head still bent down, but the eyes dull now, the light in them gone out. Yet when she had smiled for a moment he saw that girl in her again. Perhaps a little ease, a little self-indulgence would renew her. He wished earnestly that it might be so. Laura's hands, folded passively, lay on the table beside him. He put his own hand over them, patting them. " Miss Laura, you must learn to enjoy yourself."

Miss Parks snorted. Her thin nose went up. " That isn't very easy advice, Mr. McAlister, for someone who has just suffered so tragic a bereavement."

Mr. McAlister took his hand away from Laura's. " Quite so, quite so. But we are not meant to give way unduly to our grief, Miss Parks. As Christians irrational grief is surely selfish. And time heals many wounds." He paused, and was pleased that the woman had no reply. He turned again to Laura. " It may take an effort, dear Miss Laura, but I am sure it is your duty to see that that effort is made."

" Yes, Mr. McAlister," Laura said. But her voice was colourless. *She has not the faintest idea what I am talking about,* he thought, with irritation. *I was wrong. That glimpse of the girl I saw was just an accident, a trick of the memory.* But he still persisted, " I should go away, if I were you—right away."

" You mean—leave Belfast ? " She was gaping at him now. *Women should never leave their mouths open.* He wished the whole business were over and done with. He was tired. There had been a sharp breeze in the cemetery. He wished he were home at his own fireside. If it were not for George Percival and that woman Miss Parks, he would have left it at that. But the ghost of the girl still lingered.

" Of course Mr. McAlister doesn't mean he advises you to leave Belfast, dear," Miss Parks said soothingly.

" Not necessarily to leave it permanently," he snapped, " but until you have decided what to do, Miss Laura. Take a sea-trip, see the world, or if you feel like something less ambitious, go to a good hotel somewhere in the South of England and have a thorough rest."

George lit a cigarette. " Lonely affairs," he volunteered ; " hotels are lonely, even at the best of times." He blew the smoke out across the table and looked at Mr. McAlister through it. All right, the older man thought, a three-cornered scrap with this passive woman in the middle. Well, for the sake of his professional pride and for the girl he remembered, he didn't intend to let them get away with it. " Torquay is a nice spot," he told her ; " always something to see at Torquay. My dear wife and I spent a very pleasant holiday there once, just before her last illness. Do you know that part of the world at all ? "

" No—I don't think I do."

How would she, poor soul ? She hadn't known much recently outside the four walls of Marathon.

" Your sister never cared for these large seaside resorts," Miss Parks was telling her now, " but of course she was very selective."

Before Mr. McAlister could come back on this George leaned over the table to Laura, as if the two of them were the only people in the room. " I think you'll only be miserable going away on your own, Laura. Why not do as I suggested before, and come to us ? "

She turned to him, all eagerness, but there was something pathetic, almost grotesque in this girlish middle-age. " George, I should love that, really I should. But—are you sure ? Would it be convenient for you to have me ? What will Amy say ? "

" Amy will say the same as I do," George said, with confidence. He would see that she did.

" Would there be room for me in your house ? "

He laughed affectionately, easily. " My dear, the house isn't very large or very grand, but of course we could find room for you till you get your feet under you."

" That would be lovely," Laura said ; there were tears in her eyes.

" And if you decide to come to us permanently——" George hesitated for a moment, and to Mr. McAlister's dismay Laura rose like a flash.

" Oh, of course if I were coming to you permanently then you'd need a bigger house, and that's where I could help."

" Well, we should have to think about that," George demurred.

"Of course you wouldn't have to think about it,"
she insisted; "that's what the money's for—isn't it, Mr.
McAlister?"

Her face was unbecomingly flushed. She looked eagerly
to Mr. McAlister to endorse her scheme. Foolishness in a
girl has a kind of charm. Foolishness in a woman irritated
him unbearably. He washed his hands of her.

"That's just a matter for yourself, Miss Laura," he said,
not troubling to keep the disapproval out of his voice.

Her flushed face deepened. "Oh. Oh, I see," she said,
in the flattened voice he had so often heard her use to Mildred.
"I see what you mean."

George's voice sounded out brazenly in the darkened room.
"He means can you square your conscience to subsidise the
black sheep out of the family fortune?"

"That is not what I said."

"But you implied it."

Miss Parks drew in her breath with pleasure and excitement. She glanced from one man to the other. Laura put
the palms of her hands against her cheeks as if to shut out this
friction. She looked at no one.

"You implied that, Mr. McAlister."

"Frankly I did."

"May I ask why?"

"Certainly. Quite frankly, Mr. Percival, I should hesitate
to advise your sister to come to any financial arrangement
with you because of what I have heard and known of your
reputation." That was straight enough, but the fellow had
asked for it. Mr. McAlister leant back in his chair panting a
little. He was too old for this direct attack, besides he needed
his dinner.

"What do you know of my reputation?"

"I know that as a boy you had every opportunity your
father's money could buy for you. That as a young man he
took you into the business with him, intending that you should
succeed to it, but that he found you were—unreliable, and
that shortly afterwards you left this house and haven't been
living at home since. I didn't see you at your father's
funeral. Your name didn't occur in either his will or that
of your sister Mildred. You'll agree with me that that is not
encouraging."

"And now you suspect me of having designs on Laura's fortune?"

"George!" This from Laura. "Of course Mr. McAlister wouldn't think that." She turned now to Mr. McAlister and laid a hand on his sleeve. "Mr. McAlister, tell him you wouldn't."

The hand on his sleeve trembled. He patted it and set it on her knee again. Emotion would get them nowhere. She had been sated with emotion. It was reason he wanted to make his appeal to. Reason would return when the emotion was spent. "All I'm trying to point out, Miss Laura, is your obligation to your sister in the matter. It does call for a little consideration."

"Oh yes, of course," she agreed at once, and her eyes flickered over to the sofa in the window.

"It would be a pity to do anything in a hurry, Laura," Miss Parks put in.

"Take your time by all means," he said, without glancing in that lady's direction, "but I don't think it would be very good for you to stay long in this house by yourself."

"Oh, but she needn't be by herself; there's no reason at all why I shouldn't stay," Miss Parks said hurriedly, "no reason at all—that is, if you'd like to have me, of course, Laura."

"That's very kind of you, Miss Parks," Laura said. It was the automatic reply that comes from extreme weariness. It meant nothing to Laura, but everything to Miss Parks, and she was quick to follow it up.

"Not at all. I wouldn't be in the way, you know that, don't you? And I really think Mildred would have expected it of me. A sudden decision would be such a mistake, and I can easily arrange to stay for another few weeks. Or longer if you like—just as long as you like, Laura—as long as ever you like."

Mr. McAlister looked up and met George's eye. She has you beat, George was telling him. And you too, his silent glance replied to George. First round to Miss Parks. Let it go at that. He felt old and tired and hungry, and he needed his dinner.

Chapter Six

LAURA slept long and deep that night, and woke at last to hear Hannah draw the curtains back from the windows. They had been in darkness for three days, but now sunlight, shining up the Lough, sprang into the room. Laura knew by the angle of the light that it was late. " Hannah, you've let me sleep."

" Didn't you need it, well ? "

" Yes. Oh yes." She remembered yesterday, and drew a long breath that that day was over, divided from her by a night's sleep, the sharp edges of recollection already dimming a little. The thing had happened, it was over. Hannah brought her a breakfast tray, and she ate and drank slowly, savouring the moments with deliberate indulgence. Mr. McAlister had said she must learn to enjoy herself. He was an old friend of her father's, he would not tell her anything that was wrong.

Presently she rose and went across to the window, and stood looking out. The morning was clear and bright. Across the Lough wisps of white mist still clung to the folds in the Antrim hills, but the sun would soon have them. The Lough was still, and almost empty of traffic. The cross-channel steamers would be past long ago, and their passengers in Belfast by this time. Laura was well acquainted with the times and seasons of the steamers. In the isolated life she had led their coming and going was a welcome contact with the outside world. She was comforted to watch the rows of moving lights going down the Lough on winter evenings, and was always up in time to greet the incoming boats in the morning. There were other people in the world besides herself and Mildred. Now there was only herself, and the boats had gone by. But there was George ; he had come yesterday, and he would come again. He would surely come again, and when Mr. McAlister and Miss Parks were not there. The sun shone in at the window and she felt the warmth of it on her bare feet, and turned at last to dress and meet the day.

On her way downstairs she noticed that the door of Mildred's bedroom was open, and she hesitated, reluctant to go past it. But there was a noise of cheerful activity coming from the room, and the clatter of tongues. It was Hannah, and the daily woman who came in to help her, Mrs. Ritchie. Laura only knew Mrs. Ritchie as a large amorphous silent woman who retreated into doorways when discovered at work, but it seemed that the freedom of Mildred's bedroom had transformed her. The vacuum cleaner was going, and above its noise Mrs. Ritchie was relating some family catastrophe with huge enjoyment. Hannah was commenting sympathetically. Outside the door lay a pile of invalid equipment, to be sorted and disposed of—some medicine bottles, a stack of papers, faded flowers, a pile of linen. Laura was filled with admiration for these two women. If the room could ever become again a normal habitation, they and the sunlight would do it between them. She paused unobserved for a moment to watch Mrs. Ritchie prop her large bulk against the bottom of the bed and hitch her sagging stockings. She did not think Mrs. Ritchie had ever been in the room before, but already she dominated it.

Downstairs there was no sign of Miss Parks. Laura thought she heard a sound in the kitchen, and wondered if she should go back and fetch her breakfast tray—one must always save trouble if one can—but she put the thought deliberately aside, and walking boldly through her father's study went by a side door into the garden. She knew well where she was going—down the side of the long border where the earliest spires of lupin were already showing colour through their green, into the orchard spattered over with apple blossom. It was here—here—that Tom had been lying that first day that George brought him to the house, lying full length in the grass with a half-eaten apple in each hand.

He had risen when she came, threw one apple over the hedge and then stopped short in surprise, and they laughed at recognising each other before resuming their interrupted handshake. It seemed rather a ridiculous gesture, this shaking hands. George was amused to find they knew each other already, Laura confused that her two worlds had thus suddenly converged. She stood for a moment, talking— she could not remember what they found to say—and the

wind had blown her hair against the lowest branch of the
apple tree where it caught and held fast. She tugged it
free, and in doing so jerked the branch and a hail of ripe
apples fell round them. They laughed, and the dry dust
of the lichen on the apple bark got in their nostrils and made
them cough. As soon as she could Laura excused herself
and left Tom and George together. She did not quit her
own room again till tea-time, and by that time Tom had gone.
Mildred was in the house, but made no comment.

Next day at the Art Class Tom greeted her with his usual
nod. It was half-way through the period, when she was
bent over her own work, that he paused with a brush up-
lifted and accused her. " You didn't come back yesterday."

She did not know what to say, and for lack of something
better stammered, " I thought I might have seen you at tea."

" You might—perhaps—if your sister had asked me to
stay."

She was deeply embarrassed. " I'm sorry. You see—
we don't have many visitors."

He didn't answer, and she ventured, " Have you many
brothers and sisters ? "

" Not me. I am the only son of my mother, and she is
a widow." He went back to his work for half an hour.
Presently he threw at her, " My father was killed at the
Somme," and when she murmured some conventional phrase
of sympathy he said, " Not at all. My mother is a Merry
Widow—a very Merry Widow," and the rest of the period
passed in silence.

All through that winter it was like that, a few words tossed
to her before he bent again over his work, and she saw nothing of him but the humped shoulders and the springing black
hair. She was glad he didn't talk any more. He alarmed
her a little. His directness frightened her. At Marathon
they took pains to disguise their feelings, to move under
cover of conventional behaviour. With each member of
the family so acutely aware of the other this self-isolation was
the only way of behaviour possible—any lack of control
was self-exposure. But there was a certain code of careful
politeness to be observed, it oiled the wheels. This young
man had no use for oil ; if he was angry he spoke with anger,
if she said something when he was absorbed in his work he

did not trouble to answer her. He was without pride—false pride. His work was good—he knew it. " What would I be here for if it wasn't ? " George would have demurred, expressed surprise, accepted praise with charming diffidence. This young man demanded praise if it was due, and told her not to be a fool if she spoke highly of anything that was below the high standard he set for himself.

He came to the house again a couple of times by George's invitation. Mildred didn't like him ; she was silent when he was there, but missed no opportunity of disparaging him when his name was mentioned. " The boy with that extra-ordinary hair "—" George's friend with the peculiar accent." Mr. Percival said nothing. He was a sick man that winter ; his bodily wretchedness had blunted the edge of his intoler-ance. Although Tom appeared indifferent to Mildred's silent hostility, Laura was glad when each visit was over. Before Christmas Laura was ill with influenza, and in bed for four days. George told her Tom had been enquiring for her. When she was well enough to resume her classes Tom asked if she was better and seemed glad to see her. He was work-ing on a sketch she had not seen. They had always criticised each other's work, and she was surprised when he demurred at her examination of it. It was unlike his usual vigorous thrusting style : a tender Nativity sketch, the young mother's downbent head lit by the beauty of the child at her breast. The face of the Madonna was her own face. While she fumbled for words he picked it up. " Pretty," he said, " isn't it ? " She agreed that it was. " That's what's wrong with it," he said, and tore it in two.

Later that winter he was painting a portrait of his mother. Laura was too shy to venture any comment, but he asked for it.

" My mother," he said. " What do you think ? "

" She's—very beautiful," Laura said hesitantly.

" Always has been—still is, poor dear."

" That isn't a thing to pity anyone for—being beautiful."

" It doesn't matter to a small boy whether his mother is beautiful or not. He doesn't love her for that."

" Do you think beauty must—matter to someone ? "

" Of course."

" It mattered to your father."

" He died before I was born."

" I wonder your mother didn't re-marry."

Tom laughed. " So does she," he said, " but of course she had her duty to me," and he turned abruptly to his work and didn't talk to her any more.

In the early spring of that year the Art Master planned an excursion for the class to Newcastle, to sketch in the Mournes. They went by bus, through country crowded with small farms, all astir in the spring sunshine. The newly ploughed land was purple-brown, the larch trees' film of green threaded over the woods, the whins were ablaze.

The bus stopped in the main street, and they all spilled out, laden with sketching kit and overcoats. The seaside town was empty of visitors—they would come in their thousands from June to September—but it looked as if every landlady in the town had chosen this day to start her spring-cleaning. Blankets billowed on scores of clothes-lines, eider-downs lay across windowsills, and there was a rhythmic beating of carpets from every house that had a garden large enough to beat them in. The class separated, some to climb up into the bowl between Donard and Commedagh, some into the woods on Drinahilly, some to the Harbour.

Laura hesitated which group to join. She had made no friends among the girls in the class, and Tom was the only man she had ever spoken to. Coming down in the bus she had been sitting beside a girl with a large heavy face who seemed as friendless and silent as herself. Now Tom came and took her elbow. " Come on, we'll try the shore," he said, and together they went onto the wide stretch of pale sands. The tide was half-way up the beach and was coming in, a lazy tide, hardly troubled by waves. Each wave was just a bar of darker grey that resolved itself slowly as it neared the beach, and then hung suspended for an infinite sunlit moment before it came down in foam and was sucked back again. The hills too were tranquil, rising one above the other into the sunlight. Between hills and sea the busy seaside town laboured, and the smoke rose white from a hundred chimneys.

Tom was making a water-colour of the sea. He was obsessed by the effect of light on water, intent on capturing it on the unmoving page. He worked with that fierce concentration she knew so well in the classroom. Laura watched the humped shoulders, listened to the grunts of self-criticism which always accompanied his painting, and wandered off into the sandhills on the edge of the golf links where she found some primroses, a few pale scentless violets, and buds of the little low wild rose that grows there, with the prickles so fine that they are like coarse fur on the stems. When she came back with them Tom hadn't noticed she had been away. The few yards of sand on either side of him were ploughed up by his pacing feet. There was no one else on the wide beach, and no sign of anyone, only the tracks of their own feet that had brought them there. She sat below a breakwater and sketched her flowers till Tom turned to her and together they came back to the town.

They all had tea together at one of the boarding houses where the landlady, having as yet no regular visitors, was glad to suspend her spring-cleaning and cater for them. It was a noisy, cheerful party, the spring sunshine had made everyone hungry. Over the passing of cruets and bottles of H.P. sauce tongues were loosened. Laura had never been in such company before. The meal and the friendly talk made her sleepy and happy. Afterwards the two of them wandered again down to the shore till it was time for the bus to take them back to Belfast. But they hadn't the place to themselves this time. The warmth, the good food, the fellowship, all conspired to bring most of the class down, to sit around in chattering clumps, the young men tossing banter to the girls, who ignored it or returned it with interest, and were rewarded by gusty laughter. Several pairs of lovers sat silent, apart a little from the others, hand in hand. It was a golden evening : the year at the dawn, the ageless hills, the young men and women who could never grow old. Someone called that the bus had arrived, that it was turning. Reluctantly they got up, brushing sand from their clothes, unwilling to relinquish the enchantment.

Tom laid his hand for a moment over Laura's. As if the words were compelled out of him against his will he said, " I never told you I loved you," and then pulled her to her feet. They joined the chattering crowd. At the door of the bus the young men stood back, to allow the girls in first.

Laura joined the group of girls, and Tom made no attempt to detain her. Once inside the bus she discovered the large heavy girl had kept a place for her and was beckoning. Laura sat down.

" Hasn't it been a lovely day ? " the girl said.

" Lovely," said Laura, and was surprised that her voice didn't sound like a peal of bells.

" I went up into the woods. Mr. McConachie came with us," the girl volunteered. Mr. McConachie was the teacher.

" He's very nice when you get to know him," the girl went on ; " it was lovely in the woods."

Laura glanced at her. The heavy profile was unchanged, she was not transfigured. The two girls sat in happy silence while the bus carried its load of immortals through the spring dusk, past hedges shining palely with blackthorn, back to Belfast.

They had seemed immortal, but they were not. George had told her yesterday that Tom was dead. Ten years ago, George said. She knew she should have been able to feel grief, but since she had excluded Tom from her thoughts for so long, and he was already dead for ten years, she could not feel anything. She had felt so much during the last few days that she could allow even the news of Tom's death to drop into her mind without being hurt by it. It was possible, she had learnt, deliberately to numb oneself. George's coming had touched her, not Tom's death.

Why should it touch her ? Tom had married, George said, married soon after he reached America. He had a son, no doubt the darling of his widowed mother. The boy was an artist too. Laura hoped the boy's promise of artistic talent had been evident early enough to give Tom pleasure. She would go and see the boy's pictures herself, George had suggested it. Perhaps she would see the boy. A current of excitement ran through her. She was surprised to feel it.

She had reached the top of the garden now, and stood looking back at the house, at Marathon—at her house. It was not easy to realise. Mr. McAlister had said it was her house. She came up through the orchard slowly, across the lawn and onto the wide sweep of gravel. The gravel was made of rounded pebbles, larger than most gravel, and noisy under the feet. Laura usually liked to skirt it by walking along the grass verge as far as it was possible. But now she trod boldly out into the centre of the drive, and scorning the side door by which she had left the house came round to the broad front step, and into Marathon by her own front door.

Miss Parks was in the hall. She was wearing an apron, and carrying a small watering-can with a long spout. Laura greeted her. " That's a lovely morning, Miss Parks."

" Oh, there you are, Laura."

" I've been out in the garden. The crab apple's in full bloom, and the sun's quite warm. You really should come and see."

" Shortly, dear, shortly, when I've finished." Miss Parks carried the watering-can over to a row of plants that stood in ornamental brass pots at the back of the hall. " I shall come when I have time. I'm just watering the plants." A few drops of water from the can fell onto the tiles. Miss Parks set down the can and mopped at the water with a cloth. I am nothing if not efficient, her action said. See how careful I am in the performance of this self-imposed duty. Laura's pleasure evaporated. She said, " I'd forgotten it was Thursday."

Miss Parks nodded, and moved the nozzle of the can to another plant. " I thought you had when I saw you going off into the garden when you came downstairs."

" But, Miss Parks, why didn't you remind me ? "

Miss Parks kept her eyes on her work, so much for each plant and no more. " Why should I remind you, dear ? "

" I could have come and helped you."

" Why should you ? I just thought to myself when I saw you going off, if she's able to forget for a while, how fortunate she is."

Miss Parks' hand trembled with evident emotion ; the can shook a little, and again water was spilt and the cloth brought into action.

All Laura's composure seeped out of her. " I—I only forgot it was Thursday."

Miss Parks sniffed. She could not wield a watering-can, a cloth and a handkerchief, so sniffing was the only course open to her. " Mildred liked routine so much, didn't she ?

Everything done at the proper time—and in the proper way, of course. It meant a great deal to her, didn't it?"

Laura did not need Miss Parks to tell her that. Mildred's illness had come on her slowly, over the last six years. A less resolute spirit than hers would have taken to her bed much sooner. But to Mildred, the human body was a piece of machinery which the mind was forced, during its earthly stay, to inhabit, but a piece of machinery which the mind could and should control and direct. It was nothing to be proud of, this body, still less to take pleasure in, but simply an enforced point of location. If she had not ignored the recurrent pain so long she might not have been beyond surgical help when at last she had to consult her doctor. But she was not so much afraid of illness as embarrassed at this evidence of her own frailty. Gradually her sphere of activity narrowed. She could not visit the houses of the few friends who had survived from her schooldays, her attendances at church and at church meetings were less regular, she was not seen so often in the garden at Marathon —it was not possible to walk smoothly and without pain on that coarse gravel. She gave up her regular visits to the kitchen—Hannah knew her work, and in any case could be summoned to the drawing-room to listen to a complaint. Mildred's day was divided between the drawing-room and her bedroom, with the difficult business of the stairs that lay between. But the care of the plants in the hall and in the drawing-room was the last household responsibility that Mildred relinquished. Every Thursday while she could still move about Laura had attended her—Mildred with the watering-can, Laura with the cloth—and Mildred gave the plants water and picked off the dead leaves. Her interest in the plants' welfare became almost an obsession. She took no pleasure in their beauty, but only in so far as they were hers, dependent on her. Every new leaf they put up was at her ordering, every flower a direct compliment to her. If one of them did not thrive it was a matter for concern and speculation. Every Thursday they were watered. Laura had done the watering herself once Mildred could not leave her bed, reporting to her sister on each individual plant, but never missing a Thursday. And now, because Mildred was dead, this Thursday, this first Thursday, she had forgotten.

Miss Parks was glad she had forgotten. In fact Miss Parks had been waiting for her to forget. Mildred had been one of Miss Parks' pupils at school, and though not particularly intimate—Mildred made no close friends—Miss Parks had persisted in the acquaintance in later years, and during Mildred's slow illness had visited her regularly. She was the only visitor who had stayed the whole course, swallowing Mildred's criticisms, choosing to ignore Mildred's lack of cordiality. Miss Parks had a reason for this persistence. She had given up her school-teaching early in order to keep house for her bachelor brother, the Reverend Cuthbert Parks, and had enjoyed the status of minister's wife without the usual quiver full of encumbrances. She had presided at Committee Meetings, opened Sales of Work, visited hospitals, poked a privileged but oh so dutiful finger into many a family's private concerns. She was a wonderful woman, and she knew how many of his flock told her brother that he was fortunate to have her. Then the blow fell. Whether the Reverend Cuthbert grew weary of this universal commendation, or whether he preferred a wife to a wonderful woman, he decided to get married, and chose a plump and comely woman whose services had been enlisted to teach the Sunday School children choral speaking for the Missionary Tableau.

Miss Parks had to recreate her world. She moved out of the Manse before the bride arrived, found herself a bedsitting-room at the opposite end of Belfast—this meant she had a legitimate reason for changing her place of worship, and would not be obliged to go every Sunday to hear her brother preach and see his wife ensconced in the Manse pew. She did a little private scholastic coaching to spin out her small income. And she visited Mildred.

At Marathon the large rooms and the unhurried pace, the respectful servants and the many luxuries of life that were not luxuries here but everyday necessities were balm to her distressed spirit. She tolerated Mildred's tongue and bided her time. Little by little Mildred came to rely on her. Little by little Miss Parks assumed small duties and responsibilities and was never found wanting. Her manner with the servants was beyond reproach, never familiar, but as one who is accustomed to have servants about. She was careful not to overstep the mark, not to forget that Laura was Mildred's sister, whereas she was only her devoted friend. During the last month she had come to live at Marathon. At whose invitation it was difficult to say, but she had moved in, and was established before Laura had realised it. Mildred made no protest, nor expressed any gratitude. And still Miss Parks had bided her time.

Yesterday, after the funeral cortège had left the house Miss Parks had her first taste of power. It was at her reminder that the blinds had not immediately been drawn up, it was her refusal to drink tea at an hour when Mildred never drank it that had made Laura refuse tea also. And again, this morning, she had watched with satisfaction as Laura made her escape into the garden, and then put on Mildred's apron, filled Mildred's watering-can, and taken over the duty of watering the plants. She did not wish to return to her own small bed-sitting-room in Ashley Avenue. It seemed possible, probable even, that she would not have to do so.

So she watched the brightness fade out of Laura's face, and when Laura murmured again, " I'm so sorry, Miss Parks. I can't think why you didn't tell me," she replied kindly, " My dear, why should you be sorry ? I've enjoyed this little task, and it makes me feel I'm still just the tiniest bit of use in the house, even though dear Mildred has gone."

" Oh but, Miss Parks, of course you are. You've been so kind, so very kind. I don't know what I should have done without you."

Miss Parks smiled. " It's fortunate then for both of us, isn't it, that I don't have to rush away at once and leave you ? "

Laura said something Miss Parks didn't catch, but she chose to translate it as an agreement.

" I've come to feel so very much at home here, dear Laura, you must know that."

Laura's reply was again inaudible. She blinked, swallowed, and turned to look out of the window. She will come to it, Miss Parks thought, there is no sense in forcing the issue, gently does it. She stooped again over the plants, her manner was maternal.

" Ah, Laura ! Look ! Just look what I've found."

Laura came to see. Together they bent over the pot. " I declare—yes, it is—a bud ! I don't think I ever saw this plant flower before. Does it have flowers often, Laura ? "

No, Laura could not remember that plant ever having borne a flower.

" Well, I declare ! Think of that ! I wonder how long it will be before it comes out. Not very long. I shall watch it carefully—and of course water it regularly—and in a few weeks, Laura, we shall see ! "

It had never flowered for Mildred. It was going to flower for her. Surely a fortunate omen ? Miss Parks was filled with delight. Her delight was short-lived. The bell rang and Hannah came to answer it. As she crossed the hall the two women moved into the drawing-room. Shortly Hannah came in to announce, " Miss Laura, Master George is here asking to see you."

Laura's joy was evident. " Oh thank you. Will you just ask him to come in, Hannah."

Miss Parks said, " You didn't tell me you were expecting your brother, Laura."

" No, I wasn't expecting him." Laura had turned to the door, she had already forgotten Miss Parks, her own neglected duty, the auspicious bud on the barren plant. She was listening to George's footsteps coming across the hall.

Miss Parks knew she had lost ground, but she gathered herself for an orderly retreat. " Then I'll just leave you alone, shall I ? You won't want me."

Laura did not contradict her and George came in.

" Good morning, Laura."

" George dear." She was holding her hands out to him, he was kissing her cheek.

" Good morning, Mr. Percival."

George drew away from Laura. " Oh good morning, Miss Parks. Glad to see you've got the blinds up. Makes things look more cheerful, can't think why you didn't have them up yesterday, Laura. And that's a beautiful morning."

" So Laura tells me," said Miss Parks. " I haven't had time to go and look at it yet. Well—I'll leave you." And she turned for the door.

Chapter Seven

GEORGE had not intended to come back to Marathon quite so soon. When he had reached home the previous evening, after the funeral, he found Amy and Kathie had had their tea. Kathie was sitting at one end of the table in the living-room with her homework spread out all round her. How much the room had shrunk since he had left it this morning! How low the ceiling, how flimsy the door that he closed behind him as he came in out of the narrow hall. A couple of hours at Marathon and all the old standards had re-asserted themselves. Doors were solidly-built affairs with panels of carefully matched grain and brass finger-plates and doorknobs; they swung heavily behind you, and they closed easily and conclusively, and stayed closed. They were not like this door—an ill-fitting shutter of warped wood whose latch was temperamental and whose small handle did not fill the hand.

Amy was in the scullery, standing at the gas cooker, busy with the frying-pan. She turned her head for a moment, and spoke above the hiss of the hot fat. " Well ? " she asked. He knew what she meant, but pretended not to know.

" Tea nearly ready ? " he said. " Good, I'm hungry. Had a busy day."

Amy speeded up her cooking, and it was not until she had made his tea and dished up his kippers and laid them before him that she repeated her query, " Well ? "

" It all went off," he said, " according to plan."

Amy did not know what to make of this. Levity when it came to funerals was not the thing, not the thing at all. You only died once, when all was said and done. One spoke with respect of the dead, no matter how one spoke of the living. She herself made a monthly pilgrimage to the City Cemetery to lay flowers on the grave of her old ruffian of a father, who was commended to his Maker by the headstone in no uncertain words of praise. Yet here was George, her husband, able to sit at the table with his mouth full of kippers, announcing in that mocking voice of his (how she loved his voice) that his sister's funeral had ' all gone off

70

according to plan '. She had her own private views on George's sisters who lived in that big house and never paid any attention to him, but she kept them to herself. Her intuitive wit told her that George was happier with her than he had ever been with them, and she didn't propose to argue with this. But no matter what Miss Mildred Percival might or might not have been while she was living, it was a different matter now that she was dead. Convention demanded a measure of loyalty to the departed. All the same Amy felt full of admiration for this fine fellow of a husband of hers who could come back from his sister's funeral, sit down to a good tea, stretch his legs under the table and say, " It all went off according to plan."

" How did you find your other sister, poor soul ? " she asked.

" Very nicely, thank you," George said, and then as always unable to let slip the chance of a compliment, " Do you know, I think she was glad to see me."

" Of course she would be glad to see you. What did I tell you ? A woman needs a man about the house at a time like what she's been through."

George stirred his tea and ate his kippers and thought what an excellent woman his wife was. She said the things he wanted to hear her say, and it didn't matter in how common a voice she said them. Actually it hadn't all gone off according to plan. He'd been more than a little upset at old McAlister taking the offensive like that. Good God, was he always going to be judged on his merits or demerits of twenty years ago ? And he didn't like Miss Parks any more than he liked her twenty years earlier when she used to come to Marathon to Mildred's tea-parties. But Laura's welcome—that at least he had counted on, and he hadn't been wrong.

" Poor little Laura," he said, " she's had a tough time, I'm afraid."

" That's sickness for you—as bad for them that's doing the nursing as it is for them that's lying."

George wondered if it had, in fact, been as bad for Mildred. He found himself hoping that it had.

Amy came and sat at the table, hoping the warm food would loosen his tongue. " Was it a big funeral ? "

" No, very small."

" I suppose they would carry the coffin the length of the tramlines ? " In Amy's circle the respect one bore the dead was measured in yards by the length for which the coffin was carried shoulder high from the house before it was finally put into the hearse. George did not intend Amy to know he had not actually followed the funeral, but he remembered that the hearse, as it passed him on the corner, was travelling at a moderate speed, so he said with confidence, " Oh no. Which of us do you think Mildred would have trusted with that ? "

Amy looked frankly shocked, and Kathie let a giggle out of her and glanced up from her books. " When do we move in, Pop ? " she asked.

George told her sharply to get on with her lessons, and he himself finished his tea without any further confidences. He was a little worried about Kathie. When she was small he had been delighted with her quick mind and her pert tongue, but he was realising that they might prove inconvenient. A cute child is amusing. But Kathie would soon be a woman, and he liked his womenfolk as comfortably stupid as Amy—and as devoted. There was more of himself in Kathie than he cared to see. And yet what had the child said that was wrong ? Why should she not expect that they might ' move in ' to share this big family house with his sister ? It was the obvious conclusion : the child had seen it, it must be obvious. He would assume that it was obvious, and would pay Laura another visit in the morning.

Even so it was with some misgivings that he presented himself. When he had said to Amy, ' Laura was glad to see me,' he had meant a great deal more than that. Laura's delight had been most touching. He didn't want it to be like that. He disliked a show of emotion in other people as much as he mistrusted it in himself. Laura's welcome had wakened a response in him. He remembered many things he had forgotten about her : Laura, white-faced but loyal during those interminable meals where the tension round the table made eating almost a physical impossibility, Laura sitting in the orchard once when Tom had been there, when her pretty soft hair had got tangled in a drooping branch, Laura in her blue dressing-gown, standing at the top of the stairs on that night when he had come home in the full glory of whiskey, and her look of pity and horror as the light faded out of him, and he was filled with sickness and self-disgust. In maintaining his dislike for Mildred, George had forgotten that he had been fond of Laura. He did not wish to become fond of Laura. It did not suit his plan of action. Nor did he wish Laura to be uncontrolled in her expression of affection for him. He was glad to accept Amy's love because it was rooted and grounded in pleasure and admiration of him. But Laura knew him for what he was really like, and her love had its roots in pity. It would not help George to have Laura pity him. She held the subtle advantage of having known him in his immaturity. There is a nakedness in nursery recollection that to a man like George, who had put on his manhood with difficulty, was quite unbearable.

If he could believe that he, George, was coming back into Laura's drab life to give it a little brightness, that was all right. 'Poor little Laura, she'd had a pretty tough time.' But if Laura was taking back her failure of a brother and his unfortunate family into the old home out of the kindness of her heart—well, the little house at Ballydrum had its points.

So it was with the determination to act the part of the large easy, friendly—not too friendly—brother that he came to Marathon that morning. It was in the same spirit that he greeted Laura, commended the sunlight streaming into the room, and deplored the blinds of the previous evening, and did not contradict Miss Parks when she said that she would leave them as they would not want her.

He waited till the door closed behind her. " How long is *she* staying here ? "

" Miss Parks ? I don't know."

" I do. She's staying until you kick her out yourself."

" George, how could I ? She's been so kind, I don't know how I could. At all events not immediately."

" Why not ? That's why I came round again this morning. Laura, you've got to make your mind up what you're going to do with yourself. Otherwise you'll find you're being run into some plan before you know where you are."

" I don't want to be hurried, George."

He put his hands on her shoulders and gave her a little shake.

" I don't care what you want ; you're going to be hurried."

" I don't think you've any right to hurry me, George."

" Because I haven't been near you for twenty years ? My quarrel was with Father and with Mildred—never with you.　Surely you know that."

" Oh, George, of course I do."　The easy tears rose in her tired eyes.　He was annoyed to feel his own eyes prickle.

" Poor Laura.　I would have stayed if it would have helped anybody.　But there was nothing but trouble when I was at home."

For a little while the years were forgotten, and they were just George and Laura, remembering and regretting things that had happened while they were still young enough to be cruelly hurt by them.

" Oh, Laura, the rows, the endless rows—and the silences. I don't know which were the worst.　Even today do you know I was glad the study door was closed when I came through the hall.　I shouldn't have liked coming past if it had been open."

" Do you feel like that too ? " Laura asked.　" I keep that door closed."

" You don't blame me for clearing off?　Wasn't it better to admit that the thing just didn't work and clear out ? "

" I suppose it was.　Have you ever been sorry ? "

" Only when I've wanted something for Amy or Kathie and they've had to go without it."　That was a stupid thing for him to say.　Honesty might be disarming up to a point, but might it not also forewarn ?　There was one question he must ask.　He would ask it now and be done with it.

" Did Mildred ever talk about me ? "

" No."

" Not even—— ? "

" Not once."

At least he had asked, and he had had his answer.　He put an arm round her shoulders, but she moved away, a little uneasily.　" You mustn't be too sorry for me, George."

" Mustn't I ?　Why ? "

" After all I was only doing my duty."

Laura said it without a trace of self-righteousness, but it annoyed him at once, broke the spell of friendship which for a few moments had surrounded them, and to which he had allowed himself to surrender. Duty! George had no use for duty. Why couldn't Laura admit it had been a hell of a life, that she'd been a fool to get run in for it, that at least it was over now, and they could congratulate each other and thank God together?

" Your duty! Is that what you call it? "

" But it was, George." Her small colourless face was turned to him, imploring him to agree with her. " After all, Mildred was my sister."

" Your sister? Yes, so she was. She was your sister, so she was able to keep you here out of a sense of family obligation—she was your sister so she could nag and nag and know you would hold your tongue—she was your sister so she could say the small things that she knew would hurt the most——"

" Stop! Please don't talk that way, George. It hasn't been like that at all."

" Hasn't it? "

" No—you are not to think it has been like that."

" Laura, don't be absurd. It's no use pretending to me, I know what Mildred was better than most. Besides I've been talking to Miss Parks, and she says——"

" Miss Parks has no business to tell you anything."

" No business," he pressed, " no business perhaps, but there is something to be told."

" Mildred was ill."

" All that time—for twenty years? "

" George, don't shout at me. I was ill for a long time myself, just after father died."

" I know," he said, " I heard about that. Poor Laura! What was wrong with you? "

" I was—just ill."

All right, thought George, she doesn't want to tell me.

" I was a long time getting better. Mildred looked after me. It was for several years."

" And then you turned round and looked after Mildred."

" Yes, that's right." Laura smiled. It is all quite easy, her smile said. It is all quite easy when you explain it like that.

"But why did you give up your friends, Laura—and your painting? You say you hardly ever go out."

"How could I" she said, "when Mildred was ill?"

We are going round and round in circles. "I know what it's been like, looking after Mildred," he said, "you needn't think I don't. Mildred always bullied us. But you never gave in to it before like this. Do you know how much you've changed?"

Laura said, "I'm older, of course."

She acknowledged her worn face, her lack of beauty with such simplicity and meekness that George was angry. It was wrong that any woman could speak like that. Women were beauty—or at all events they should imagine themselves to be, so that men might tell them so. When Amy was eighty, and as bent and raddled as they make them, she would still lift her eyelids in the old way to demand her due of homage. Thank God for it! She'd get it, too.

"I know I've changed, George; but I'm older."

"That isn't what I mean." He gripped her by the arms, peering pitilessly into her drab face. She didn't even try to avoid his gaze. "Why did you let her do it to you, Laura?"

"I had to. There was no one else."

George skipped the thought that there might have been himself. He said deliberately, "I didn't know your attachment to Mildred went as deep as that."

Suddenly her face crumpled and became unbecomingly flushed. She twisted away from him and went to the window; she was breathing quickly. "You mustn't say that. I wasn't attached to her."

I've done it, George thought. I've broken her.

"*What* did you say?" he asked. He wanted to make her say it again.

"I wasn't attached to her. George, I—I hated her! I hated her, do you hear? I've hated every day of every year I've lived here since you went away. I've hated everything I've had to do for her, every little thing!"

George did not answer directly. He could not. Those were the words he had wanted to hear her say, had compelled her to say, but now that they were spoken he was shocked by them, and at the bitterness with which they were spoken. They were unbecoming words for any woman to speak, least of all Laura.

Gentleness was the attribute with which in his imagination Laura was chiefly endowed. She wasn't made for hating. Shame for his own shirked responsibility stirred in him uneasily. Laura was still standing at the window; he couldn't see her face. He didn't think she was weeping, he wasn't sure. If it had been Amy he would have known what to do, but with Laura he felt out of his depth. He would have slid one clever arm round Amy's waist and turned her towards him. He knew the words to use to Amy and the voice to speak them with. They would both have been the better of it : Amy with her grief comforted, he reassured by his power to comfort. But Laura—no. That wasn't the way.

"I hated her, George." She wasn't crying. Her voice was low but controlled, frightening in its intensity. She had hated Mildred, he knew that now, without any doubt.

"Then why in God's name did you stay ? Why didn't you get out, Laura ? You needn't have stayed when it was like that."

"I had to."

"I don't see why."

"What else could I have done ? Where could I have gone ? And she looked after me while I was ill. I had to stay with her and look after her. You do see, George, I had to."

She spoke with peculiar emphasis. It is tremendously important to her that she should believe she had to stay, George thought. She knows how much she lost by staying, and she wants to be persuaded that it was the only course open to her, and that she did what was right. It is the only comfort she will have for the memory of all those pitiless years.

She looked up into his face, compelling him to agree. He could not refuse. "Poor Laura," he said, and watched the ugly anxiety fade from her face, "of course you had to stay."

"You see, George, I owed it to her."

"And she saw that you paid it."

"I did, George, didn't I ? The minister said that I did."

She is like a child, thought George, a middle-aged child, pathetic and transparent. She had never learnt to put on the protective armour that he had been at such pains to assume. Mildred had seen to that. He was filled with anger and disgust that Laura should have been brought to these straits.

" You heard what the minister said, George ? "

" Yes, I heard. You did a grand job, Laura. You repaid all you owed to Mildred. You have that to remember."

Let her have all the assurance she needs, he told himself. If she believes strongly enough then little by little as the years slip past the bitterness will wear thin in remembering how well she paid her debt. It is all she has now, husband, home, children to her, this service that she did for Mildred. All right, he wouldn't grudge her the glory. She was welcome to it. Besides if she knew the debt to be paid in its entirety it would serve his own purposes better.

" But it's over now, Laura. That's what you've got to remember, paid up to the last halfpenny. You've got only yourself to think of now."

She smiled rather vaguely. " I know, George. It seems so odd."

" I expect it does. But you'll get used to it."

" You will have to help me, won't you ? "

" Of course I will." He wondered if she guessed how readily he gave that assurance.

" The money, George," she said, so unexpectedly that it startled him ; " the way she left the money to me ' In Trust ' —that means I'm still under an obligation to her where the money's concerned. I must use it in a way she'd have approved ? "

George would have preferred not to have this question asked nakedly like this, or at least to have had notice of it.

" That was Mildred's idea. That was why she worded the will in the way she did. But it doesn't really bind you in any way. The money is yours now, whatever you choose to do with it."

Laura didn't answer at once. When she did she spoke with difficulty. " It seems—a more shocking thing to disregard a person's wishes after they are dead."

George put a finger under her chin and turned her face

up to him. With Amy the gesture would have been instinctive and easy, and Amy's response immediate. With Laura it was experimental, but she did not draw back.

"Laura, look at me," he said, in full seriousness. "Mildred *isn't here* any more. Neither here lying on the sofa, or upstairs in her room. She's dead, Laura. She simply does not exist any more. She has no wishes. Nothing you can do now will hurt or please her."

The gravity of what he was saying bore down on them both. She looked at him earnestly and then suddenly self-conscious drew away. "I know. I know you think me stupid. But it's odd, you see. She knew everything I thought and everything I did. If I said one thing and was thinking another, she *knew*."

"Then she knew that you hated her?"

She turned to him quickly, appalled. He knew that she had as yet barely realised Mildred's death. Mildred was still at her elbow.

"George! You don't really think that?"

"It doesn't matter whether she knew or not." He spoke with deliberate bluntness, trying to shock her into realisation. "It doesn't matter a tuppeny ticket. That's what I'm trying to tell you. Mildred's dead, and—whether she knew you hated her or whether she didn't—it simply doesn't matter now."

She received this calmly. "I see. I think I see. I must get used to being on my own, that's what it is."

"Not quite on your own, remember," he teased her gently, "not as long as I'm around."

"Oh, thank you, George. You have been so kind."

"And don't you forget you have a duty to your brother. You hadn't thought that one up, had you?"

"No, I hadn't." She laughed uncertainly.

"You've been neglecting me shamefully, you know. So you make up your mind to come and stay with us for a while till you think things over and decide what to do with the house."

"Shall I?"

He had no intention that she should settle down with them in Ballydrum, but his real plan could be expounded later when she had seen the little house and had had time to compare its shoddy cosiness with the solid comfort of Marathon.

"We'll go about a bit, shall we?"

"Oh yes."

"Where would you like to go?"

"I don't know. I haven't been anywhere for ages. George, do you think we could go to see that exhibition of pictures—by Tom's son?"

"Of course we will. There are lots of things we can do. And Amy'll take you shopping. You can buy some clothes."

"I don't think I really need any more clothes."

"You may think that, but wait till Amy gets her hands on you. She'll teach you how to spend your money." Perhaps that wasn't a wise thing to say. Amy knew how to spend, and how not to spend her money. It was he who needed to learn. But the words came out of him in that easy flush of self-confidence, that sudden camaraderie, that necessity to say what the other person wants to hear. His elation at the easy victory possessed his tongue.

Laura was laughing. "Oh, George, you are silly."

It was good to hear her laugh. It was good to stand here in the drawing-room at Marathon, with his elbows on the broad mantelpiece and one foot on the brass fender, to hear Laura laugh and to laugh himself, and to plan that his wife should take Laura on a shopping orgy to spend some of Mildred's money. It was what Laura needed, he told himself. Of course it was what she needed. Poor little Laura.

Laura gave a long sigh of pleasure. She came and stood beside him and put one hand on his. "Oh, George, looking back on it all now I feel—I feel as if I'd been in prison as long as I could remember."

"Well, the door's open now, and you just walk out."

"Is it as easy as that?"

"Just as easy as that."

"Oh, George," she said, her face transfigured with relief and gladness. "Oh, George, I believe it is."

Chapter Eight

FRIDAY was a difficult day at Marathon, as if the household, after meeting the emergency of Mildred's death and her funeral, found it difficult to adjust itself to life again. So much of the day had revolved on Mildred and her necessities, so much of the conversation turned on her condition, whether she had slept well or badly, whether the doctor would come before lunch or after, whether the new drug was preferable to the old, that bereft of all this the hours limped past. Miss Parks had hoped that Laura would have taken the chance of a day in bed—she must be tired, she must need the rest, and it would provide Hannah and herself with a pivot for their activities—but Laura had risen for breakfast and declared that she had slept well. Miss Parks felt annoyed. Laura was slipping up badly on the finer points of behaviour. It would have been much more becoming for her to have lain in bed. A week ago she would have made the suggestion herself, and Laura would have agreed meekly. Miss Parks had looked forward to assuming the role of chief support of the household ; she would have consulted Hannah over the question of meals—light but nourishing—have answered the telephone, received any callers.

There were, in any case, no callers, for the household had exhausted its slender stock of friends during the previous few days. The telephone rang twice. It was Mr. McAlister the first time. Miss Parks thought it unnecessary of him to ask to speak to Laura personally—she could quite well have given her his message—but she gathered that Mr. McAlister was coming to see Laura the following afternoon. The second time the phone rang Miss Parks was up in Mildred's room, sorting through some of her personal belongings. Laura had welcomed her suggestion that she should do this, but had shown no inclination to join her. Instead she had gone off into the garden by herself (so unhealthy, this quiet brooding, Miss Parks told herself, but what could you do ?). Miss Parks was glad to have the chance of handling Mildred's clothing and her shoes and hats. It gave her a sense of power that the disposal of them should lie with her. And it would add greatly to her prestige at her new church when she was able to give so fine a contribution to the Jumble Sale. But she was sorry that she had not been downstairs to answer the telephone herself. It was Hannah who answered it, and Miss Parks heard her calling Laura in from the garden to take the call. Laura spoke for a long time. Twice she laughed. At last the telephone was replaced, but Laura went out into the garden again and did not come in till Hannah called them both for afternoon tea, nor did she make any reference to the call. Miss Parks could have asked Hannah, but she knew better. Hannah was a servant of the old-fashioned school, with old-fashioned ideas and codes of behaviour. If Miss Parks were to succeed with her she knew she must not overstep the boundary laid between mistress and maid. So she must be content to remain ignorant of who it was who had called Laura on the phone.

Laura came in to tea with an air of excitement. She ate and drank, and talked without prompting. She had lost the numb look which she had worn during the last weeks. She could even give an opinion for herself.

"Do you think, Laura, dear, you should order some printed cards thanking your friends for their letters of sympathy? I could see to it for you?"

"There haven't been so many letters," Laura said, regarding Miss Parks over her teacup.

It was unnecessary for her to put this into words; indeed there had been few letters, pitifully few, but she need not have said so.

"You mean you will answer them all personally?" Miss Parks said. "Of course that is the best way if you feel you can do it. People do appreciate a personal reply, and I am quite sure that is what Mildred would have wished herself."

"We'll have the printed ones," Laura said at once, and Miss Parks was too shocked to furnish an immediate reply.

Laura's mood of mild elation lasted into the following day. "I'm going into town," she said at the breakfast table. "I shan't be in to lunch." She turned to Hannah who was serving them. "You can look after lunch for Miss Parks, Hannah."

"I can do that," Hannah said, with no show of enthusiasm. "You will be in for lunch, Miss Parks?"

" Well—yes, I suppose I shall, Laura dear.   We are not all
as fortunate as you are to have a luncheon appointment."
Then in case she had spoken too pointedly—she was moving
warily with this new Laura—Miss Parks added, " Of course
I don't want to be any trouble.   Anything at all will do for
me.   Hannah knows that, don't you, Hannah ? "

Hannah was not to be enlisted either.   " Mrs. Ritchie'll
be here, and she'll be wanting her dinner anyway.   You
can't be cleaning on an empty stomach," was all she said.

Miss Parks was defeated.   She was to have a share of the
servants' meal, even though she did not have to work for it.
That was what it amounted to.   She did not look forward
to her solitary lunch, served in the dining-room with the
kitchen door opening and shutting on Mrs. Ritchie's chatter.
Miss Parks hadn't felt so unsure of her ground since she
had come to Marathon.   It was all proving much more difficult than she had anticipated.   To make matters worse the
morning paper had borne an announcement that she had
expected but hardly braced herself to see—the birth of a
son and heir to her brother, the Reverend Cuthbert, and his
plump-voiced wife.   Miss Parks had heard the baby was on
the way, had caught a glimpse of the expectant mother
shopping in Royal Avenue, large and well pleased with herself
in an ample swagger coat, like a laden ship in full sail.   She
knew she must call at the Manse, express her good wishes,
deliver a gift of pale blue knitting, smile her pleasure at the
event to any of the parishioners she met, and it would not
be easy to do.   Her own old bedroom, she supposed, would
be the nursery now.   She could have done it if she could
have said that she was now established at Marathon—helping
Laura Percival, poor Laura, you know how nervous she
always was, and of course since her sister's death she has
become almost an invalid herself and needs care and sympathy till she is on her feet again—but it looked as if Laura
needed neither sympathy nor care, and that Miss Parks might
find herself back again in the bed-sitting-room in Ashley
Avenue.   So she sat a little longer than was necessary over
her breakfast, listening to Laura crossing the hall and going
up the wide stairs, and at last to Laura's door closing.   Laura
had somewhere to go.   She hadn't said where she was going,
or asked Miss Parks to go with her.   Long purposeless

weeks stretched in front of Miss Parks in her tired imagination—weeks unpunctuated even by a committee meeting, nothing for which her continued existence mattered. She made an effort to shake the mood off her, and rising to her feet commenced to clear the remainder of the breakfast dishes away with fussy zeal, in an effort to prove, to herself at least, that she was indispensable.

Laura took her own time to prepare to go to town, and it was well after half-past ten before she came out of her room. The door of Mildred's bedroom was closed—she was glad of that. Hannah and Mrs. Ritchie had cleaned it out, Miss Parks had made a superficial survey of the contents of the wardrobe, and the door was closed. She came downstairs slowly, like a child coming to a party, savouring the moments when the waiting is over and the pleasure is part of the here and now, yet not already begun.

The drawing-room door was open. There was no sign of Miss Parks. Laura thought she must be in her own room. From the kitchen came the clatter of dishes as Hannah and Mrs. Ritchie prepared their eleven-o'clock tea. Laura halted for a moment in the hall, just outside the drawing-room door. She could see the sofa in the window. Laura could not remember any time since she had been a girl that she had set off on an errand in town and had gone past the drawing-room door without entering. A month ago Mildred would have been on the sofa. Laura would have crossed the hall in small steps, trying to hush her footsteps on the tiles.

" I'm going now, Mildred."

Mildred would have turned to her slowly. Laura waited for her scrutiny. Slowly the head was turned and the eyes looked at her.

" You're wearing that hat."

No criticism would be offered. But the comment was implied that it seemed an extraordinary hat to choose, an unbecoming hat to the wearer, and a hat unsuitable for the occasion.

" Yes." Laura admitted it.

Mildred would sigh deeply. If that was the hat Laura chose to wear—well, that was all there was to be said or done about it.

" You'll take an umbrella ? "

" Yes."

" You have the list of messages."

" Yes." Laura would open her handbag, and the list which had been there as she left her room would momentarily disappear as she fumbled for it. Then she would find it. " Here it is."

Mildred would smile but say nothing.

" Turn round."

This was the most humiliating moment of all, a slow revolving on the heel while Mildred's eyes examined her from top to toe for straying wisps of hair, a sagging skirt, uneven stocking seams. It was a survival of the years directly after Laura's illness when she could not have faced the outside world and its terrors without the assurance which Mildred's scrutiny gave her. Mildred rarely had any comment to make now, but Laura was conscious of her slow sick eyes travelling over her body, from the unfortunate hat to the calves of her legs which, thinning as she got older, did not now fill the thick silk stockings that covered them.

At last a dismissal and the escape to the outer world, but with all confidence gone and a bad taste in the mouth, and Mildred's eyes still following her from the window as she went down the drive. Laura knew the exact turn of the drive when she would be no longer visible from the window. After that the moments were coloured by the necessity of a punctual return.

But not this morning. This morning Laura paused in the hall just long enough to assure herself that she was not hurrying past the door, then called down the passage in the direction of the kitchen, " I'm off now, Hannah," and went out through the hall door and down the drive. Once she stopped and looked back at the house. Yes, the sofa in the window was empty.

George was waiting for her at the hotel. He had gone there early because he wanted to have time to spend, savouring the hotel and its appointments. It was the hotel to which his father had always come when lunching in town, to which George had accompanied him during the short spell of his apprenticeship in the business. It had been badly damaged during an air raid, and George had not been in it since it had been rebuilt and redecorated. While his father was

alive he had avoided it. Once he had married Amy it was
far beyond his pocket—when she joined him in Belfast during
a day's careful shopping they lunched at Woolworth's
Snackery—but for the same reason that he wished to reassert
himself at Marathon George had invited Laura to lunch
with him at this hotel. His father had looked on it as almost
his own personal property—had received like services in it
—but it was no place for his fool of a son. And now the
fool of a son had come back to it, and was enjoying a lazy
cigarette in the foyer as if he had never left it.

George sat and watched the people threading through the
foyer, people with an air of money about them, people to
whom this hotel furnished a meal that was adequate but not
extraordinarily lavish, who would not feel their pockets
noticeably lighter after it. He did not feel out of place in
this company—after all, it was his birthright. He hadn't
ordered himself a drink although he wanted one, because
he knew just how much money he had in his pocket. He
was relying on Laura to pay for the lunch—she would have
the sense to suggest it, wouldn't she? He would make
some play on his own poverty during the meal to bring the
necessity home to her. If she didn't, of course, he had his
month's cheque in his pocket, he could always ask them to
cash it; but that would be more than ordinarily awkward.
Amy expected to have that cheque passed on to her un-
broken. It was a humiliation to which he had submitted
rather than fight about it. He recognised its necessity and
handed over his cheque to her every month, and she made a
just and fair allocation of the money to him. He hardly
minded doing this now. Amy knew enough to accept the
cheque in a way that made him feel his own magnanimity.
"There you are, gold-digger," he would say, "it's all yours."
He had come almost to enjoy the gesture. But it would
be a different matter to give her a collection of pounds,
shillings and pence, along with an explanation.

There were a couple of girls at the other side of the foyer,
drinking sherry, glancing at him. George appreciated their
interest. He had kept his looks, thank God. He was probably better-looking now in the early forties than he had been
at twenty. His slightness and extreme fairness of hair and
complexion gave an impression of youth which he used to

resent. But now the fair hair concealed the greying temples, the face was more firmly modelled, and the small moustache he had grown since he left the navy added distinction and strengthened the line of the indeterminate mouth. He let his glance rest a little longer than was necessary on the two gossiping well-dressed young women, then beckoned in a passing waiter and ordered himself a drink.

Of course Laura would pay for the lunch. He hadn't anything to be afraid of there. He took his drink, waving away the change, and drank it with slow enjoyment. He could see himself in a long mirror across the way. He settled down comfortably in his chair to wait for Laura, one ankle resting on the other knee, very much at his ease. Of course she would pay for the lunch. If she didn't—what the hell? He searched—and found—expert reasons to offer Amy for lunching Laura in this extravagant manner.

The place was more full of mirrors than he remembered it. There had been a lot of changes. Chromium plate and glass had replaced mahogany and brass, walls that had been covered with sombre encrusted wallpaper were colour-washed, strip lighting had succeeded massive electroliers. Where pictures of race-horses had hung—barrel-bodied animals with spider-thin legs—there were curious daubs that he could not interpret, in shades of lemon-green, sugar-pink, and an oddly aggressive blue. George thought he had preferred the old décor. Still the mirrors were welcome. Amy had made a good job of pressing this suit ; it looked quite presentable. Of course a lot depended on how a suit was worn. And he had kept his figure.

His drink was finished. He wondered if he had time for another one. Of course Laura would pay for the lunch. Here was Laura, coming in through the swing door. He was glad to see she appeared presentable, though unremarkable. He must get Amy to teach her to use a little make-up. It would furnish her small defenceless face whose nakedness embarrassed him. He rose to greet her.

Laura, it seemed, had been shopping. " I didn't buy very much, George, but I looked about."

" You'll have to fix up a day with Amy."

" That would be lovely." No, she wouldn't have a drink. They moved into the dining-room. " Lobster, George. I haven't had lobster for ages.   Mildred couldn't eat anything like that."

Of course she would pay for the lunch.

" What are you going to do afterwards ? "

" I don't know, really.   What time is it ? "

" A quarter past one."

" Oh lovely."

" Why ' lovely ' ? "

" Just asking the time and knowing it doesn't matter what the answer is.   You see, George, I've hardly ever been in town since Mildred was ill—only to the library, or something like that.   And I've always had to hurry back to be in time to bring her in her tea—you know, she liked it at four o'clock."

" I suppose she gave you hell if you were late."

" George, you really shouldn't say things like that."

" Why not, when they're true ? "

" I never was late.   But I was always afraid I might be."

" Couldn't Hannah have taken in her tea ? "

" She could, of course, but Mildred always waited for me. She used to lie on that sofa in the window, you know."

" I know."

" There's a turn in the drive where she could see me coming in—I know just where it is.   I always looked at the window when I got there, and she'd have the curtain pulled aside and be watching for me and waiting."

" Well, there's no one waiting today."

" Except Miss Parks."

" Her !   You don't care about her, do you ? "

" Oh no, of course not."

Good brave little Laura !   Miss Parks wasn't going to be any obstacle.

" We'll have liqueurs with our coffee."

" Oh, George, I don't think so.   I don't think I've ever had a liqueur.   I mightn't like it."

" You'll like the one I choose for you."

Of course she would pay for the lunch.   Of course she would.   He ordered liqueurs.

It was three o'clock before Laura left the hotel.   She hadn't really enjoyed the liqueur, but she did not like to say so to George.   The talk, the food, the crowded room, had made her feel a little confused.   Perhaps it was the liqueur.   She wondered if her behaviour was strange. She thought George had looked oddly at her when she bid him good-bye. She hoped she had thanked him adequately. It was really very good of him to entertain her to lunch—such a good lunch, too. She would have liked to offer to pay the bill, but of course George would have been offended at that. It would imply that she remembered what he had done with his money when he was a young man and that would be to take an unfair advantage. After all, he wouldn't have invited her if he hadn't been able to afford it. Of course he wouldn't.

The fresh air of the spring afternoon and the liqueur now made her bold to do what she had intended to do since she had left the house that morning. She had done a little shopping before lunch, it was true, small inconsiderable trifles, but more important she had discovered where the exhibition was, had walked past the poster once, just glimpsing the name ' Terence Richardson ', and then after standing gazing into the music shop until the surging of her quickened pulse had steadied, had walked past the poster again, and read it through, deliberately. Now she crossed Donegall Place, and without trusting herself to look at the name again stepped off the crowded pavement, and up the quiet stairway, feeling her way round the corner with eyes half-blind after the spring sunshine, and was in the large light room where the walls were hung with pictures, and people moved about, talking quietly, moving and talking.

After the noise and movement of the street this remote room with its glass roof and leisurely-moving soft-spoken people had an air of unreality, as if the room were a tank, the people slow-swimming fish whose mouths opened and shut silently, and the pictures brilliant strange submarine growth. Laura felt a moment of panic and turned to the door.

" Would you like a catalogue, ma'am ? "

A uniformed man sitting at a table handed one across to her.

" Oh, thank you. Thank you very much."

" One shilling, please. Thank you."

Laura paid her shilling and, holding her catalogue, joined the crowd. She must stay for a moment or two, appear interested just for a little while. Then she could find the street again. It wouldn't take her long, but for a little while she must stay.

A quick glance at the walls reassured her. She could safely look at these pictures without being reminded of Tom. In whatever other ways Terence Richardson might resemble his father he had not learned anything of painting from him. That gave her courage. She had no knowledge of contemporary art, since her illness she had not lifted a brush or looked at a picture. There was much here that she did not understand ; forms with an unfamiliar rhythm and difficult significance, a harsh almost brutal use of colour, a technique that seemed deliberately to ape the nursery, and yet a sincerity that came through it all and gave purpose and weight to the work. Without understanding it, she felt the sincerity of the painter, his youth, his arrogance, and his humility.

She stood longer than she had intended, studying first one canvas then another. The crowd had thinned, the light overhead faded a little, the colour in the pictures seemed to burn from the walls. She was turning at last to go when she saw him coming in. There was a chair against the wall a little way from where she was standing. She reached it safely.

He was of a slighter build than his father—Tom's size and bulk dominated any room—but this man, this boy, was no taller than his fellows. His clothes had that unmistakably foreign look about them, but he wore them as if he enjoyed them, not like Tom to whom clothes were only a social convention and a protection against the cold and the rain. This boy's mother, Laura thought, must have taught him to care for his clothes. But his face was Tom's—the high forehead with the white skin stretched tightly over it, the deep-set eyes, bushy eyebrows, black springing hair. He was leaning over the table talking to the man in uniform. He used his hands as he talked, the same thin wrists, bony wrist bones, emphatic manner. The room was quiet now, and his voice, though not his words, came to Laura's ears. The clipped American accent, the slick easy phrasing seemed so wrong that she wanted to rise and say, " No. No, not that way ; not like that at all."

He had turned and was coming towards her. She fluttered the pages of her catalogue desperately. He had stopped in front of her. " You're tired, ma'am. You're not sick, are you ? "

"Oh no. No thank you. I'm quite all right."

"Would you care for a drink of water?"

Laura realised he was as embarrassed as she was.

"Water? Oh, do you think I could?"

"Sure." He called down to the man at the doorway.

"Thank you. That is kind of you. It's just—I've been shopping this morning—and now—standing about more than I should——"

"I guess I know."

"And then—the pictures."

"What do you think of the pictures?"

The man had brought the water. She sipped it gratefully. The room had emptied now, only the two of them left.

"I—I hardly know what to think. I'm afraid I don't know much about modern art."

"What brought you here then?"

That was like Tom—the direct question, asked sharply, disconcertingly, without any attempt to oil the issue.

"I used to draw a little myself," she said. She watched him smile. The smile said 'funny old dame, she used to draw when drawing was a young lady's accomplishment', but she didn't resent it.

"Then you don't understand work like this?"

"No. I'm afraid I don't." She handed him back the glass. "But I'm glad I came." She wanted to say that much.

"You think the work's—interesting?"

"Oh yes, very interesting." She was sorry to give that bleak unproductive answer. She knew the creative artist's passion to discuss and deliberate on his art, to argue, elaborate, analyse. She was afraid he must despise her, and determined to go before she wasted any more of his time.

"What did you draw, when you studied drawing?"

He was being kind, of course. She didn't think young people nowadays were kind. "Designs from flowers, chiefly. I studied botany."

Again he smiled—a safe tidy study for young ladies his smile said, botany, the birds and the bees, nothing more disconcerting. Of course she had studied botany. She knew this young man, and what he was thinking, knew him quite well. Or was it Tom she knew—Tom—Terence—she

found it difficult to think clearly.   She must go, go now, right
away ;   she must get out of this into an open quiet place
where no one would notice her and she could sort things
out in her mind.

"I'll have to go."   She rose and fumbled with her gloves
and handbag.   He stooped to lift the glove she dropped.

"Wait a minute.   Don't go straight away.   There's something I want to show you, something you'd like better than
these pictures.   Come over here, they're in this."   He drew
a dark portfolio from behind the table, opened it, spread
out the contents.   "There—what do you think of these ? "

"Oh !   How lovely !   You do landscapes as well, then ? "
Laura was glad she had the edge of the table to hold on to.
She bent over the paintings to hide her burning face.

"Those aren't mine ;   those are some of my father's."

She could say nothing for a moment.   A tear dropped on
her hand, another on the painted scene.   She stooped low,
wiped it off and said, "Yes, I see it isn't your signature."

"He was ' Tom '," the boy said.

"He painted these some time ago ? "

"About twenty years ago, I guess, before he left Ireland."

"He was Irish then ? "   Laura marvelled at the ease with
which she pretended she didn't know.

"Yes.   He came over to settle in the States just after."

"They're beautiful," Laura said.

"I fancied you'd like them."

"Does he—did he—make a great success of his painting
in America ? "

"He didn't try."

She turned to look at him.   That was what he had said,
"He didn't try."

"You mean—he didn't paint at all ? "

"Nothing to signify.   He was too busy trying to make
a living—and he didn't make much of a hand out of that."

She knew from the bitterness in his voice that he was
speaking the truth.   Neither Tom nor his son would make
any pretence about it.   Tom had failed.   She had opened
a door she should not have opened.   She didn't want to
find out anything more, and to prevent the boy from telling
her, she asked, "Does your mother live in America ? "

He laughed.   "I wouldn't know."

" I—I don't quite understand."

" I wouldn't know about my mother. She walked out on my Dad when I was a fortnight old. He said maybe she didn't like the look of me."

" I'm sorry," she said, feeling how inadequate the words were. Then anger compelled her to persist in her questions. " What are you doing over here ? "

" Trying to work my way round Europe. There's a lot to be seen over here."

" Why did you come to Belfast ? "

" Sentiment, I guess. Anyway, Ireland's on the way."

" Have you—met any of your father's old friends ? "

" No. I wrote to a couple of them—I found the addresses on some old letters of his—but they didn't answer. Why would they ? Twenty years is a long time."

" Your father was fond of Ireland ? "

" I wouldn't know that either. The way I remember him he wasn't very fond of anything."

He spoke lightly enough, but Laura wasn't deceived.

" Are you selling these pictures of his ? "

" Not unless I have to."

She wondered what it was that kept him from selling his father's pictures. If Tom had been—that kind of a father —why should the boy hesitate ? In her heart she was grateful to him for hesitating.

" They're good, aren't they ? " he was asking.

" Yes, they are." She spoke with authority. He noticed it. His manner towards her changed, he had the artist's respect for knowledge.

" Yes, they are good," Laura said, and took one picture carefully in both her hands. Even after twenty years the paper felt familiar. " This one is good." She wondered if her voice was steady.

" I don't know anything about that kind of picture," the boy said. " Everything's there, isn't it—sky, clouds, hills, water, just the way he saw it ? "

" Yes. That was how he meant it to be."

He took the picture from her, handling it with new interest. " Funny way to paint. It all comes in at your eyes and goes out again at the tips of your fingers."

" They have to be the right kind of eyes and the right

kind of fingers." His hands were like Tom's hands, she noticed—the same long fingers, the black hair lying over the prominent veins.

" There wasn't anything the matter with his fingers," the boy said, and his voice warmed to a new enthusiasm. " What time of the year would you say it was when he painted this ? "

Laura didn't have to speculate. She said, " The third week in April."

" It's going to rain in a minute," he said, holding the picture at arm's length. " Look at that sky."

" It never rains long, not in April."

" Do you know where it was painted ? "

" Down by Lough Neagh, past Ballinderry."

He did not question her reply. The two of them were alone, spanning twenty years in this quiet room. She spoke what she knew and he accepted it.

" Is that far from here—Ballinderry ? "

" Not very far."

" I'd like to go some time and have a look at it for myself. Do you know the place ? "

" I've been there." There was no need for caution in this timelessness.

" I don't know my way around. Do you think, maybe, if we could get a day when it didn't rain you could show me the place ? "

This direct request broke the spell. " I don't know," she said, realising suddenly how ridiculous a proposition it was, and wondering how he had come to make it. " I don't know really."

" I'd be very much obliged to you if you would show me the place. I'd like to see it."

" I must be going, really I must. I'd no idea it was anything like as late."

He fumbled in his pocket, handed her a scrap of pasteboard with printing. " Look, this is where I'm staying. See if you can't fix it up, and phone me, will you ? I'll be here for another week."

Laura put the card into her bag. She could not remember how she made her adieux, but at last she was on the stairs, and then in the street again.

In her relief at being under the open sky she did not notice

which way she went, but allowed herself to be carried by
the crowds, borne along by them, chivvied from this side
of the pavement to that, herded off from a shop window,
shouldered and hustled, until she came to the front of the
City Hall, and stood for a moment with her back to a doorway, deciding what to do. She could not immediately return
to Marathon, she must first sift and assimilate the events
of the past hour, sort them and lay them aside for future
remembering. There was so much she did not want to
lose ; she must lay hold on it before she went any further.
She crossed over Donegall Square, and sat for a while on
one of the seats among the flower-beds. It was quieter
here. In any case her legs were shaking, she could not
have walked further. A few old men thumbed their newspapers on seats beside her, housewives set down their shopping
baskets and rested their aching feet. An African student
chewed a banana and read a book. Beyond on the broad
pavement the flower girls lifted great bunches of spring
flowers—daffodils, mimosa, tulips—to brandish at likely
purchasers. A cloud of starlings chattered on the windowsills of the Scottish Provident Buildings. Among so much
life she could safely be alone and have time to think. For
so many years so little of any value or significance had happened that the last week, Mildred's death, George's return,
the meeting with Tom's son—it was all too much to be easily
borne.

She sat there for half an hour, unremarked and unremarkable, and then rose determined that before she caught
the bus home she would go round to the Technical School,
and for pure sentiment's sake stand again on the wide steps.
It was an indulgence which in these bleak years she had
never allowed herself. But so many unusual things had
happened already that one more would make no difference.

She hurried up Wellington Place, but once opposite the
Technical could not find the courage to cross the road and
stood looking up at the array of tall windows. Young men
and girls were coming and going through the gateway ; she
noticed the ironwork had been painted an unusual shade of
blue. She searched the faces of the students, as if she
should recognise them, and then suddenly realising her
absurdity, felt herself conspicuous and moved on aimlessly

up Great Victoria Street. She could not go back to Marathon, not yet. She must wait a little while longer, till she was sure her face would not betray her.

There was a crowd in front of the station. Inside a band was playing. Something unusual was afoot. People paused to look, crossed the road to enquire, and Laura, unresisting, was carried over with them.

It was the departure of an immigrant train, bound for Cork, carrying passengers who would there board the liner for the United States. The platform had already been screened off, but people were lined up outside the gates, shamelessly watching the drama that was playing itself out. The band was grouped together on the far side of the bookstall. "Come back to Erin, Mavourneen, Mavourneen" was the air, played wooingly but discreetly, the brass subduing its exuberance to suit the occasion. "Come back to Erin"—would they come back? And if they did, would not they and their native Erin be changed?

Only the relatives of the passengers had been admitted onto the platform. There was a mother with two children clutching at her knees, and one in her arms, bidding good-bye to a husband whom she hoped to join when he had made a home for them. They had no words left. All their good-byes had been said before they left their home. They stood dumb in the chattering crowd. The man stooped suddenly to pick up one of the toddlers and hide his moving face in the hollow of her soft neck. The child laughed and clung to him. A man of eighty, holding his great shoulders erect with a mighty effort, was shaking the hand of a lump of a lad, his youngest son, whom he could hardly hope to see again. A young girl, advanced in pregnancy, went up the platform alone to find her place on the train. She walked slowly and proudly, neither looking to left or right. Her face was unmoved. Whatever Irishman had fathered her child, she would see to it that, when it was born, it would know little, and care less either for him or the land that bred him.

Round one carriage stood a group of wedding guests, conspicuous in their finery, but their gaiety was wearing thin, and their buttonholes beginning to droop. Framed in the window were the bride and her young groom, their

radiant faces oblivious to everything—the station, the farewells, the crowd—they were not saying good-bye to one way
of life but standing on the threshold of another. They would
not be sorry when the train drew out. Further up the platform a dignitary of the Orange Order, wearing regalia and
supported by two of his brethren, was bidding a formal fare-
well to a worthy gentleman of his persuasion. They prolonged their handshake to give a press photographer a chance.
This picture of goodwill would be circularised in the papers
next morning. There was no press photographer to record
the group of black-clad clerics in the next carriage who
crowded round to press the hand of a silent young priest
with a pale dedicated face.

" Come back to Erin, Mavourneen, Mavourneen " wailed
the tactful brass. But the sadness of the air made it tragic-
ally certain that to come back would be to court disappointment. An Irishman on his native soil will no more
talk of his love for his country than he will of his love for
his wife, but when he is away Ireland is immediately coloured
in his imagination with picture-postcard hues, wrapped in a
perpetual mist, romanticised out of all recognition. Once
across the Atlantic he will turn to look back at his own particular spot of Ireland and see sprouting whether from Protestant
or Catholic soil shamrocks of impossible size and vigour.
He cannot go, and hope to return to find both himself and
his homeland unchanged.

An air of excitement spread up the platform. The relatives
had said their last farewells and were drawing back ; officials
were going up and down the train closing carriage doors.
The band gave up its effort to remain subdued and with
some relief broke into " The Minstrel Boy to the War is
Gone " and the brass stretched its legs over the noisy flourishes.
At least the noise drowned the grief of those who were by
now weeping openly, and lent an air of helpful unreality to
the whole proceedings.

These last farewells—they were only gestures. The passengers for America had all said their farewells a hundred
times since their minds were made up and their tickets
bought. That boy from the farm—for the last month the
lane up to his home has been holy ground and he has trodden
it devotedly. The last meal he ate this morning in the

farmhouse kitchen—the last farl of soda bread from his mother's griddle—has been a sacrament. He will be glad now to get away. Already he feels self-conscious in his native land, his nationality has become a burden, the daily event nothing but a procession of good-byes. When he put off his working clothes last night he put off the old ways, and there is no going back for him.

Yet every traveller takes with him one part of Ireland which in memory becomes a shrine to which homesick thoughts return when return is itself impossible. To each the shrine is different : to this man the quayside at Porta-ferry, to this a pub up the Shankill Road, perhaps the broken crab apple tree that overhangs Fiddler's Green above Rostre-vor, or a grave out on the hillside at Carnmoney, or a whinny field, more rock than soil. Perhaps in later years the traveller will come back, larger than lifesize, more Irish than the Irish. But he is doomed to disappointment, for he will find the men he knew smaller than he remembers them, the grass less green, the crack not so good. Nor will he be able to leave off his expansive American ways and be one with his fellow countrymen again. It is good-bye indeed.

Nineteen years ago Tom had gone to America. He had sailed from Southampton, and there had been no one there to see him off. He hadn't come back. But Laura knew what picture of Ireland he had carried with him. She had handled it that afternoon.

" I never told you I loved you," Tom had said that spring afternoon on the shore at Newcastle. And Laura was thrown into a sweet confusion of spirit that upset her world. " I never told you I loved you," he had said, and yet in the months that followed, all through that lovely spring, the words were not repeated, nor did he make any effort to con-firm them. They met at the Art Classes until the term was over. Tom's manner was unchanged, they greeted each other, discussed their work as before ; on the last day when they were gathering up their gear he nodded a good-bye to her, expressed some wish that she'd have a good holiday, and took himself off. " I never told you I loved you." Laden with brushes and sketches Laura had followed him into the street and stood for a moment on the steps, her eyes blinded with tears, until she could trust herself to go down to join the hurrying crowd. " I never told you I loved you." That was honest enough. He had never told her. That meant he did not love her. " I never told you I loved you." She remembered his hand laid on hers, and the warmth in his voice. He was gone now, and whatever way he had meant her to interpret his words, she must wait until the autumn term recommenced. The long aching summer days stretched ahead in her imagination—days when nothing could happen, days which must be lived through until the autumn, until she would see Tom again.

But much did happen that summer. On the day before they were due to set out for the family holiday at Bundoran —the cases were packed, the car ordered—Mr. Percival took a slight stroke. There was now no question of a seaside holiday. The cases were unpacked, a nurse installed ; Mildred rose magnificently to the occasion, Laura grew listless at the inactivity which her sister's efficiency imposed on her. There was nothing for her to do. The sight of her father lying motionless on his bed day after day terrified her. His huge body had become his prison. Though he did not move, the eyes under the half-closed lids saw everything that went on in the room. If Laura were asked to perform some small duty for him she became so nervous that she did it clumsily. To go into the room was an effort ; once inside she lost all control of herself in horror and pity for the man on the bed.

George, on the other hand, seemed to flourish on the responsibility that his father's illness had shifted to his shoulders. He was up early in the morning, was never late leaving for the office, came home in the evening apparently confident and well-satisfied. Sometimes he didn't return until bedtime—working late, he told the girls. But everything at the business, he said, was under control. He told his father this too, speaking the words slowly and emphatically with his mouth down at the level of the pillow, but did not know if they had penetrated, or if they had, whether his father would believe them.

For six weeks Mr. Percival lay without moving. Then one day he stirred, the next was sitting up. The following morning he dismissed the nurse, put on his clothes, and coming downstairs with slow determined concentration, ordered the car to take him to the office. Mildred's entreaties had no effect on him. Laura had watched her father's slow descent of the stairs from the door of her own bedroom, and was lying on her bed shaking with nervous fright. George, of course, had left for the office directly after breakfast.

It was surprising that that first visit to the office was not Mr. Percival's last. Perhaps the shock of finding what George had been doing in his absence acted as a tonic on him. At all events he came back in the evening tired, but with the air of a man who has had the satisfaction of proving that he had fathered not only a fool but a knave. George did not come back. His father made little comment on his absence. Any strength he had was spent straightening the mess that George had left. For George had done well for himself in the limited time. The old man took a bitter satisfaction in unravelling all the ingenious extravagances. He derived from it a twisted pleasure, and dealt personally with the procession of trades-people who presented bills incurred by George during his father's absence. The greater the cross, the greater the glory. The old man thrived on the exposure of his son's iniquities.

So Laura had no seaside holiday that summer. The long weeks were spent in nervous inactivity, anxiety for George, apprehension for her father, whose pleasure in this business seemed to her most horrible, and at the back of it all was the dull ache for Tom. She rarely went further than the garden, and earned sharp criticism from Mildred for what seemed morbid mooning, though Mildred never asked for help or made any suggestion how she could better employ her time.

There was some question whether she should resume her classes at the Art School in the autumn. For a week the debate went on over her head between Mildred and her father, while Laura experienced a suspense of suffering which made her sleepless and stupid. Now that George had left home, Tom wouldn't be a visitor at Marathon again. If she were not allowed to join the Art Class, there was no reason why they should meet. " I never told you I loved you," he had said. It seemed then that he never would.

The crowd on the station was turning now, as the last carriage of the train disappeared far up the platform. With the relief that comes when they are delivered from some strong emotion that has been too long prolonged, people turned to laugh and chatter, and find their way out of the station and take themselves on their journeys homeward. Laura turned home too. She did not know what time it was. Time did not matter, nor was there anything to bring her home. But there was nowhere else where she could go.

Chapter Nine

MISS PARKS and Mr. McAlister faced each other in the large drawing-room at Marathon. She knelt to poke the fire. It required no poking, but it helped to establish her position in the house that she should kneel to poke the fire. The clock in the hall struck five. Mr. McAlister fidgeted with some papers on his knee.

It had annoyed him to find this woman so firmly installed in the house when he had called an hour earlier. He had gathered during the funeral that she was a friend who had come in for the emergency, but he did not expect still to find her there. He had anticipated with some pleasure an evening with Laura. Although since Mr. Percival's death he had not been a frequent visitor to the house he was constantly there during Mr. Percival's lifetime—had been at his side during the early days of his tragic widowhood, had been almost as interested as his friend in the upbringing of the young children. Mr. McAlister and his wife were childless, and so he had no practical advice to offer, but the two men read and discussed together the books on child psychology which Mr. Percival brought to the house. He had been shocked and disturbed at George's stormy youth, and felt the disgrace almost as keenly as George's father. Since Mr. Percival's death he had only been at the house a couple of times to discuss the transaction of any legal business. This was soon done—Mildred had the mind of a man and no hesitation in declaring her decisions. He had seen little of Laura during these visits—it seemed she was ill. Of course she was always highly strung as a child. But the glimpse he had caught, or

thought he caught on the day of Mildred's funeral, of the shy
girl he remembered had persisted with him during the following days.   Since his own wife's death Mr. McAlister's house
was ruled by an efficient housekeeper who alarmed him.   He
would like to dismiss her, but did not know how to set about
it.   He despised himself for his inability to send her packing,
and endured the bleak meals, the small fires, the self-righteousness of the woman.   When he could conveniently do so he
dined at his Club.   This evening he had arranged to dine
there with a couple of old friends, and to make the evening
more perfect had arranged first to spend a couple of hours
with Laura, here in the familiar drawing-room at Marathon,
the two of them comfortably arrayed in front of the fire while
he explained to her the intricacies of the will.   Warmed by
the fire and Laura's gratitude and respect for his knowledge
he would then proceed to the Club and dine slowly with his
friends, postponing as long as he could the hour when he must
return home to the woman who dared him to find fault with
her ordering of his house.

Now this was all upset.   He had been at Marathon an hour
and there was no sign of Laura, although he had made the
appointment by telephone the previous day.   He had not
even had the satisfaction of sitting alone in the room, dozing in
the heat, recalling old friends and other days.   This thin-
nosed woman, Miss Parks, had greeted him, ushered him into
the drawing-room, fretted at Laura's absence, played hostess
to him.   She reminded him of his housekeeper.   He would
have been happier left alone.

Miss Parks finished her show of business with the fire.   " I
can't think where she has got to," she said, rising and resuming
her seat.   " It's too bad of her to have kept you waiting like
this."

Mr. McAlister had no intention of showing the woman that
he agreed with her.   " Don't upset yourself, Miss Parks, it's
quite all right.   I only want her to sign these papers.   There
is nothing that cannot wait till some other day."

Miss Parks eyed the papers longingly.   " There's nothing
you would like me to explain to her."

" No thank you.   Everything is perfectly clear."

" It's too bad of Laura not to be here when she was expecting you."

"Anything may have happened to detain her."

"And it's so unlike her to go off and not say where she is going."

This woman is taking too much on herself, Mr. McAlister thought. Dislike for her grew in him as the minutes ticked over. He didn't reply, and she took up the lament again. "If she had only said where she was going——"

"Oh come, Miss Parks. She can't be expected to report all her comings and goings, can she?"

"Oh no, of course not." Miss Parks' nose went up. "Now that dear Mildred is gone there's no reason why Laura shouldn't please herself, I'm sure. But it's not like her, that's all. I know Laura better than you do."

Mr. McAlister determined that Laura must be delivered from this woman. He said, "I expect Laura has shopping to do, and other arrangements to make before she goes away."

"Oh she has no intention of going away, not for some time, at any rate," Miss Parks said with decision. "Laura will need a chance to pick up her strength again before she's able to travel—if indeed that is what she decides to do. She has never been very strong, you know."

Her manner hinted at the more obscure female complaints and made it impossible for Mr. McAlister to reply. Miss Parks realised she had the advantage, and made haste to secure it. "Of course," she went on, fussing with the hearth brush, "she may be with that brother of hers."

Mr. McAlister leant forward. "Oh. Do you think so? Has he been here again?"

"Oh yes," said Miss Parks, preening herself at her more intimate knowledge. "He has been most attentive. Yesterday he phoned her just after you did." This was a guess, but Miss Parks felt she was safe in making it. After all, who else could it have been?

Mr. McAlister thought rapidly. It would be easier for Laura to extricate herself from the attentions of this woman than from those of her brother George. He would have to disguise the dislike he felt for her in order to get the information he wanted. There was a phrase for it—ah, he had it! "Adversity makes strange bedfellows." It wasn't an expression he cared for, but it was appropriate, and in a twisted way, amusing. He took another look at Miss Parks, sneering privately at her plain face and lack of charm. 'Strange bed-fellows' indeed!

"George Percival never came to the house when Miss Mildred was alive, did he?" he asked.

"Oh no, never." Miss Parks drew her chair a little closer. "At least he was never here during the latter years of her illness. I was in her confidence, you know; she would have told me if he had been. Mr. McAlister—perhaps you can tell me—what does Mr. George do exactly?"

"After he left home he ran through a variety of jobs. Sometimes I don't think he had a job at all. He managed to keep his movements very much to himself. He was always better at spending his money than earning it. But since he married he must have been managing his affairs better, certainly he's been in no conspicuous trouble. I know he's been with a firm of wholesale seedsmerchants for some years back. He seems to have settled down. It's wonderful, Miss Parks, how even the most unreliable of us can mend our ways when we get a good woman behind us."

He arrayed his heavy features to register a compliment, and was amused to see her smirk back at him.

"I feel sure," he went on, "that the less Laura sees of her brother while she is making up her mind how to adjust herself to things the better."

She beamed her agreement. "Oh, Mr. McAlister, I feel quite sure you're right."

Then her eye, always alert, caught some movement on the drive; she sprang to her post at the window. "Here she is. Laura at last."

Mr. McAlister tried to soften the irritation in his voice. "I shouldn't let her see you at the window, Miss Parks. It might look as if you were spying on her, and you don't want that. After all, she isn't a child any more."

"Oh, Mr. McAlister!"

Her consternation made him forget his scruples and he joined her at the window. "It isn't Laura—look who it is."

He looked. George Percival was coming up the drive. George was coming up the drive as if the place belonged to him. By his way of thinking it did—or should have—or soon would. Still, he would have been just as glad not to have come on this particular errand. Laura hadn't paid for the lunch. She'd thanked him and taken herself off. They'd cashed his cheque for him all right, and he'd paid the bill. All the confidence and poise that had brought him to the hotel had ebbed out of him as he pocketed the remaining notes and silver. He'd whistled an air under his breath as he crossed the foyer and navigated the swing doors. Then he'd gone into a pub to have a drink he didn't want, couldn't afford to pay for and couldn't do without, while he meditated on the kind of fool he had been.

He had been this kind of a fool so often he ought to have been wise to it by now. The well-appointed hotel, the expert service, the good food, the drinks, the two interested young women, Laura's obvious pleasure in his company and her admiration of his ease in these surroundings—all these had given him the build-up he needed. He'd been a king for a couple of hours, sure of himself and his ability to please, wearing the charm he enjoyed as lightly as only he knew how to wear it. He wished Amy could have seen him. Life was good and he was its equal. For two hours the magic was on him, and he couldn't put a little finger wrong. He couldn't make a mistake.

It was Laura who made the mistake. When the lunch was over she should have thanked him prettily and quietly pushed a fiver across the table to him. He would have demurred, of course, but she would have insisted. He would have made a little on the fiver—you couldn't offer Laura the change. But Laura had thanked him prettily and had gone, and he was left to pay the bill.

The bubble broke ; he'd been the same fool again, the same old fool. He looked at himself half an hour later in the glass wall of the pub—not the same fool, a different, older fool. The face was tired and old and weak. He avoided his own eyes in the mirror. He felt sick to the bottom of his soul.

In the ordinary way if something had happened to rob him of his self-confidence he would have gone back to Amy. She had the blessed gift of restoring his godship. She knew how to do it. She didn't see through his act. He wanted her now fiercely but knew that this time it was no use wanting. Sooner or later this evening she would ask for the cheque and he would have to fiddle through his pockets and pull out the notes and the silver and lay them down in front of her. It was a long time, years now, since he had handed her less than the whole of his pay. He had grown to enjoy the gesture—what was money to him? But there was no deceiving Amy where money was concerned. She didn't pretend to despise it. She was a businesswoman to the tips of her little painted fingers. She wasn't ashamed to know all the prices, down to the nearest halfpenny. Lunch, drinks, tips, it wasn't going to be easy or comfortable accounting for the hole in his wages. Ten to one Kathie wouldn't have gone to bed; he'd have to give an account of himself in front of her. When she was a little girl he knew that Kathie found him faultless. He'd a suspicion she was growing out of this. " How soon do we move in, Pop ? "—that was what she had said when he came back from Mildred's funeral. He fancied she might have some remark to make this evening.

So he sat in the pub and ordered himself another drink and made up his mind to go up to Marathon and ask Laura for the money.

The drink put a swagger on him coming up the drive. When he found Miss Parks and Mr. McAlister in the drawing-room, and no sign of Laura, he was angry, cheated by these two of the effort it had cost him to come. Miss Parks asked him to sit down. He resented being invited to sit down in his own drawing-room. He kicked at the fire, emptied the remaining coals over it, rang for Hannah to bring more, behaved with a boorishness of which he was secretly ashamed.

" I suppose you've come to see Laura on business," he barked at Mr. McAlister. " Easy way you solicitor fellows make your money."

Miss Parks shrank as he turned on her. " I didn't realise you'd still be here," he said. Miss Parks bit her thin lips, but could offer no justification for her presence. She walked over to the window again. It was really very vexing of Laura to go out like this and leave her to deal with these two men.

A heavy silence fell on the room. Hannah had piled the fire high, and it made the air uncomfortably warm. Mr. McAlister rose from his chair and joined Miss Parks at the window.

" Any sign of her ? " he asked.

" No," Miss Parks said, " but she can't be long now, really she can't."

She put out her hand and drew back the curtain from the window, as if to hasten Laura's return by making it evident a second or two sooner.

" Oh ! " Her sharp cry brought George to stand beside them.

" What is it ? " he asked.

" Laura—she's come. But—why—whatever is the matter with her ? "

The three of them crowded in the window peered out at the figure that was coming up the drive. It had paused just beyond the laurel bush, as it came into sight, and the small face was lifted enquiringly for a moment towards the house. Then the figure halted abruptly, stiffened, and the hands were gathered over the mouth, as if to stifle sounds that could not be checked. Her eyes were wide and stared straight at them. One shaking hand was raised and pointed uneasily at the window.

The three turned from the window and met Laura in the hall. She was standing still, her eyes looking beyond them, to something that lay inside the open drawing-room door. At last she spoke.

" She was there—in the window—watching for me as I came in."

Miss Parks approached her fussily, but Laura pushed her off. " I saw her—it was Mildred—she was there."

Miss Parks stumbled against the hall chair and sat down on it abruptly. Her mouth fell open, she was bereft of speech or action.

" She was there," the voice persisted.

George found he could not look into the drawing-room where Laura's eyes were looking. It was Mr. McAlister who first moved. The old man stepped forward and took Laura's elbow. " Come and see for yourself," he said, and walked with her slowly across the hall.

For a long moment Laura stood beside him, staring into the empty drawing-room. When she turned again the mask had fallen and there was an ugly flush rising on her face. She pointed to Miss Parks. " It was you," she said, " it was you."

Miss Parks loosed a babble of commonplaces ; of course they had been expecting her. Mr. McAlister had called.

Mr. George had called. They were naturally wondering what had happened to delay Laura. Laura would not listen. "That was her place," she said, in a hard condemning voice. "You know that was always her place. What business had you to be watching for me there?"

Miss Parks fumbled again for words, but was cut short by an ugly torrent of weeping from Laura. The harsh sobs shocked the two men, who turned away to avoid witnessing this added shame. The sound brought Hannah from the kitchen, and it was she who caught Laura against her ample bosom as she fell.

Laura lay at last in her bed, her small body straight and rigid, her hands flat out to the finger-tips, pressed against the sheets in that extremity of exhaustion that cannot yet relax. The room was dark, but for the light at the bed-head, the curtains were closed. It must be towards evening. She could not remember how she had come at last to her bed, or who it was who had undressed her and put her there. She hoped it had been Hannah. She would not like her body to be touched by Miss Parks. She could see that her clothes were folded and laid on a chair. The house was quiet. She could fancy she heard the roughness of male voices from the drawing-room. Slowly the events of the crowded day and the evening came back to her. Carefully she put into words what had happened. "I came up the avenue and saw the curtain pulled back from the window. I was so used to seeing Mildred watching for me from that window that for a moment I forgot that Mildred was—dead, and I thought it was her. I would not have forgotten if I had not been so tired. It was not Mildred, it was Miss Parks. George and Mr. McAlister had called too, and I was late coming home, so Miss Parks went to the window to see if there was any sign of me. That was why she pulled the curtain to one side. It was not Mildred. Mildred is dead. It was Miss Parks."

This deliberate analysis was a help. The small body surrendered a little to the soft bed and the warmth. With the body's immediate need met, the mind became more active. I knew Mildred was dead, and yet I thought it was Mildred. The reason I thought it was Mildred was because I had been thinking about Tom, and because I had been to see Tom's son. Mildred knew. She was the only other person who knew. No, Mildred cannot have known, for Mildred is dead. Her body is dead and her mind is dead. She could not have known. But if she did not know then why did I feel as I did ?

It had always been difficult to tell how much Mildred knew. How much had she known, for instance, of her affairs and Tom's during that long winter after George left home for good, and while his anger at his son's failure seemed the only fire that kept Mr. Percival's body alive ? Not that there was much to know. Laura remembered with sadness the poverty of that winter. After some debate it was decided that she should resume her classes at the Art School, but her friendship with Tom had not blossomed. At every class they exchanged greetings, sometimes discussed the lecture or each other's work, but beyond that there was nothing. Tom had soon discovered, of course, that George was not attending his classes, and Laura had told him the reason. But even Tom's concern at this was unproductive. It seemed that their acquaintance had come to a standstill.

But it was this acquaintance that made the winter tolerable for Laura. It was her only escape from the constant tension at home. Mr. Percival was not content to accept the fact that George had left home, he could talk of nothing else but the son who had so cruelly disappointed him. Mildred was an able and willing chorus. Torn between hope that George would come back and fear lest he might, Laura's nerves were frayed with the continual uncertainty. Odd scraps of news reached them as to how and where George was living. The weeks were punctuated with alarms and possibilities of reconciliation. The sick old man could not leave the subject alone ; he debated it endlessly, keeping his finger deliberately on the old sore. One of the cousins from Armagh had seen George peddling brushes round the doorsteps of a provincial town— a schoolfriend had passed him in the street and asked if he had been ill—he spent a night in a lodging house in the city, and one of the doormen recognised him and reported it to Mr. McClintock the minister. Mr. McClintock was to be sent for if he turned up at the lodging house again. He didn't turn up. A girl he used to take out told Mildred that he had met her and asked her for money. She gave him some and promised him more. He didn't come to collect it. It was small wonder that with this current of emotion running so strongly at home Laura's personal unhappiness passed unremarked.

Perhaps trouble sharpened her sympathies, for it seemed to her that Tom too had a private load of trouble. He was preoccupied, he wasn't working so well. Sometimes he didn't lift his head to answer when she spoke, and yet she knew his work wasn't absorbing him. He wasn't the popular figure that he had been with the other students. His brusque criticism, offered too readily, more often offended than it amused. Laura's heart yearned over him, watching the bent shoulders, the nervous thrust of the head, the tightened mouth. In her concern for him she succeeded in shedding, to some degree, the weight of each week's uneasy passage at home.

Christmas passed, a miracle of sustained civility which they were all glad to have done with, and the four empty holiday weeks went over. During the spring term the students were exchanging views on jobs and future plans, once the year's course was finished. Tom, it seemed, was giving up Art Classes to take a post in a linen business. He would keep on the evening classes in industrial design.

"But your painting, Tom!" Laura said.

Tom frowned. "I've got to earn my keep, haven't I?" he said roughly. "My keep and my mother's. After all she's been keeping me for a good many years."

Laura hid her despair as best she could. She counted the weeks until the summer term would be ended, and did not dare to look beyond. "I never told you I loved you." It was nearly a year now since Tom had said that. If he had wanted to tell her, why had he waited so long?

Early in the spring term Tom came over to her desk as the class was dispersing. "I'm going into the country for a day's sketching," he said. "Would you like to come?"

It had all been ridiculously easy. Mildred and Hannah were in the throes of spring-cleaning. Mr. Percival had gone with Mr. McAlister to spend the weekend at Cushendall. Laura heard herself explaining to Mildred that there was to be another expedition with the Art Class. Yes, they would take sandwiches; no, they wouldn't go if it was wet.

It wasn't wet, not until Laura and Tom had got off the bus at Ballinderry and were walking along the straight narrow

laneway that led from the main road to the Lough shore.
Then a flurry of wind and rain came suddenly out of a clear
sky and sent them to shelter in the hedge. This was soon
over and the sun came out stronger and fuller, and the puddles
in the lane reflected back the blue of the sky, while the stones
on the ditches steamed and paled as they dried. Chaffinches
sang their interminable light-hearted jangle, a lark rose above
them, pollarded willows on either side of the road were torches
of pale gold. They passed low prosperous farmhouses, where
the hens ran and scraped among the daffodils in the untidy
gardens, and plump children waved at them. A man hoeing
in a field of early potatoes straightened his back to call a greet-
ing. A woman with her mouth full of clothes pegs paused at
her washing-line till they had gone past.

At last the road came to the shore of Lough Neagh. In
spite of the sun a sharp wind was whipping up the surface of
the water into small crests, and on the finely gravelled beach
where they sat down to eat, little inland waves gathered and
fell, and left behind them a creamy scum on the stones.
Tom told her that George had called at his house. He was
in a job, not much of a job. He wouldn't say anything about
it, but it kept him fed and housed. He made Tom promise
not to tell anyone but Laura.

" I suppose he wanted money," Laura said.
" Yes."

After they had eaten Tom made some colour notes and
sketched the little stony beach, the farmhouse on the green
field that rose to the left of it, the dim outline of the Sperrin
Mountains across the great expanse of water. Laura did not
take out her sketching book. She lay on one elbow, contented
in the sufficiency of the moment, in the luxury of knowing that
just by turning her head she could see Tom beside her, feeling
the sun warm on her skin, hearing the waves. Here was
richness. She hoarded every moment as it went by, each
chaffinch's flourish, each small lazy wave. It would have to
last her a long time.

" Do you think George will come back to your house ? "
she asked.

" I expect he will."

" I can give you some money for him."

Tom turned round to her and snapped the elastic that

secured his pages.   " I'd better not take it in case he doesn't
come till after I have gone away."

" I didn't know you were going away," Laura said carefully.

" I have to."   Tom was looking out across the water,
avoiding her eyes.

" Where are you going ? "

" To America—as far as I can get—to paint."

She waited a moment.   Then she said, " I thought you said
your mother needed you at home ? "

He put his head back and laughed.   It was an ugly sound.
" No, it's not me she needs."

Then he told her about his mother.   He was an orphan ;
this much she already knew, his father had been killed before
he was born.   His mother and father had been deeply in love.
In her grief she had vowed to devote her whole life to the
unborn child, for the sake of his father.   From his earliest
years Tom had loved her with his whole heart.   She had been
a beautiful girl—still, in her early widowhood, was little more.
Her gaiety and love had been the touchstones of his childhood.   They had been true and loyal companions.

It wasn't a lonely house.   His mother had other friends,
many other friends.   Mostly gentlemen, if the small boy had
noticed.   He called them ' Uncles '—it was his mother who
told him to call them that.   They laughed and joked with Tom
and brought him presents.   Of course they joked and laughed
with his mother and brought her presents as well.

His mother's beauty hadn't diminished with the years, but
it had hardened.   Her laughter had hardened too.   Tom
knew no transition period, but one day in his late teens realised that his mother wasn't the gay creature of sympathy and
grace that he had shared his childhood with, but a woman on
the verge of middle-age, still pitifully beautiful, desperately
lonely, hoarding her beauty that had never been any use to
anybody but one small boy who was now almost a man.   For
the succession of ' uncles ' had dwindled.   They had been
harmless enough friendships, lonely men glad to assert their
manhood by paying attentions to the beautiful and lively
young widow and her small son.   Now in her early forties,
with her boy on the verge of making his own life, Tom's
mother looked back on the sacrifices she had made for him.
Scanning her own face in the mirror, she grudged each

deepening line. Her loveliness, unspent and useless now, reproached her.

Tom watched her with pity and dismay, saw each small trick to retain her youth, the sprightliness that had lost its spontaneity, the winsomeness that had soured. She dressed in a manner to challenge attention, she was moody, extravagant, short with him, gushing to outsiders. To the few men who came to the house, the doctor, the minister, even the trades-people, she was coy, sometimes almost arch. The whole proceeding made Tom very uneasy. He saw with the discerning eyes of youth what had happened. His mother had given up her beauty's birthright to make him happy, she had battened on the memory of her dead husband when her whole body cried out for the embrace of warm flesh and blood. Now that she had reached her goal, and he was ready for the world, the body's hunger was still unsatisfied though the body itself was ageing. He knew the debt he owed to his mother, and reproached himself for despising her in this extremity.

There was a new visitor to the house, a commercial traveller, recently a widower. He was plump, common, loud-voiced. Tom's mother had bloomed afresh. Tom believed that it was only shame at what her son would think that prevented her from accepting him. It was unlikely she would have any other offer of marriage. He would be good to her in his aggressive hearty way. She might find peace. Tom was going to clear out to America to leave the way open to him.

Laura didn't interrupt as Tom told her his story. When he had done she laid her hand on his arm. " Oh, Tom, I am sorry."

He shrugged her hand away. She could not see his face properly, he was staring out across the grey water. Words came from him now like a torrent.

" I hate the sight of him. If you could see them together, Laura, giggling and leering. He's fifty if he's a day. When he's coming she spends hours upstairs, dressing for him. You can hear her singing and laughing about the house. She can't sing now, not like she used to. She doesn't seem to know that. I always go out when he comes. Sometimes I wait for ten minutes first, just to watch them growing impatient, wondering if perhaps I'm not going out after all.

You should hear her voice when she asks me if I really *must* go. Sometimes I just walk the streets, and when I come back his car's still in front of the door."

Laura didn't know she was crying until a tear splashed onto her hand. "Oh, Tom, I am sorry," she said again. Her breast ached to draw his rough head down to her, but she knew better than to stir.

"She tried to tell me about it the other day," Tom went on. "She said she needed—love." He spoke the word with disgust.

"What did you say?"

"I said I expected she did. Then I went out into the garden until I stopped feeling sick. When I came in they were in the drawing-room together, I could hear them laughing."

Neither of them spoke for a while. The small waves came and fell on the stones, washing away some of their unhappiness.

"I never told you I loved you," Tom said, still staring out across the water. "How can I tell you, if that's what love is?"

Certainty in Laura rose, surmounting all her inexperience. "Tom, of course that isn't what love is."

And turning urgently to search each other's face, they had discovered that Laura was right.

Chapter Ten

MISS PARKS had helped Hannah to put Laura to bed on the evening when she had collapsed. Afterwards she came down to the drawing-room with all the self-importance and authority of a Vestal Virgin coming off her spell of duty. The rebuff she had suffered when Laura had pushed her away in the hall was expunged by this office. George and Mr. McAlister were both still waiting.

"Oh, we're much better now, thank you—much calmer. All tucked up in bed, and we'll feel quite like ourselves again when we've had a little sleep."

'Vestal Virgin' was wrong, thought George. That is the midwives' plural she is using ; he must remember to tell Amy about it when he got home. She wouldn't appreciate it, but he would enjoy telling her. Or would he ? No, he wouldn't be in a position to enjoy telling Amy anything until the hole in his salary had been mended.

He said : "I'd like to go up."

Miss Parks frowned and pursed her lips. "Oh, I don't think I would, Mr. Percival ; not tonight—not when she's so nicely settled."

"I'm sure she'd be better undisturbed," Mr. McAlister seconded ; "a sleep will do her good."

George resented this. Who were they to dictate to him whether he should or should not visit his sister ? "If she's asleep," he said, "I won't waken her. If she's awake, I have a feeling she'll be glad to see me." It was getting late. Amy would wonder what was delaying him.

"But, Mr. Percival, your sister's quite happy in her mind now about everything. I can assure you I explained it all to her—it was my fault, I said, my fault entirely. I should have realised that the sofa was dear Mildred's place, and that you wouldn't wish anybody else to be there. I should have known, I said, how you'd feel."

Miss Parks was enjoying this generous self-depreciation. "You can be sure, Laura dear, I said, that it won't happen again. Everything will be just as Mildred always had it— you can be quite sure—we shan't change a thing."

"I don't know that that was quite the wisest thing to say," Mr. McAlister put in. "After all, Laura must make her own life now."

But Miss Parks hadn't finished yet. "You mustn't blame me, I said, for being just a tiny bit anxious about you this afternoon. It was only natural, I said, that I should have been wondering where you were. Mr. McAlister was waiting for you quite a time, I said—and your brother George."

George said bluntly : "Look—I'd like to see her."

"But there's no need to worry, Mr. Percival, none at all. She quite understands now just how it happened. She'll settle much more easily now if she's left alone. I—I understand her fairly well, you know." She smirked at him.

"She's very highly strung," Mr. McAlister said. "Always

was, from a girl.   I remember after your father's death she
had a regular nervous collapse.   She was more or less of an
invalid for a couple of years.   Of course, you mightn't have
known that."

I know what you're getting at, thought George.   I should
have been at home, shouldn't I?   "How could I have
known?" he demanded.   "I wasn't here."

"No."   But Mr. McAlister hadn't finished with him yet.
"I remember your sister Mildred, how wonderfully she
managed with all the responsibility on her shoulders—first
your father lying unconscious for four days, and then poor
Laura collapsing completely when she came home.   It was
a terrible house."

Thank God I wasn't in it, thought George.   He said: "I'm
sure it was," and left it at that.

"So we must be particularly careful with Laura now,
mustn't we?" Miss Parks suggested.   "You could ring up
in the morning, couldn't you, and see if she feels well enough
to see you then?"

"I could," said George, "but I'd rather go on up and see
her now.   It's all right, you needn't come with me.   I *do*
know my own way."

He felt pleased with himself as he left the drawing-room
and crossed the hall.   He could handle them all right.   There
wasn't anything to fear from that pair.   The buoyant assurance took him up the wide shallow stairs where his hand felt
for the familiar curve on the banisters before his mind remembered it.   He crossed the landing and knocked lightly on
Laura's door.

"Come in."

Laura looked very small, very childish, lying in bed with
her hair braided over the pillow.   She turned her head.

"Oh, George, it's you!   I am glad to see you."

"I told the old she-dragon you would be.   She said you
were asleep."

Laura giggled a little.   In that soft light, with her hair
that way, it didn't sound a ridiculous noise.

"George, you are awful."

He sat on the end of the bed.   A warm flood of affection
for his sister filled him.   It was all so friendly and casual.
She had been glad to see him.   It pleased him that she

had been glad. Then he remembered his errand, and was suddenly ashamed of the shabby business. He wondered if perhaps he couldn't cook up some story that would get past Amy. But he pulled himself up in time. It was an old trap, how often he'd fallen into it. The desire to please— he'd made a fool of himself often enough that way. It would be fun to sit here with Laura and crack jokes at Miss Parks and forget all about touching her for a fiver. But it had to be done, whether he liked it or not. He had to have that money. She looked small and frail in the bed. But that was just the way the light was shining. What he was feeling was sentiment, not affection. Why shouldn't he borrow money from his sister ? Borrow, of course. She was rotten with money anyway—Mildred's money. The fact that it was Mildred's money made it easier.

"Are you feeling better ? " he asked. "You gave us all a horrid scare."

"I'm sorry." Her small face lost its gladness. "It was terribly silly of me. But you do understand how it happened, don't you ? "

"Of course I do. It could happen to anyone." Laura's hands, lying on the counterpane, might have been a child's hands, little, slight, with plain unvarnished nails. Amy took her shiny pink fingernails to bed with her. She never looked like a child in bed.

"Are you sure you understand ? " Laura was asking.

"Of course—and I don't blame you either. I told you Miss Parks was a silly old fool. It's no wonder you got the creeps when you saw the curtains move."

Her handbag was lying on the dressing-table, a small plain bag that contrived to look unobtrusive and expensive. Amy could have put a price on it even across the room, though it wasn't the kind of bag she'd have bought, even if she could have afforded it.

"It wasn't just that, George. There's more to it than that. You don't know where I went this afternoon after I left you ? "

"No. Where did you go ? "

She said she'd been at the Bank in the morning, he remembered. That meant she'd be bound to have the money on her. She'd looked at the shops, but said she hadn't bought much.

" I'd been—to the Picture Gallery—to see Tom's son."

She had, had she ? He'd never have thought it of her. It was probably his liqueur that had given her the courage to go. He'd been a fool to buy her that liqueur. He'd been all sorts of a fool. Oh well, once he had the fiver everything would be squared up. The lunch had been a treat for Laura anyway, and she'd enjoyed it.

" What was he like—Tom's son ? " he asked, postponing for a little longer the request he must make.

" Like Tom—except for his voice, of course."

" Were his pictures any good ? "

" I don't know ; I don't understand that kind of painting."

He'd have to hurry. Amy would start to fuss if he was any later. " Oh well, it was decent of you to go along anyway. Look, Laura——"

" But you see that was why it happened, George—because I'd been to see Tom's son."

George wondered if Miss Parks were right. Perhaps he shouldn't have come, perhaps Laura was feverish. She seemed to be worked up over very little. She was sitting up in the bed now, her fingers gathering up the edge of the sheet in a succession of little pleats.

" You see, George, she *knew*."

" Laura, what on earth do you mean ? "

" Mildred knew. She knew where I'd been this afternoon."

" Look, Laura——"

" I never told you, George, but—I loved Tom."

He put his head back and laughed. " And why wouldn't you ? He was a darn good chap. I always thought he had a fancy for you too. Look, Laura, we hung about over our lunch so long this afternoon that I missed a couple of calls I should have made—chaps that were expecting me. Oh, it'll be all right, I'll see them tomorrow or next week, but in the meantime I'm down a little. Could you be a good girl and lend me a fiver ? "

" Yes, George, of course. That was why I thought it was Mildred at the window when I came back. She wouldn't have liked me to go to see the exhibition, you see."

He moved to the dressing-table. " In here ? "

She nodded and he opened the handbag. There were some notes in the pocket at the back—yes, there was a fiver.

" That was what made me feel she was watching me, you see."

" Oh, I wouldn't say that. More force of habit, I should think." He took out a five pound note. " Thanks, Laura. Thanks a lot."

" Oh, George, not from that pocket. Take it from the little wallet—that's my own money—the other's——"

She stopped short.

" It's all your own money now, my dear child."

" Oh. Oh yes, I suppose it is. It's just that I used to keep my own allowance and—Mildred's money separate, you know."

" Well, you don't need to do that any longer. Now if I stay here another minute I'll have Miss Parks making a scene ; she didn't even want me to come up and bid you good night, but I told her where she got off."

" Oh, George, did you ? "

" Yes. I'll be up again soon. Take care of yourself, Laura. Good night, my dear. It was fun today, wasn't it ? "

" Oh it was."

" We'll have to do it often."

He kissed her cheek and left the room. Once on the landing he took the fiver out of his pocket and put it carefully into his notecase. Then he went downstairs, whistling under his breath. It had been easy, too easy. Perhaps that was why he hadn't really enjoyed it.

Laura lay quite still, listening to him going downstairs. How kind George was, how good of him to come up this evening. She couldn't remember why he had come, he hadn't known that this was going to happen. But his being there had taken the edge off the horror. How comfortable it had been, having him sit on her bed, listening to him talking. He lent a cheerful sanity to things which, she realised, had long since become distorted. A gentle peace enveloped her. She wished for nothing better than to lie there remembering that George had kissed her good night and said that he would come to see her again soon. It had helped her to tell George that she had loved Tom. It was odd, though, how calmly he had taken it. He could not have known—Tom and she had determined to keep it from everyone, even George. It had been a secret which she had so long cherished with guilt that she had expected George to show a more definite reaction. But of course he didn't know everything. No one did now, no one but herself. Tom was dead, Mildred was dead; there was no one left but herself.

Lying suspended between sleep and waking Laura suddenly remembered what it was that had brought George up to the house that evening. She slipped out of bed, crossed the room to the dressing-table and opened her handbag. Then she took five pounds out of the little wallet and put them into the pocket at the back of the handbag, and having made this adjustment went back again to her bed and fell asleep.

Miss Parks was glad to see Mr. McAlister when he presented himself at Marathon the following morning. It was Sunday, but she had not gone to church. She disliked the old gentleman, and suspected that he disliked her, but the events of the last few days had shown that it was necessary for them to work together to save Laura from the influence of George. What Laura's ultimate destination would be when the salvation was effected was another question, and she was ready to believe that Mr. McAlister would have widely different views on it from her own, but first things must come first. Laura must be delivered from George's clutches before she could be surrendered to anybody else's. Miss Parks was glad that Mr. McAlister had been there the previous evening, and that it had been in defiance both of his expressed wishes and her own that George had gone upstairs to visit Laura before he left the house. There was no need for her to tell Mr. McAlister what they were up against.

" Come in," she said, " how kind of you to call. I'm sure Laura will be very glad to see you. Yes, she had a quiet night, and is much more like herself this morning. She's still in bed, of course, that's why I haven't gone to church myself. I put my foot down—breakfast in bed, I said."

She rang for Hannah. " Hannah, will you ask Miss Laura if she will see Mr. McAlister ? " She enjoyed ringing and asking the servant to do an errand that a week ago she would have done herself. It gave her confidence, and it allowed Mr. McAlister to see in what capacity, and to what a degree, the household at Marathon had accepted her.

Laura was not sure that she wanted to see Mr. McAlister.

The tranquillity that she had felt the night before had deserted her. Last night she had been tired, tired and confused, and to yield to the unfamiliar feeling of security had been the easiest way out. Now her body was rested, and her mind refreshed after a night's sleep, and already she mistrusted last night's easy conclusion. What actually had happened yesterday? She had not passed so eventful a day for years. Lunch with George, the visit to the Art Exhibition, the scene at the railway station, the nightmare return home, all these had succeeded each other too rapidly, and had become a jumble of half-remembered incidents and impressions, of thought and reality, and now her restless mind nagged backward and forward through the hours, remembering, half-remembering, unable to remember. She could not leave the day alone. Her own behaviour on reaching home stood out with horrible clarity. It was sharply and unpleasantly reminiscent of much that had happened during the years of her illness, years which she had learned, through sheer necessity, to forget. Mildred's death had not solved the problems which she had expected it to solve. Living was not yet any easier than it had been then. While Mildred was alive she was the only person with whom a relationship was necessary, the only guide to Laura's conduct. Now she was dead, but Laura had no sense of liberation. Already she was involved in a tangle of duties and obligations —Mr. McAlister—George—Miss Parks—Tom's son. And meanwhile Mr. McAlister was asking if she would see him.

" Oh, Hannah, do you think I should ? "

" It's for yourself to say, Miss Laura."

" I don't know. I don't really want to see anyone. Miss Parks was vexed with me for talking so long to Mr. George last night."

" She's below in the hall with Mr. McAlister now, well. I heard her say she knew you'd be glad to see him."

" Oh dear—did she ? "

" Never you heed what she says, Miss Laura. She takes a lot on herself, that one."

" She has been very kind, Hannah." The implied reproof was mechanical, Hannah knew that as well as she did, but convention demanded that it should be made.

" She had the queer clear-up out of Miss Mildred's room yesterday."

" But I told her to take anything she liked, Hannah. It was good of her to go through Miss Mildred's things for me. There wasn't anything I wanted to keep, and Miss Parks takes a lot to do with Missions. Miss Mildred would be glad to think her things would go where they were appreciated."

" A whole taxi-load of stuff there was that went off."

" Oh, was there ? " Miss Parks hadn't said anything about this.

" It went off while you were away down the town in the afternoon."

" I expect she just forgot to tell me. She didn't know I was to be out in the afternoon anyway."

Hannah was not convinced. " The taxi came at the time you would have been taking your rest, if you had been here," she said.

Laura was secretly glad that the taxi had gone without her knowledge, that the house was freed of so much that would have reminded her of Mildred, and that it had all happened and could not now by any means be recovered. The stuff was gone. She had told Miss Parks to take it away. She was glad it had gone. Yet it had been a little high-handed of Miss Parks to get to work so quickly Mildred would not have liked it, Miss Parks must have realised that. Miss Parks was a comparatively new addition to the household. She must have been sorting and handling personal things of which she had no knowledge.

" Mr. McAlister, Miss Laura," Hannah reminded her. " What'll I tell him ? "

" Oh yes, of course. All right, Hannah, please ask him to come up."

She heard his slow careful foot on the stairs, and his discreet knock.

" It is good of you to see me, Miss Laura," he said, and established himself in the chair beside the window.

" It was kind of you to come," she said, wondering suddenly what it was that had brought him.

" You wanted to see me on business ? " she suggested.

" I do, I do, but business can wait. I came because I was anxious to learn how you were, my dear. You gave us all a fright yesterday, you know."

" I'm afraid I was silly—very silly."

" My dear, you mustn't think that. It was a very natural thing to happen."

" Oh. Do you think it was ? "

" Of course it was. The kind of thing that might happen to anyone who has been living under the strain that you have. How are you feeling today ? Better ? "

" Oh much better, thank you. I'm really quite all right again, but Miss Parks insisted I should take the day in bed."

" Well, perhaps she was right. I should be inclined to be as lazy as you can for a little while. You're very pale, you know."

Laura put her hands up to her cheeks. " Oh. Am I ? I'm so sorry." She seemed genuinely concerned.

The old man laughed. " Come come, my dear ; it isn't a crime to be pale."

" No, of course not," she agreed ; " it's only that—that Mildred never liked it if I looked off colour. It depressed her, she said."

Mr. McAlister drew his chair nearer. " Don't let that worry you. You have my permission to be as pale as ever you like."

Laura laughed. " Oh, Mr. McAlister, how kind you are ! "

Mr. McAlister picked her hand up off the counterpane and set it down again. " My dear, I want to persuade you to be a little kinder to yourself. Do you understand what I mean ? "

Laura had been embarrassed by his touch. She wished he would go back to the place at the window. " I—I think I do," she ventured.

" You've got into the habit of unselfishness," the old man went on ; " it's high time you got out of it."

" But, Mr. McAlister——"

" I know what I'm saying. Consider yourself for a change. Do whatever you want to do. Don't take anybody's advice."

" Everybody has been most kind," Laura ventured. She wondered if he would notice if she edged her small body to the far side of the bed, further away from him. She supposed he would and lay still.

" They may mean to be kind, I've no doubt they do, but don't you take advice from anybody—not from Miss Parks, or from your brother—or from me, for that matter."

" I don't know what I would have done without George,"
she said.

He left the bed now and returned to the window.   She let
herself lie slack again.   He was playing with the tassel on the
blind.   " You must have been very glad to see your brother,"
he said, without turning to look at her.

" Oh, very glad."

" He came at once ? "

" The very day of the funeral—you remember, he was here
when you got back."

" Yes, so he was.   You sent for him, I suppose ? "

" No, I didn't.   I wanted to, Mr. McAlister, ever so often
I wanted to, but—well, you know how it was.   He didn't get
on with father or Mildred.   He hadn't visited the house for
years."

" He knew Mildred was ill, surely ? "

" No.   He didn't know anything about it.   It was the
notice in the paper he saw, and then of course he came right
away."

" Really ?   When I saw him here I assumed you and he
had kept in touch."

" Oh no.   But—well, George and I were great friends when
we were children, Mr. McAlister.   He guessed I'd be glad
of his help."

Mr. McAlister turned round and looked at her directly
from under his heavy brows.   " It's just a pity he waited
so many years.   You'd have been glad of his help before
this."

Laura didn't like him staring at her like that.   " I told you,
Mr. McAlister, it would only have made trouble if he'd come
up here before."

" You mean your sister wouldn't have made him welcome ? "

Why was it necessary for him to put it into words ?   " I
suppose that is what I mean."

" I see."

" But he's been so kind, Mr. McAlister.   They're not
well off, you know ; in fact I rather think they've been having
a difficult time, but he offered me a home—you heard him,
didn't you ?—and his wife is going to help me to do some
shopping."

Put in so many words George's sudden solicitude for her

welfare seemed transparent enough. Laura did not like putting it into words, but she could not keep herself from babbling on.

" I'm going shopping with his wife."

" Yes. Yes, you were saying so. I expect she'll enjoy that, won't she ? Have you decided yet whether you will go and live with them ? "

" Perhaps. I don't know. But they really do want me, Mr. McAlister. And of course I shouldn't be a burden to them. I shall pay my way."

" I quite realise that, my dear. And I'm sure they realise it too."

She knew what he meant by that, and wished she had checked her nervous chatter. His veiled accusations seemed to call forth confidences she had not wished to make, and to force her to declare decisions which she had not yet reached herself.

" Of course I wouldn't dream of going unless they allowed me to contribute to the household. I told them so—but that was after they had asked me. They suggested my coming first ; you see they do want me. It's so nice to go where you're wanted, isn't it ? "

Mr. McAlister didn't answer for a moment. He stood considering her, as if undecided what to reply. Then he sighed deeply and said, " Don't make up your mind too quickly, will you, Laura ? You may have—other invitations."

" Other invitations ? " she laughed. " Oh, I don't think so. And George wants me to decide quickly. He says it will be lonely for me living here all by myself. He's coming up soon to see what I've decided." What other invitations could she have, she wondered. She wished Mr. McAlister would share with her the pleasure she felt in being welcomed into George's family circle. He might have done that much. He knew how drab her life had been. Hadn't he been telling her she must please herself now, and do what she wanted to with her own life ?

" I hope your brother will not try to rush you. You lunched with him yesterday, didn't you ? "

" Yes, I did. It was lovely. We had such a lot to talk about."

" I'm sure you had, especially when you hadn't seen each

other for so long. It must have been odd meeting again. You would be almost like strangers after all these years."

"Strangers! George and I strangers! Oh no, George and I have always understood each other."

He stood looking down at her and frowning. "I hope you do understand him, Laura."

Laura avoided his eyes and said stubbornly, "Yes, I understand George." The old man didn't answer, and she made an appeal for his approval. "Mr. McAlister, I must have someone to rely on."

"Yes," he agreed heavily, "yes, of course. That's why he comes so often, I suppose."

"Yes, I suppose that's why."

There seemed no more to be said, or rather no more that either was willing to say. He concluded the small amount of legal business and bade her good morning.

Laura lay still for a long time after he had gone. She felt childishly angry at this lack of sympathy. Happiness, life had taught her, is a matter of degree, to be measured against the suffering or anxiety or boredom that preceded it. After the barren succession of years that she had lived through, George's return and their renewed friendship were poignant and heart-warming. She knew as well as anybody else—as well as Mr. McAlister anyway—that he hadn't made a success of his life, but must she wait for pleasure until the perfect circumstances presented themselves? George had come home —she had a brother again—his family would welcome her— here was richness! And here was Mr. McAlister at such pains to warn her against the first real joy she had had for years.

Her anger made her bold. She knew Miss Parks expected her to stay in bed for lunch, so she got up and dressed, and came downstairs just before one o'clock. Miss Parks was surprised to see her.

"Laura! My dear! I thought you were having your lunch in bed."

"No, I got up."

Miss Parks was anxious to wipe out the memory of her mistake of the previous evening and the snub she had received.

"I've had such a busy morning, my dear," she said, "sorting the last of the things out of Mildred's room."

" I thought you got them all cleared out in the taxi yesterday," Laura said bluntly.

Miss Parks was disturbed. She did not know Laura knew of the taxi. " Oh no. Those were only the clothes, the things you so generously promised me for our Mission work. Such a welcome contribution, they will be greatly appreciated, you may be sure. No, today I was busy at her own personal things, her papers and her jewellery, things like that—things you wouldn't wish anyone outside the family circle to handle. They are all in order now, waiting for you to see what you wish to keep."

" Burn the papers," Laura said, " and sell the jewellery, if you want the money for your Missions."

Miss Parks gaped at her. Laura was behaving in a very odd and difficult manner ; perhaps she was still far from well.

" Laura, are you sure you should have got up ? "

" Quite sure, thank you."

Miss Parks' nervousness made her voluble. " A beautiful room, your sister's room. I quite enjoyed working there this morning—the sun was streaming in. It's quite the nicest room in the house. The little room I have gets no sun, you know. But it was beautiful in Mildred's room this morning."

" I'm sure it was," Laura said, " and it has been good of you to stay long enough to sort things out for me. It has been a great help. I hope you will still come and visit me sometimes."

Miss Parks accepted the inevitable. It had come so quickly out of so blue a sky, that she had no defence prepared. Next day she went and packed her small suitcase. She thought Hannah smiled faintly when she asked her to order a taxi. She would have preferred to travel home by bus, for it was necessary now to start counting the shillings again, but Marathon demanded a departure by taxi—and by five o'clock she was climbing the stairs to her own flat in Ashley Avenue.

She called it a flat. It was two rooms on the third floor of a small ugly house. The lower flights were occupied by a dressmaker—her fitting rooms were on the ground floor, and she lived on the floor above. Most of the ladies the dressmaker worked for came from houses on the Malone Road, and she had a veneration for the upper classes. Miss Parks had

hoped to impress her by an account of her stay at Marathon—
"With my old friend, Laura Percival "—and with a casual
mention of the ménage and its sober lavishness.   She had
planned to do it very cleverly, as if it was the most natural
thing in the world.   But there was a smart car outside the
door, and the lights were on in the fitting room.   Miss
Jordan had a customer—a client, she called it.   A voice
whose accent spelt wealth and ease came from the fitting-
room door, and Miss Jordan's voice, respectfully imitative,
answering phrase for phrase.   But as Miss Parks carried her
suitcase up the stairs Miss Jordan opened the door for a
moment, and put out her head, with her mouth full of pins.
"You're back," she said, tight-lipped, preoccupied.   Miss
Parks nodded confirmation and went on.

It was some weeks since she had quitted the flat to go to
live at Marathon.   She had left hurriedly, eager to seize the
opportunity offered by Mildred's serious condition.   She had
not taken the trouble to leave an address to which her letters
might be forwarded.   It was not likely there would be many
letters.   There were three.   They lay at the back of the door
as she pushed it open, and when she had lit the gas-fire she
sat down to study them.   There was a free coupon for a new
washing powder, the gas bill, and a cordial invitation from the
Minister and Kirk Session of her brother's church, to attend
the Annual Congregational Social.

Miss Parks sat studying the invitation.   Two years ago,
before the Reverend Cuthbert had married and while she was
still occupying the position of Minister's wife in congregational
affairs, she would have filled in the names on these cards, and
when the evening came, have sat beside her brother on the
platform.   Now here was a card with her name written on it,
in the bold sprawling hand which she recognised as that of her
supplanter.   It was customary for the church to send out
these special invitations to some of the people who had left
the neighbourhood and joined other churches as she had done
—in fact it was the cue for one of her brother's little jokes,
"And now I must extend a special word of welcome to some
of the old—or should I say *former* members of the congre-
gation who are back with us again this evening."   Now she
was one of those who would be expected, from a humbler seat
in the hall, to raise a simper at this pleasantry.   She kept the

coupon for the washing powder and the gas bill, and put the invitation into the waste-paper basket.

The room was cold and smelt damp. She noticed that the dark patch at the side of the window had got darker, and that the wallpaper was peeling again below the picture rail. The gas-fire hissed and spluttered ineffectually. She thought of the broad grates at Marathon, with coals that one could poke, and solid polished fire-irons. On the table sat the bowl of daffodils that had been blooming when she went away. She had planted them herself, and they had made quite a show. They had grown taller than she had expected, and she had stuck a knitting-needle in the fibre, for a stake, and tied them up to it with wool. How proud she was of them as they came into bloom. She counted each one, and quoted Wordsworth to herself as she watered them. Now they were limp and withered, the wool had broken and the leaves sprawled onto the table while the flowers, still erect, were brown and dry. At Marathon there were hundreds and hundreds of daffodils on both sides of the drive.

She was hungry, and there was no food in her larder. She went downstairs again, softly, so that Miss Jordan would not come out, and bought herself a loaf and some food at the little shop on the corner. The woman who served her did not seem surprised to see her. Evidently her absence had not been remarked. She procured an evening paper and came back again, softly up the stairs, and made a meal for herself. She wondered if Hannah had sounded the gong for Laura's evening meal.

As she ate her meal, Miss Parks studied the paper. Scanning through the obituary notices she came on one which arrested her attention. It was the death of the mother of one of her former pupils. Miss Parks recalled the lady as a loud-voiced interfering parent, who had never any hesitation in saying what she thought and coming to the school to say it. She had even, on one occasion, said it in front of the class. The girl, Monica, was like her mother, shrewd and thrusting, lazy unless it suited her to be otherwise, always sure of popular support from the back of the classroom when it came to a battle of wits with one of the staff.

The family lived in Wellesley Avenue, just across the Lisburn Road, a street of small red narrow terrace houses that opened straight onto the pavement. They were in poor circumstances, Monica was the eldest of the children. Miss Parks remembered the others as noisy ill-mannered little boys. She could remember nothing that could commend them to her. But when she had finished her meal she rinsed the dishes and put them carefully back on the shelf, and without unpacking her suitcase, walked out into the darkening evening, and round to the house where the family lived.

The blinds were drawn, the lights lit behind them. The funeral, the paper stated, had taken place that afternoon. The front door stood open. A few visitors were saying good-bye. The last of them lingered in conversation with a lanky girl whom Miss Parks recognised as Monica. Monica was wiping her eyes and the lamplight showed that her face was pitiful with weeping. She clung to the departing visitor. Miss Parks slipped into an entry and bided her time.

" Good-bye then, Monica. I must run on," the visitor was saying.

" Oh, Auntie, must you ? " the girl entreated, twisting her handkerchief. " Could you not just stay overnight ? "

" I would if I could, you know that. But haven't I my own at home to do for ? "

" I'll never manage," the girl wailed.

" Indeed you will. I'll be round whenever I can to see how you're getting along." The visitor was impatient to be off, and embarrassed at the girl's lack of control.

" It's that lonesome," wept Monica.

From the house behind her came the wail of a young child, and the voices of older boys raised in dispute.

" Lonely ! Haven't you lots of company in the house there ? "

" Do you hear them ? They're at it already. I'll never manage them, and there's no company in the house without Mammy ! " She cried unashamedly out in the street.

The visitor made an effort to calm her, and at last was off. The girl stood looking after her, her thin shoulders humped in the black frock. The uproar from the open door increased. The girl turned and went in slowly.

Miss Parks waited a moment, and then made up her mind. There was no comparing this house to Marathon, but the empty flat daunted her. Here at least she would be needed. She hurried hopefully to the house of mourning and rang the bell.

Chapter Eleven

HANNAH made no comment that evening as she served Laura's supper at one end of the long dining-table. Laura ate it slowly, glad of the good food and that she was alone to enjoy it. When she had finished she went into the drawing-room where a small fire was burning. Hannah came in to draw the curtains and then took herself off.

There were a few letters on the mantelpiece that she should answer—letters of condolence from old acquaintances. She looked through them idly, but made no move to the writing-desk. She was elated at Miss Parks' departure, but the effort it had cost her to bring it about had made her tired. She wanted nothing better, she told herself, than to sit by the fire, in this familiar room, knowing that no demands, physical or emotional, could be made on her. There was nothing now that she must do or leave undone, nothing she must be careful to say or leave unsaid, or consider in what way she should say it. She did not need to adjust herself to anyone. She could think, do, feel as she pleased. It was so new a luxury she did not hurry to embark on it. It was enough to realise that the freedom was there.

She could not remember sitting alone in this room in the evening. This was what she had imagined it would be like after Mildred's death. But since then Miss Parks and George and Mr. McAlister had crowded in on her so persistently that she was rarely alone, and what solitude she had had been employed in sifting each day's events. Miss Parks had gone now ; George would be glad to hear that. Mr. McAlister, she suspected, would be glad to hear it too.

It was a quarter to eight. A few months ago, before she had finally taken to her bed, Mildred would have been sitting over there in the big chair—she moved from the sofa to the fireside chair in the evenings—turning the pages of a book, and wondering aloud what sort of taste the Librarian thought she had to send her rubbish like this to read, and why Laura had not refused to carry it home. Or she would have had her embroidery frame in her hand, stitching at it with that pitiless precision that characterised everything she did. And Laura, pretending to read, or trying to hide her inexpert knitting, would see it was a quarter to eight, and would think—three-quarters of an hour before Hannah comes in with the weak tea and the biscuits, three-quarters of an hour while I must guard my tongue and suffer whatever Mildred chooses to say, accept her sour opinions as the truth, swallow whatever veiled rudeness she may have to make. Three-quarters of an hour and then tea, and after that the slow procession from the drawing-room to the bedroom, the painful climbing of the stairs. Half-way up the flight the pain would grip Mildred, and she would stand, rigid and silent, holding onto the banisters. Laura would stand beside her, turning her eyes away, over-come by a physical repugnance of which she was deeply ashamed and a pity for which she could find no expression. When the pain had finished with her Mildred would be the first to speak. "Now, Laura, shall we go on, if you are ready?" There was always a sneer at Laura's vulnerability behind the words—if I can stand it, why can you not? So the progress to the bedroom was recommenced.

Then the business of helping Mildred to bed. How Mildred hated to be helped, and how much she found to criticise in Laura's service! It would be half-past nine before the ordeal was over, the light adjusted, the extra sleep-ing-pill laid beside her—" just in case, Mildred, you know the doctor says it will do you no harm "—the hot bottle that had cooled filled again, the window opened, closed, and opened again, and sometimes the clock in the hall would be striking ten before Laura, limp with nerves and smarting under Mildred's tongue, wracked with pity for the pain her sister must suffer and yet unable to utter one word of compassion, was at last released to find her own way to bed, consoled that at least another day was over.

The clock in the hall now struck eight o'clock, and Laura, alone in the drawing-room, sat on, the letters in her hand. She remembered that after Mildred had been confined to her bed, when the illness had her defeated, the night-nurse would come downstairs about this time, and sit a minute before the fire, chatting, yawning, enquiring if there hadn't been a phone call for her during the day. Then she would go upstairs to take over, and the day nurse would drop in on her way to bed, to report on the invalid's condition, the prospects of a good night, the state of her own stomach (the day nurse suffered from chronic indigestion) and any other topics that might crop up. Those blessed girls in their white uniforms, how Laura admired them! They could say 'so long' and trot upstairs humming the latest tune, and after an airy tattoo on Mildred's bedroom door, enter the room with no more to-do than if they were coming in for a cup of tea. They could handle Mildred's sick body with skill and confidence and yet smile and chat over the top of it, and turn a deliberately obtuse ear to Mildred's most acid comment. They were full of good nature and pity, and yet oblivious to atmosphere. They knew nothing of the fumbling ineptness that overcame Laura when she must do a service for her sister, or the dumbness she felt when Mildred spoke to her. It had been a revelation to Laura to discover that Mildred's influence was not universal.

It was now ten minutes past eight. It was wonderful how slowly the time went when one was alone, when there was nothing against which one must spend the empty minutes arming oneself. Laura opened her handbag to search for her pen. Perhaps she should answer a couple of the letters. There would be time—more than time—before Hannah brought her her tea. At the back of the handbag was a square of pasteboard. She picked it up and studied it. It was the address and the telephone number that Tom's son had handed to her before she left the Picture Gallery.

He had asked her to ring him up. He wanted her to go with him to see where Tom had painted that picture. It was a ridiculous proposal, of course. And yet—was it? At the time she had been flustered by the crowded room, the novelty of the experience, the boy's likeness to Tom. She could not remember what excuse she had given him, if indeed she had made any coherent excuse, but at least she had not made any arrangement to go with him. She wished now that she had. Why should she not go? She knew with what cold scorn Mildred would have dismissed the idea. Mildred was dead. George and Mr. McAlister had said she must please herself now, do what she wanted to, enjoy things. She would enjoy going with this boy to revisit the little stony beach at Lough Neagh.

She wondered if the boy would be at the address now if she rang him up. It was hard to decide to do it. She wished there was someone to whom she might mention the enterprise before she embarked on it. She remembered it had been George's suggestion that had sent her to look at the boy's pictures. "We owe that much to Tom," he had said. It would be a kindness to take this boy into the country. She would mention it to George. She hadn't really expected that George would call yesterday. It was Sunday, he would be at home with his wife and daughter. And all day she had deliberately tried to avoid listening for the door-bell. He had said he would come back soon. That should be enough.

It was a quarter past eight when the telephone rang. Hannah answered it and told her that George was on the line. She crossed the hall in a flutter of delight.

"Hallo, old girl. Did you think I'd forgotten you?"

"Oh no, George."

"I knew you wouldn't want me yesterday, and I had rather a rush of work today, and just couldn't make it."

"Of course I understand."

"I'll bet Miss Parks has been wondering what has happened to me?"

"Miss Parks has gone; she went this afternoon."

"She did? Ah-ha! Good for you, Laura! How did you pull that off?"

Laura was a little diffident about the telephone. It was a medium for communication, not for confidences. "Oh, she —just went."

"And I'll bet you're not sorry?"

"It's—quiet without her."

"I'm sure it must be. Look, Laura, that's why I rang up. Amy wants you to come up for your tea tomorrow."

"Oh—does she?"

"And young Kathie's dying to meet you. You will come, won't you?"

"Well, it's very good of her to ask me."

"Good my foot! Isn't she your sister-in-law? And don't you want to meet your niece?"

"Of course I do."

"Well then, you'll come along—common or garden high tea, you know—we don't run to dinner."

He would be offended now and think her stiff if she refused. "Thank you, George, I'd like to."

He gave her the address and said good night. Coming back across the hall she thought, I shall ask him tomorrow about going to Lough Neagh with Tom's son. He's bound to think it a good idea, and then I shall enjoy going so much more.

It was twenty-five past eight when she sat down again at the fire. In five minutes Hannah would be bringing her weak tea and the plate of biscuits. There was not now long to wait.

She went to the little house at Ballydrum next evening for her tea, and when it was time for her to leave for home George said he would walk to the bus with her. It was quite a journey across Belfast back to Marathon. He wanted to call a taxi for her, but she insisted she would go by bus. She said good-bye to Amy and Kathie, and set off with him down the road.

"You should have let me get you a taxi," he persisted.

"Of course not, George. It would have been a dreadful waste of money."

"Are you all right for money, Laura, until the will is through?"

"Oh yes. Mr. McAlister has seen to that. He's explained everything. He's really been awfully kind."

"There's every reason why he should be—it's his bread and butter, isn't it? An easy way of earning it, if you ask me."

"Still, he *has* been good. There's really been no need for him to come up as often as he does."

"Keeping an eye on you, is he? Or on me?" George laughed. "Well, don't you let anybody boss you about. And I'll tell you another thing—you ought to get a car."

"A car!" If he had said an aeroplane she could hardly have sounded more startled.

"Why not? You could get around then and see places. You'll have lots of money, you ought to run a car. I could give you a bit of advice what to choose—run it in for you, if you like."

" But I can't drive."

" Nothing to prevent you learning. I could teach you, and chauffeur you a bit until you get used to it."

They were on the Shore Road now, waiting to get across the stream of quickly-moving traffic to reach the bus stop.

" I would like to get into the country sometimes. George —you remember I told you I'd been to see those pictures of Tom's son's ? "

" Yes, you said you'd been there."

" Did I tell you I'd met the boy ? "

" Did you ? " George didn't sound very much interested. There was a lull in the traffic now, and he took her by the elbow.

" I liked him, George. We talked quite a lot. He hasn't been to Ireland before."

" No, I don't suppose he has."

" He wants to see something of the country before he goes, but of course he doesn't know his way about."

George's grip on her elbow tightened and they began to move across the road.

" He showed me some of Tom's sketches—of places that I recognised. He wanted to know how to get to them. He suggested I might go with him."

George didn't answer till they were across the road and safely landed on the opposite pavement. Then he said, " Very nice for him, perhaps, but surely just a little bit ridiculous for you."

Laura gave a little gasp and stood still.

" Come on, Laura. Bus stop's over there."

Still she didn't move. " Laura, come on. What is it ? People are looking at you."

" What you said just now," Laura answered ; " it was just what Mildred would have said to me—and the way she would have said it."

" I'm sorry, Laura. Forget it. Forget the whole thing. Look, there's your bus, you'll have to hurry for it. Good-bye now, it's been grand having you."

" Good-bye, George—thank you."

Her pinched face, those bleak words, they haunted him as

he waved at the bus and turned on his heel for home. He could have kicked himself for striking this discordant note at the end of an evening which had, he thought, been otherwise an unqualified success. But to be accused of thinking and speaking like Mildred in the middle of the Shore Road was unnerving. In a way it was also insulting. True, it was he who had suggested Laura should go to see the boy's pictures. It had been something to say, a way of establishing a footing on that first difficult evening when he had come up to Marathon. Since then he had learned from Laura that she and Tom had been in love. He had always guessed that Laura entertained a sentimental weakness for his friend, but her words had affirmed something much more real. He was uneasy at the way she had confessed it, and next day had been himself to see the boy and his pictures. He seemed a likeable enough youngster. But if Laura still cherished romantic ideas about Tom there was every reason why she should cultivate a friendship with Tom's son—and every reason why George might stand to lose by that. Women of forty were tricky, they did unreasonable things on an impulse. Laura would need watching. It wouldn't suit him if Laura went chasing over the countryside with this youngster of Tom's.

Still on the whole the evening had gone well—or so he thought until he let himself into his house again and went through to the small kitchen where Amy, an apron tied over her smart cheap frock, was stacking dirty dishes. She didn't turn when he came in.

"Well, that was a pleasant evening," he opened up. "I think Laura enjoyed herself."

Amy was scraping the remains of the meat and salad off the plates. "Small thanks to you then," she said.

He said, in tones of outraged ignorance, "What on earth do you mean by that?"

"It's well your sister enjoyed herself anyway, let alone what the rest of us thought about it."

He threw his hat down on a chair and went to her. "Look, Amy, what is all this?"

Amy turned quickly with a couple of dirty plates in her hand, holding him off with them. "You know rightly what I mean."

She must be really upset, George thought.   She always lets her careful imitation accent slip when she's upset.

" I wish you'd tell me what it's all about."

Across the protecting plates Amy told him.   " If you'd wanted me to make coffee, why didn't you say so ?   If that's what your sister's used to I'd have made it and welcome. You had no call to apologise for a good cup of tea."

Amy couldn't make coffee, but no matter.

" Why did you have to bring her out into the back garden through the scullery ?   Couldn't you have gone round the front way ?   You know yourself the back's never fit to be seen when there's a big meal getting.   And telling Kathie to take her aunt up the stairs to see her room !   Kathie's room's nothing to write home about—you know I would have had it papered in the autumn only I couldn't gather the money. It's only a wee cupboard, the way it is.   And when you were out in the garden, what for did you have to start up cracking with Mr. McGonigal from next door ?   You know well he's no class—and the common way he has of talking ! "

Amy's resentment had not been suggested in her manner to Laura.   She had remained a courteous and charming hostess—a little effusive, perhaps, but Laura was nervous herself and wouldn't have been likely to notice that.   Now, however, the stream of injuries, swollen by delay, flowed from her and George could find no reply.   Besides, the couple of dirty plates that she held between them had him stymied.

The door opened, and Kathie came in, Kathie arrayed in tennis shorts and a T-shirt, both of which were skimpy on her, and her healthy budding figure would have looked less ridiculous had she been naked.

" See," she said, pirouetting comically, " they'll neither of them look at me.   They were tight enough in the autumn, and they're worse again now."

" What are you doing ? " her mother demanded.

" Trying on my tennis things," the girl answered.   " I said they'd be too small for me, and so they are."

" More money," said George.

" I don't know where it's coming from," Amy lamented.

" Well, I can't play like this," said Kathie, displaying a generous glimpse of the obvious.

" But if you have to get a racquet as well——"

" Not now. I'm getting my racquet."

" What do you mean ? "

" I'm getting my racquet.   It's only the clothes I'll need."

" Where are you getting your racquet ? "

" From Aunt Laura. She's going to buy me one—and it'll be a good one, if she goes and buys it."

Amy and George said nothing for a moment, but looked first at each other and then at their daughter.

" How did your aunt know you needed a new racquet ? " George asked at last.

The girl avoided his eyes.   " Oh, I just happened to say."

" And when did you ' just happen to say ' ? "

" When I was showing her my room—you remember, Pop, you told me to take her on up to see my room. My old racquet just happened to be lying out on my bed, and well— she could see it was an old one, couldn't she ? It's no use to anybody the way it is."

" Kathie, you'd no business to tell your aunt you needed a new racquet," Amy started, but George cut her short.

" You didn't lose much time before you were on the make," he said.

Kathie stuck out a rounded underlip.   " Listen who's talking," she said.

George, for once, was at a loss for words.   He took a couple of steps at Kathie who turned around to beat a retreat, and caught her a smart slap across the inadequate shorts before she reached the door.   She gave a yelp and disappeared, and her bedroom door banged behind her.   George looked round at Amy for support. But Amy was again engrossed in her dishes, and ostentatiously preoccupied. George knew that this time the two women in the house were against him.   He picked up his hat and went out into the narrow strip of back garden for a breath of air, and to give himself time to think.

The Cave Hill was dark against the darkening sky.   A train went past, a moving belt of lights, with the glow from the funnel lighting up the travelling pillar of smoke.   Over the garden fence the regrettable neighbour, Mr. McGonigal, was scraping his tools and packing them away in the little garden shed.

Amy was right, of course. He was a common old man.

She had been right about the other things as well. George
had apologised for the teapot on his table instead of the more
refined coffee pot, in a way that was quite unnecessary ; he
had deliberately escorted Laura through the messy littered
scullery on her way to the back of the house ; he had purposely
accosted Mr. McGonigal and drawn him into conversation.
But it was all with a purpose. He was anxious that Laura,
while appreciating Amy and Kathie, should realise the inconvenient little rabbit hutch of a house for what it was, their
neighbours for the ordinary folk they were. He knew he
could rely on Amy and Kathie to behave impeccably. Laura
would like them. She would, he hoped, be drawn to the
child. The expedition up to see her bedroom had been pro-
posed in order to give them the few moments together when
a confidence might be ventured. And Laura would see the
poor little room the child had to do with.

When she had seen all this, what could she do except
suggest that the family remove themselves wholesale to
Marathon, where there was room and plenty for all of them,
where Amy would learn to give a perfect imitation of a lady,
and Kathie would grow into one without self-consciousness ?
He had no intention of Laura joining the family in Ballydrum,
but every intention of the family migrating to join Laura.

He had made a mistake, of course, in underestimating
Amy's sensitivity. Thank God, at least, she had given no
sign of feeling hurt while Laura was there. But the child had
cashed in on her aunt, the tennis racquet had ' happened ' to
be lying on the bed—George could imagine only too vividly
how it had been managed ; it was, after all, his own particular
line of country. And Kathie knew that—" Listen who's
talking ! "—and Amy hadn't checked her for it either.

The cool air of the spring evening helped George to readjust
things, to twist them, as he so often did, until it seemed as if,
after all, what had happened had been what he wished to
happen. He smoked an extra cigarette—that little bit of
licence restored much of his self-esteem. Then the light
went up in the bedroom—Amy had gone to bed. The rosy
square of light—Amy's bedroom was pinker than any orchard
of apple blossom or the most strawberry of ice-creams—drew
him indoors. He could make his peace with her now. He
smiled to himself ; he knew well how to make his peace.

Half-way up the stairs he saw the light still on under the door of Kathie's little room. He would enjoy his recon-ciliation with Amy much more if he could go to her knowing that he and the child were friends again. So he opened the door and went in.

He was immediately unsure of himself and sorry he had come. As a child Kathie had adored her father; she accepted him at his own estimation of himself. He was a god, kindly, jovial, omnipotent, a jester, exquisitely funny, a safe refuge. But now he felt himself out of his depth. She was sitting at the chest of drawers that served her for a dressing-table, wiping cream from her face, and studying her reflection in the little mirror hanging against the wall. She turned round, cotton wool suspended. Her hair was drawn back off her face, her skin shiny and pale under the single bulb, the cheek-bones protruding. She didn't look like a child at all.

"Hallo," George said, "what's this? Next year's Little Mo putting in her beauty treatment?"

Kathie didn't smile. "Yes," she said, and finished her job with the cotton wool.

"All fixed up for the night? It's time you were in bed, young lady." A couple of years ago he would have carried her there, and tickled her till she was helpless.

"I'm just going. You might fix the window for me, would you?"

George crossed over to the window. When he turned back she was in bed, the clothes drawn tightly across her shoulders.

"Not as wide as that—the middle catch." George ad-justed the window to suit her, and turned again to the bed.

"Good night," he said. She didn't move. He aimed a kiss at her unresponsive forehead, feeling her eyes on him all the time, and was glad to be again on the other side of the bedroom door. The child was changing. She didn't look like herself, somehow, not with her skin shiny and her hair drawn back. It wasn't just the hair and the skin though. She reminded him of someone. He'd never thought of it before, but now it hit him like a stone—she had a look of Mildred!

George would have been less happy about the success of the evening had he realised its impression on Laura. She went home tired and excited, but delighted to have spent an evening with George and his family, charmed by the welcome, by Amy's kindness and Kathie's interest in this new relation. She had not noticed the tawdry little house, Amy's ' off the peg ' dress, Kathie's shabby crowded bedroom, or if she had noticed them, had thought them all part and parcel of this friendly household in which she had suddenly been made welcome. The light-hearted banter between George and his daughter, the obvious affection of his wife (Amy had hidden her irritation very successfully), her desire to please Laura and make her feel at home, these were the impressions that she carried away with her. Here were a real family, people who thought what they pleased and said what they thought. Beneath their casual chat she sensed a real and deep affection, something which she had never known in her experience of family life. Words were not carefully weighed and as carefully spoken, they were not weighed at all. The heart welled over into words, and that was all there was to it. They had accepted her into their circle without formality. She had not been offended by the untidy scullery, the middle-class pot of strong tea, or the coarseness of Mr. McGonigal. She had been delighted at the chance to offer the child a new tennis racquet. She wished she could have peeped into the third bedroom—the spare bedroom—for it would be there she would sleep when she joined the household.

For she had made up her mind to join it. Next morning, reviewing the events after a deeper night's sleep than she usually enjoyed, she did not change her mind. In the clearer light of the morning she could and did realise that George's wife was not what Mildred would have called a lady—that the house was small and flashily comfortable—that Kathie's desire to be friendly was not entirely disinterested. But she was prepared to accept these facts. They made no material difference. Her affection for George had been deepened by seeing him through the eyes of his family. She saw what he might have become in a less frigid air than that of Marathon.

Laura was not blind to George's character. She knew him to be unreliable, extravagant, a braggart, lazy, without conscience. Yet even these faults were, in her eyes, explained away, if not pardoned, by the warmth of his personality, the quick sympathy, the bravado—silly, of course—with which he matched his wits against the dull common sense of other men. Charm is an attribute which any decent Ulsterman will vigorously disown. It was George's misfortune to have been born in Ulster.

She was not blind either to the bond between George and Amy. It was beyond her experience but she could guess its strength. The bond was physical, but was augmented by a loyalty and appreciation of the satisfaction they found in each other. It had done more for George than ever his father's careful upbringing had. He had found a stability, not deeply engendered, but enough to make him and two other human beings reasonably happy. He lived a regular respectable life, earned honest money, came home in the evening to a house where he was welcomed. There had never been any welcome for him at Marathon, and the right to criticise had always superseded the right to love.

Laura looked forward now with confidence to becoming one of George's family. There was much she could do for them in the way of additional material comfort, and she knew that though they would demur prettily they would allow her to do it. She did not think she would be in the way. She had long ago learned to be unobtrusive, and she was hyper-sensitive to atmosphere. She only wanted to go to live in the small house at Ballydrum and be part of George's family. It would be possible, she thought, in that house as it had never been at Marathon, to discard the twisted past, not to try to analyse or excuse it, but simply to let it go, like a worn dress, and stepping into another to walk out a new woman.

She contrived how she could placate her conscience in taking this step. Her own small personal allowance, made over to her by her father twenty years ago and never since augmented or increased, could pay for the luxuries she hoped to buy for the family. Mildred's money—her money as it was now—should simply provide her keep. It would not matter whether she bought it in George's house or anywhere else. She must eat and drink and be housed, nobody could dispute that. As well—how much better—at Ballydrum as anywhere else.

So Laura made up her mind, reaching the decision partly in the flush of her new-found courage, but always careful to provide reasonable arguments in case that courage should desert her, and the old enemy, her conscience, begin once

again to nag. She was sorry that she had herself been
responsible for the one jarring note of the evening—when
George was seeing her onto the bus, and she had asked him
whether she should take Tom's son out into the country. and
had received his peculiar answer. She had not meant to tell
him that he spoke to her in the language and the manner of
Mildred. The words had come unprompted to her lips, and
she wished them back as soon as they were spoken. It was
not only what he said, not only his manner of saying it, but
even his face had vividly recalled Mildred's face. George
had been upset, she knew. But perhaps it was as well she
had said what she had and received his criticism. It had
prevented her from making a big mistake, she could see that
now. It would have been—as George put it—'ridiculous'
for her to go around the countryside with this young artist.
In any case, she should never have taken his suggestion
seriously. It had only been a joke. How well for her that
George had been there to put her right! She searched
through her handbag and took out the card the boy had given
her, with his telephone number.

But, holding it, she hesitated. It would be a pity that the
boy should not see the countryside his father had loved so
well. She should let him know she could not come, then he
could go ahead and make his own plans. That was only fair
to him—he might have made the suggestion in all sincerity.
Though she would much rather have thrown the card into the
fire she picked up the receiver and dialled the number. A
woman's voice answered, and asked her to wait. Then a
man's voice spoke.

"Hallo," said Laura, fighting to control a ridiculous
nervousness, "hallo, is—is that Mr. Richardson?"

"That's right," the easy voice assured her, "Richardson
here."

"Yes. Well, you won't know who I am, at least you
won't remember, or I don't think you will, but we met at your
exhibition a couple of days ago."

The young man was courteously non-committal. "Oh
did we?"

"Yes. You came and spoke to me. You were very kind
and fetched me a drink of water. I was interested in your
pictures."

" Oh yes," the voice said, and Laura heard him laugh. " I know—I'm right with you now—only it was my father's pictures you were interested in. "

Laura had recovered her confidence. The voice was so foreign in flavour and in phrase that it did not trouble her. This was not Tom's son, just a young American lad who was trying to be a painter.

" My father's pictures—they were the ones that rang the bell with you."

" Well—yes."

" That's all right, I can take it. And we're going out to see that stretch of water—where did you say it was ? "

" At Ballinderry—that's where the picture was painted, but I'm afraid I can't come after all. That's why I rang you up."

" But say, we'd as good as fixed it ! "

" I'm sorry. I'm very sorry, Mr. Richardson, but I find I can't come after all."

" Isn't there any day you could make it ? Business isn't all that brisk here, I could shut up and come right away if you say the word."

" I'm sorry, really I am."

" You know, I looked at those pictures of my dad's again after you went away. I think he's got something. I've got to take a look at that part of the country for myself before I go."

" Yes, you should try to go."

" That picture you fancied, you remember it—the stretch of water, and the stony little beach, and the hot sun. It makes you feel he enjoyed himself when he painted that."

Laura said hotly, " Of course he enjoyed painting it. Don't you enjoy painting ? "—and then stopped, appalled.

He laughed, and the slow voice answered her, " Oh, I enjoy it all right, but that's different. You didn't know my dad. Enjoyment wasn't his strong suit. That's why I'd like to see the place. It's got me wondering."

" Well, that was really why I rang you up. You can quite easily go there by yourself, it isn't difficult to get there, and if you've only got another week in Ireland you——"

" But see here, I thought we were going together."

" I know. I'd have liked that—very much. But I can't. It's just the way things have worked out."

"Not any day?" the soft voice wheedled. "Ah, come on. If I go by myself I shall get lost in one of your Irish bogs. You wouldn't want that to happen, would you?"

Laura was laughing weakly. What fun it would have been —out of the question of course, George had said ' ridiculous ', but what fun! "Don't be silly!" she said.

"And I shall get my feet wet. It says in the picture it's going to rain—you noticed that for yourself."

The silly laughter was checked, and hot tears prickled her lids. "Only for a little while, it never rains long, not in April."

"Oh please——"

It hadn't rained long. Only a space of minutes, great slow drops that quickened to a tattoo and then as suddenly ceased. Tom's coat had sheltered them both.

"Please do come!"

"I can't!" Laura cried. "I tell you I can't! Don't ask me any more—I can't!" She put on the receiver and let the tears come. The boy would have thought her odd. What did it matter? He didn't know her name. She owed it to Tom to let him know not to count on her, but to go into the country and find it for himself. He would go now. She wouldn't see him again. He had gone. Miss Parks had gone. There were only George and Mr. McAlister left. George had been quite right in his advice about the boy. She had done the wisest thing. Her heart was full of gratitude to George when Hannah came in to tell her that he was at the door, asking to see her.

Chapter Twelve

IT wasn't very convenient for George to make this call on Laura. But he hadn't telephoned to her that morning. He thought that after the unfortunate episode when they were making their farewells the previous night, a personal call would be better than a telephone conversation. It was important for him to make sure that this small unpleasantness was deleted before he continued his campaign.

He could see she'd been crying when he came in. He kissed her cheek. " My dear, you've been crying."

" I'm sorry. Only for a moment."

He held her hand. Poor Laura, her humility exasperated as much as it touched him. " Cry if you like, why wouldn't you ? "

" George, you are kind." He felt the ground under him now.

" I just popped in to see if you got back all right last night."

" Yes, I got back all right. George, I—I was so sorry I said that silly thing to you when you were leaving me at the bus."

This was better than he had hoped. He patted her hand and let it go. " Dear girl, forget it. It was just one of those things. I didn't mean to upset you, speaking as I did."

" But you were quite right, George. I rang up Tom's son and told him I couldn't go."

" Did you ? Wise girl ! I'm sure it was the best thing to do. Don't let's talk about it any more. It's over and done with. Well, what did you think of the family circle ? "

" Oh, George, I did enjoy myself. What a nice child Kathie is."

He laughed. " She's not bad. Amy's afraid you were scandalised at the awful little matchbox of a house we live in."

" Of course I wasn't ! It's a dear little house—so friendly."

" Friendly's the word. And don't talk nonsense, Laura, you know it's a ghastly hole."

" But I liked it, George, really I did."

He stared at her. There was no need to be obstinate. " My good sister, you needn't stretch politeness to such impossible lengths."

" I'm not being polite. I know the house is small, but it's quite big enough, surely ? "

He was annoyed. " Look here, Laura——"

She leaned forward, looking into his face intently. " George—are you trying to tell me you don't want me to come to live with you after all ? "

" Of course I'm not." She wanted to come as badly as that ! Poor Laura. Well, it suited him.

" I'm not sure that I believe you. Perhaps after last night Amy or Kathie changed their minds—perhaps they didn't like me—perhaps they don't want an extra person in the family. It's all right, George, you needn't mind telling me. It would be better for me not to go if they don't think it would work out."

" It isn't that, Laura, honest it isn't."

Her relief was childish. Her face was a mirror, she could hide nothing. George pitied her transparency.

" Well, George, what is it then ? "

" Sit down and I'll tell you." He lit a cigarette, and with his elbows spread wide on the marble mantelpiece and one foot on the brass fender, exhaled the smoke before he answered. " Amy and Kathie both liked you. But the house *is* small. There is a room you could have, if you came to us there, of course. But don't you think it would be better if we all came to live with you ? "

" In—Marathon ? " Her surprise was ludicrous.

" Why not ? " said George. " The house is here. After all, it is—or was—my home as much as yours. You know you don't need the half of it for yourself. It would be desperately lonely for you if you tried to live here alone. But if Amy and Kathie and I came to live here with you—well, that would suit us all, wouldn't it ? "

She didn't answer. " Don't you see, Laura ? It would be the only sensible answer. Amy'd be thrilled to bits— Hannah wouldn't mind, would she ? "

" Oh no. Hannah wouldn't mind."

" And as for Kathie—well, you saw the pathetic little cupboard of a place she calls her room, didn't you ? "

He hoped Laura wouldn't remember that it had been at his suggestion that Kathie had taken Laura up to her room. " Kathie could have the old night-nursery, couldn't she ? She'd love it. She's a nice child, Laura. There may be a lot of things about her that—that would have been different if we'd been able to bring her up in different surroundings. But she's young, Laura, she'd soon learn. You could do an awful lot for Kathie, you know. She took a real fancy to you last night."

Why wouldn't she ? Hadn't she been promised a tennis racquet ? But George could see that Laura was touched.

Emboldened he said, " We'll come and live with you here, Laura. That'll show old McAlister and Miss Parks and the rest of them." He threw the last of his cigarette into the fire and went over to the window. Sprawled on the sofa he cushioned his head on his hands and stared at the ceiling. " I shall like coming back to Marathon," he said.

Laura didn't answer. He wondered if she were crying again—tears of gratitude this time, no doubt. It had all been very easily and peaceably concluded, worth interrupting his work this morning. The personal touch—there was nothing like it.

" No, George," came Laura's voice from her place by the fire. " No. I'm sorry, but I couldn't agree to that." The small hard voice was one he would hardly have recognised as hers. He sat up.

" But, Laura—why ? "

" I'm sorry, George, I'd really rather you didn't ask me to explain."

So that was it—all right, but she wouldn't get away without having it put into the words she didn't want to hear. " So that's it, is it ? We're not good enough for you. You don't mind doing the Lady Bountiful act out at Ballydrum, but you'd be ashamed to have my wife and my daughter to live with you here."

" George, it isn't that, really."

He came back and stood kicking at the coals in the fire. " Oh, what's the good of making excuses. Amy's common—all right, I said it, you only thought it. Kathie's her mother's daughter. Hasn't Amy stuck to me when none of my family had any use for me ? Hasn't she done her damndest to keep that little place decent and bring the kid up in the best way she could according to her lights ? But you don't want her here. They can stay in Ballydrum where they belong. You'd be ashamed of them at Marathon."

Tears of self-pity brimmed up in George's eyes. He hoped Laura saw them.

Laura leant forward and gripped his hand. He wished she were less intense. Had he over-played the whole thing, and was she now going to make a scene ? He remembered how unbalanced and emotional she had always been as a girl.

" George, listen. It isn't anything to do with what I thought about Amy or Kathie. I liked them both—and I liked your house, little and all as it is. And I want so much to come and live with you there and be part of your family. But I—I can't have you to live at Marathon. You can't come ! "

Her emphasis struck him with force. There was something behind this that he didn't know. " Why ? " he asked.

She took her breath in sharply and said nothing, but sat back in her chair. There *was* something, he was convinced of it now. He would have to find out what it was. " *Why ?* " he said.

Still she didn't answer.

" Laura, there is some reason, something you haven't told me. There is some—hold Mildred had over you. I've guessed as much. Now I've got to know. She's dead, Laura. But you're still afraid of her. Why ? "

Laura turned her head away, putting up her hand as if to ward off a blow.

" Why, Laura ? "

Still she did not answer, but covered her face with her hands. He stooped down and took them away, compelling her to look at him. Her face was white, her eyes wide and haunted. He was shocked at what he had done, but there was no turning back now.

" Laura, you must tell me why."

He let go of her hands, and she sat twisting them dumbly. " You must tell me."

Still she did not speak, and the only sound in the room was the rubbing of her small fingers. Then at last they were still, and she said, " I'll tell you then. I never told anyone before. Mildred never told anyone either. Mildred and I were the only people who knew. George—it was my fault that Father died."

At first he couldn't reply. The unexpected took away all words. Then he said roughly, " What do you mean ? "

She said quietly, " It's true. It was my fault. I killed him." As if the burden of long years was at last laid down her hands relaxed and fell in her lap.

George stood back from her. " I—I don't understand. You don't know what you are saying. You're not well, Laura, I'll ask Hannah to come to you." Her sincerity frightened him, but it was plain she was ill.

" Don't send for Hannah. It is true, George."

" I don't see how it could be."

" I was staying at Hetty's—I told you that." Laura's voice was like a woman's who has told the same story to a child countless times and tells it again. " I'd persuaded Father to let me visit her. He let me go—he wasn't well all that summer, we hadn't gone away. So I arranged to go to Hetty's. After that I was going to Southampton to meet Tom. We were going to America together. We were going to be married when we got there."

" Good God! Did they know at home—about you and Tom ? "

" No. Nobody knew. It was no use my telling them. Once you left home Tom was just labelled as one of your undesirable friends. They didn't know that we still saw each other at the Art Class."

" But how can you have—killed—Father if you were away in England ? "

" I'll tell you. I was at Hetty's house for a fortnight. The day I was leaving for Southampton I wrote to Father to tell him what I was doing. I posted it that morning. When I came back from posting it there was a wire waiting for me from Tom to say that the boat was delayed and wouldn't be sailing till the next day. I didn't know what to do ; the letter was posted. I stayed at Hetty's an extra night, and the next day a wire came for me from home to say that Father was dead. He had got my letter in the morning, George—it was the shock that killed him."

" Oh, my poor Laura ! " So she was right, she had killed him. George could think of no words with which to comfort her. The whole thing was true, and yet incredible. This small middle-aged woman who in her appearance and manner bore every evidence of defeat had loved Tom, had loved him with passion, enough to make a bid to escape with him to America. But in the end she had failed Tom and killed her father. Compared with her story his own was that of a naughty child.

" I suppose it was Mildred who wired ? "

" Yes."

" What did she say ? Did she say it was the shock that killed him ? "

" Not in the wire, but I knew—she told me when I got home."

" What did you say to Tom ? "

" I didn't know what to do, or how to reach him. He had his passage booked. I had only time to catch the Heysham train. I let him go. I thought he would write from the other side and I could explain, but he didn't."

Her voice was flat and expressionless. He said angrily, " No, he didn't think it worth writing. He married the first dame he walked into. Couldn't you have had a cable waiting for him when he landed, telling him you were following ? "

" I couldn't. I couldn't cable him or follow him, not after what happened when I got home."

" What did happen ? "

She turned away, her fingers threading and unthreading again. " I don't want to talk about it."

" You're going to talk about it—what did happen ? "

" It was Mildred—the way she spoke about what I had tried to do."

" You mean running off with Tom ? "

" Yes."

" What had she against Tom ? She only saw him a couple of times when he was up at the house with me."

Laura's hands covered her face again. Her words came with difficulty. " Not about Tom, really—but—about men —and marriage. She didn't call it—love. She used dreadful words. She made it all seem so shameful. I—I was very young, George. She came and stood in my room and shouted. Her face——"

George couldn't stand any more. " All right. You don't need to tell me."

" Next day it was Father's funeral. It was the news in my letter that had killed him."

She is telling me over and over again, George thought, because for all these years the words have been there but she has never spoken them. It is a luxury for her now to speak them at last.

" Oh, Laura, my dear," he said, with pity.

" In the evening Mildred came to me and said she would never speak of it again, either to me or anyone else. And she never did. No one else knows."

" Did you *never* get a message across to Tom ? "

" I couldn't, George   I was ill after that, quite ill, for

rather a long time. I—didn't want to get better. Mildred looked after me. She made me get better. But by that time there was no way I could have sent a message."

" So that's why you were ill."

" Yes."

George had no words. What use is comfort for a thing that happened twenty years ago ? She had lived with it so long now, day in, day out, it was part of her, nothing he could say or do would alter that. He could guess what suffering lay behind her story. What could he pity himself for now ? The careful build-up he'd been at pains to cultivate, himself the hell of a lad, misunderstood misjudged—this all evaporated. He'd got away, he'd got Amy, he'd made a life of his own, some kind of a life. In his illumined moments he'd even managed to feel proud of himself. He knew what freedom meant—of the body, sometimes of the mind, occasionally even of the spirit. But Laura didn't. He was embarrassed at his inability to find anything to say.

" Laura," he attempted, " I'm sorry. I'm going now. I'll come back, perhaps tomorrow. Take care of yourself." He kissed her cheek, but she didn't turn her head or seem to notice. He went softly across the room, closing the door quietly behind him, and out through the hall door without even remembering that as he had entered it half an hour earlier he had said to himself, " Next time I come I shan't need to ring—I'll have my own key." It was the first time for years that George had been compelled to think of someone other than himself.

Laura sat still in front of the fire for a long time after George had gone. The knowledge that at last the words had been spoken, the secret shared, and that George had accepted it without condemnation made her very tired, and at the same time afforded her a spiritual peace which she had not known for years. She had hidden the secret for so long, and with it all the memories of that unhappy summer. Now the forbidden memories flooded in on her, she could not keep them back. But across the span of twenty years which separated her from them she could see them in proportions in which she had never allowed herself to consider them before. She wondered how the Laura of twenty years ago had concealed from her father and from Mildred the transformation of her world when Tom and she had discovered their love. As a girl Laura's pleasures were measured largely in negative terms, what had *not* happened, rather than what had. Father had not had a bad night, George had not provoked him at lunch, Mildred had not poured scorn on the new hat she had bought. Now from her knowledge of love given and received a radiance of positive happiness glowed from her. Tom loved her, she would see him today, tomorrow. She discovered herself to be lovely and desirable. If Mr. Percival had not been ill and bent on tormenting himself and those around him by the failure of his son, if Mildred had been less taken up with her father's ill-health, surely Laura's transfiguration could not have escaped notice ? When Tom asked her to go with him to America she agreed with joy and confidence and set about in secrecy which delighted more than it alarmed her to make her plans.

She had no qualms about selling some jewellery left to her by her mother to pay for her passage. With the surplus money, augmented by her own small personal allowance, she furnished herself with a trousseau, smuggled into the house by instalments, concealed with care. It was so easy it almost frightened her. A few well-timed headaches during the visits of the family doctor to her father gave her the excuse for a holiday—Miss Laura is looking pale, the doctor told Mildred, she should get away. She missed her holiday this summer ; unless she takes one you may have another invalid on your hands. Is there nowhere she could go by herself ? Of course there was. A letter carefully prompted arrived from her old school-friend, Hetty, giving the required invitation for the appropriate week. Without a twinge of doubt Laura made her arrangements to meet Tom in England, packed her bag, and was on the Heysham boat, sailing down the Lough, looking back at the green shore and the windows of Marathon, with the sure knowledge that it would be her last sight of them.

Tom was already in England. A letter came to her from him while she was at Hetty's house, confirming the final arrangements. She did not know what possessed her to write to her father to tell him what she intended to do. Perhaps it was Hetty's household, the shining bond of affection between Hetty and her husband, the happy household of young children, Hetty's absorbed love for them, the young father's touching compassion. This is what it will be like, she thought, when Tom and I are married and have our children. Then—perhaps it was like this between my father and mother when we were little, before my mother died. On the morning that she was due to join Tom she helped Hetty dress the two toddlers and after breakfast took them out into the sandpit in the untidy warren of a garden to play. Coming into the house again she went to the nursery. Hetty was sitting in the chair at the window with the youngest child, newly bathed, at her breast. Over his soft head and her own domed pearly breast Hetty looked at Laura and said, " Isn't it odd to think that when they grow up they won't remember anything about all this ? They'll just be up and away." If she had not said that Laura would not have written to her father. But she did write, and walked down to the post office to post the letter, knowing that when her father got it the following morning in Belfast she and Tom would be together on the liner headed for America. She came back to the house briskly. She must pack her suitcase. She was catching a midday train to Southampton to join Tom. But as she turned in at the gate she met a telegram boy and held the gate open for him to ride out on his bicycle. The wire was waiting for her in the hall, to say that the liner was delayed. She was to stay for another night with Hetty. And next morning another wire, sent by Mildred on the chance of finding her still there—for she had told her father no details of her plans—gave the news that her letter had arrived and that her father was dead. Instead of catching the train for Southampton she was just in time to catch the Irish Mail, and next day, standing on the incoming boat, saw the windows of Marathon again, and knew that, though she could not see them at this distance, the blinds were drawn.

Her decision to come home, viewed now across the years, must she thought have been based on the assumption that Tom's love and hers could stand the test of this delay. Or had she reasoned about it at all, had not instinct brought her back ? She could not clearly remember. She had no distinct recollection of the hours between the opening of the wire and the boat coming up the Lough in the early morning. Mildred met her in the darkened hall. After that she remembered nothing coherent—a series of nightmare flashes. Mildred taking her hand firmly and leading her into the room where her father lay unapproachable in the rigidity of death—Mildred's words as they stood together in that room, alone but for him, " How could you have done it ? Didn't you know it would kill him ? "—standing at Mildred's side in the drawing-room hearing her receive the mourners' condolences—her own futile replies to the sympathy that was expressed—lastly the awful nausea and headache that overcame her when Mildred was compelled to release her and Hannah had put her to bed—and that dreadful enduring memory of Mildred coming into her room when the last of the visitors had gone, unleashing all the scorn and disgust she had concealed through the day. Laura's suitcase was lying at the foot of the bed, she had not opened it since she came home that morning. Mildred saw it, and unfastened the clasps. She knelt beside it, rummaging about among Laura's pitiful hoard of finery. Laura had held the soft silks against her face, now Mildred brandished them and threw them from her like dirt. Laura said nothing, she lay on the bed and her eyes implored pity, but Mildred had no pity. She told Laura what love between men and women was—or what she conceived it to be—using shameful words with an enjoyment that was far more shameful.

Next day Mr. Percival was buried. Of that day Laura had no memories except one—the slow tread of the coffin-bearers crossing the hall. The door of her bedroom had been left open. It was, perhaps, as well that Mildred had left it open, because otherwise Hannah would not so soon have heard the screaming. The funeral cortège was on the road by that time. Mildred, closing the door as the hearse drew away from the gate, climbed the stairs in answer to Hannah's urgent call. And the doctor, returning from Mr. Percival's funeral, found another patient waiting for him in the house.

Chapter Thirteen

MR. MCALISTER let himself into his house with his key the following evening. He had come home to an empty house each night that week. His housekeeper, Mrs. Milligan, was attending a week of special services at the Salvation Hall she frequented. This concern for her spiritual welfare was a seasonal affair with Mrs. Milligan, recurring with the spring and the visit of a special preacher from across the water. Mr. McAlister recalled that for the last two years she had attended the series of spring meetings and proclaimed herself saved at the end of them. Now spring was here again, and Mrs. Milligan was off to make salvation trebly safe.

This in itself did not vex the old gentleman. This evidence of doubt and mortal fallibility in a being otherwise so confident afforded him some pleasure, and the bleak welcome she usually gave him on his return from the day's work he could readily forgo. But he was fond of his food, and the cold meal spread out under a cloth at one end of the table in the dining-room was discouraging. He lifted the cloth. Cold meat and salad again, with prunes and custard—yesterday it had been a pink blancmange. There was beetroot again. He recognised the piece of cheese. He had seen it every day this week. He sat down to the meal with a sigh.

He had more than this to worry him. He had called at Marathon the previous evening, half hoping that Laura when he told her of Mrs. Milligan's spiritual preoccupation might invite him to sup with her—Hannah was an excellent cook, he knew that from the old days when he often shared an evening meal with Mr. Percival—but Hannah had informed him that Miss Laura's brother was in the drawing-room with her, and he had told her not to announce him and had come on to his own empty house. He had called the day before that as well, only to be greeted by Hannah with the news that Miss Laura was out, visiting her brother's house. He didn't like it ; he didn't like it at all. Perhaps he had himself to blame. He had urged Laura, on two occasions since her sister's death, to make her own life, go her own way, but he had not thought this was the way she would have chosen. He had also learnt from Hannah that the woman Miss Parks had left Marathon. He disliked Miss Parks, but had hoped with careful handling that she might have become his ally in preventing Laura from committing this foolishness. Now Miss Parks had gone, and George had the way open to him.

Mr. McAlister brooded on all this as he masticated his way through the salad, and dealt with the skin of one of the prunes

which clung to his plate. The piece of cheese he ignored.
The meal over he folded his napkin and came to a sudden
decision. Sudden decisions were against his nature, but this
one was being forced upon him. It merely meant putting
forward his plans by a couple of months. With George
occupying the position he did, delay was impossible. Mr.
McAlister rose from the table and went into the drawing-
room, standing for a moment before the small fire, so well
damped down. The room had the appearance of a museum.
It had been like that since his wife died. There were no
traces of casual habitation. Any litter which he made was
firmly dealt with, either removed or else absorbed into the
orderliness of the whole. His wife's photograph stood on the
piano. He lifted it and smiled at her. When she had been
alive every corner of the house bore her mark—flowers, scattered embroidery, discarded magazines, stray gloves—her
untidiness had often irritated him. Now he longed for it.
He stared long at her picture, then set it down. She would
understand, and forgive him for what he was going to do.

A quarter of an hour later he was at the front door of Marathon. Hannah admitted him. Yes, Miss Laura had finished
her meal, yes, she was alone. There was a pleasant smell of
good food well cooked in the hall as he crossed it. Hannah
would go where Laura went, that was an added inducement.
Laura was alone in the drawing-room, sitting at the fire.

" Mr. McAlister, how kind of you to come." He noticed
that she had not been reading, and that no needlework lay
beside her chair. It was unnatural. It was time a change
was made.

He sat down. " I'm glad I found you at home, Laura.
When I called a couple of days ago Hannah told me you were
out—at your brother's house, she said."

" Oh yes." Laura smiled. " I went to visit George and
his family. I'm so sorry I missed you."

" And when I called yesterday your brother was with you,
so I told Hannah not to announce me."

" Yes, he was here. I'm so sorry not to have seen you."

" You had never met your sister-in-law before, had you ? "
" No."

" And there is a family too, isn't there ? "

" Yes. A little girl." Laura did not smile now, or volunteer any more information. She knows I disapprove, the old man thought, and she is wondering what business it is of mine. Well, she will soon learn.

There was silence for a moment. Then Laura said impulsively, " Mr. McAlister, I know how you feel, but you mustn't blame me. After all, I have no one else."

She looked very small and fragile in the firelight, and as she turned to him with this appeal he remembered again the girl he knew. That made it easier for him. He pulled his chair a few inches nearer.

" You mustn't say that, Laura, my dear. You have— someone else."

" I'm afraid I don't understand." There was no trace of coquetry in her manner, just the polite mystification of a child who waits to be instructed. He didn't like that so much. Must she remember him only as her father's friend ? He wished she had a hint of what was coming.

" Am I being stupid, Mr. McAlister ? "

" No, my dear." He laid one hand on hers. " But you mustn't say you have no one else. You have—myself."

Her fingers lay under his, and she made no move to pull them away. She didn't answer him. He looked into the fire to help her over the first embarrassment. Still she made no reply and he turned and said, " I am asking you—to make your home in my house, Laura my dear—to marry me."

At first he thought she had not understood. She looked at him without a flicker of feeling, just a dumb surprise. His vanity was hurt that she showed no emotional response whatever. He hurried on with his suit.

" We are both lonely people, Laura. I have, as you know, a deep regard for you, and a sincere wish for your happiness and welfare. I would be more than pleased if you would agree to be my wife."

It seemed at last that she had understood. She pulled her fingers away, and rising went to the window. He waited, glad that she showed some trace of feminine confusion. At last she said, " I am sorry, Mr. McAlister. I do deeply appreciate your kindness, but I can't possibly marry you."

He had been prepared for some demur, but not for this forthright refusal. He went quickly to stand beside her. " I know this has come as a surprise to you, Laura, but I am not

in any hurry for an answer—no *great* hurry that is." He
smiled at this avowal of restraint, he felt quite boyish. " I
feel sure if you think it over you will see that, for both our
sakes, it is the happiest conclusion. Two lonely people—
your father would have wished it."

He knew as soon as he mentioned her father that he had
made a mistake. Laura turned to him this time quite calm
and firm. " There isn't any question of my accepting, Mr.
McAlister. I shall not be lonely. I have made my own
plans."

So that was it. Already she had made her plans, he had
come too late. He felt old and angry, tired with the effort this
declaration had cost him, hurt at her reception of it.

" I see." He made no attempt now to keep the bitterness
out of his voice. " You're going to that brother of yours."

" Yes. I am going to live with George and his family."

Mr. McAlister wondered if she was as sure of herself as
she professed to be. " At Ballydrum ? " he asked.

" Yes," she said firmly, " at Ballydrum."

She said it not as if it were settled, but as if she wished to
believe that it were. But he saw that he had lost her. " That
will be quite a new way of life for you, won't it ? " he sneered,
raw from her refusal.

" I expect it will."

Mr. McAlister hesitated. She was obviously quite resolved, but for her father's sake, no, for her own sake—he
could not leave her like this. There was more that he must
say.

" Laura, are you sure you are doing the right thing ? "

" Oh quite sure, Mr. McAlister," she said, and turned to
him. If he had not been angry he would have thought her
confidence touching. " I have been to see them, and they do
want me to come."

" Do you know why ? " he said bluntly, impatient at her for
her stupidity, and determined to hurt her as she had hurt him.

Laura's eyes flickered uneasily away from his. " I don't
know what you mean."

" Then it is time you did know. They want you because
of your money."

" I don't think you have any right to say that."

" I think I have every right. I was your father's oldest

friend. When your mother died he confided—and I think relied—on me a good deal. I know the hopes he had for your brother, and how they were disappointed. Your brother has a slick tongue, Laura, and he's clever. But where money's concerned, he's a fool. Your father knew that. If you are honest with yourself you know it too."

"I know when George was younger he was very foolish," Laura said.

"And do you imagine he's different now? That kind doesn't change. He has no moral sense whatever where money is concerned, none. Your father knew that. Mildred knew it too. While they were alive he never came near the house. It was the day Mildred was buried that he came back —the very day. And he's been coming ever since. He didn't lose any time, did he?"

"Mr. McAlister, please——"

"Do as I suggest, Laura, and marry me, I beg—I implore you. You will not regret it. I am amply provided for, I can make you very comfortable. George only wants your money, you can be sure of that."

She had left the window now and returned to the fireplace. He followed her, thinking that after all he had gained his point. Her face was hidden, her shoulders turned away. "George only wants your money," he repeated, and took her shoulders to pull her round.

When he saw her face he was shocked. It was filled with distaste such as he had never seen on Laura's face before. "It's only your money he wants," he said again.

She leaned towards him, and through thin lips said, "And what is it you want?"

He left her at once, and picking up his coat and hat in the hall went quietly out of the house for what he knew was the last time. In his confusion of mind one impression emerged clearly—Laura's face as she spoke. He had never seen before any physical resemblance between the two sisters. But it might have been Mildred.

Hannah heard the hall door close and came into the drawing-room. "He's away," she said in surprise, "and you sitting all your lone and the light not lit." She turned on the light and tended the fire.

Laura did not stir. "Yes, he's gone," she said heavily.

She had sent Miss Parks away, she had told Tom's son that she could not see him again, Mr. McAlister had gone. There was no one left to her now but George.

Laura had been deeply disturbed by Mr. McAlister's proposal, but more disturbed at her reaction to it. She was already ashamed at the words she had spoken to him. She did not know what had possessed her to act so crudely. But since George had left her the previous day, and she had been forced to recall what details she could muster of her own calamitous love story, she mistrusted all those sweet impulses of the senses that had made her willing to go with Tom. How long had they known each other? Little over a year. What did she know of him, after all? Not much, except his unhappy home background. What had it been that she had felt for him but the body's necessity, the same hunger that drove Tom from his home, that kept George with his flashy little wife. And here was Mr. McAlister, offering it to her. The thing might be excusable in youth, not in age. She was repelled by his words and manner. She could not help herself. She had sent him away. There was only George left now. George had said he would come back. He would, of course he would.

George lay beside his wife under the pink eiderdown in the pink bedroom. She was asleep. The street lamp shining in through the curtains showed him her face, the lids closed, the mouth slightly open, the skin shiny from her evening application of cream. Her hair, he knew, was set in pins tight to her head, but these she concealed with a turban of tulle which had fallen a little awry. One end of the filmy material hung over her face and rose and fell with her breathing. Amy was always careful to preserve the conventions of the beauty parlour. If she must wear pins at night she took pains to disguise them with this transparent wisp. It didn't really disguise them, but at least it acted as an apology for the operation, and it gave George pleasure to know that after all these years she still cared what she looked like when she went to bed with him.

He wished he could sleep. Amy slept without trouble. The women's magazines recommended eight hours of sleep, and she accordingly slept for eight hours. Not that the rest of the neighbourhood was sleeping yet. The last of the children, seizing these first long spring evenings to steal some extra play on the road, had been called indoors some time ago, but there was still plenty of evidence of stirring life. The baby next door had had his last bottle and had been put down again, and was now discovering that the bottle had been too liberal, and that he had drunk it too quickly. The wail came clearly through the wall, rose to a crescendo and then sank again to a rhythmic drone as his mother commenced rocking. It must be teething again ; surely by now they were nearly all through. George had been on the High Seas while Kathie was cutting her first teeth, but he recalled she had had some trouble with the later ones. He had been conscious of the draught as Amy got out of bed. Mr. McGonigal on the far side coughed and turned the wireless up a little. He didn't sleep much, and it helped him to put the night in if he stayed up for the late news. The girl from the house opposite had arrived home from the pictures with her boy friend half an hour ago, but it was a night made for young lovers, and the two of them were still standing at the gate saying goodnight and would be another half-hour saying it unless the girl's father shouted at her from the window. George could hear their soft murmuring talk, sometimes the girl's laughter, or a stifled protest.

A couple of nights ago George had been sure that this spring would be the last he and Amy and Kathie would need to spend in this little house. Next year, he told himself, Amy and I will be in the big bedroom at Marathon, with Kathie in the old night-nursery at the end of the passage, with walls thick enough to contain each room's life, and only the distant noises from the river to come in at the windows. It irked him to live in the middle of so many other people's lives. George had always preferred to consider himself unique, and his concerns the focal point of things. All this evidence of other people living and enjoying their own lives without reference to him made his self-esteem shrink to a pin-point.

But there was more than this to keep him awake. All day he had wondered whether he should visit Laura, and if he did what he could find to say. He knew now the secret of her long captivity—she hadn't stayed at Marathon because she was too weak-willed to make a life of her own. He had always derived some satisfaction that however inglorious his own exodus he at least had gone. But Laura had chosen to stay, or had been compelled to it by her responsibility for their father's death. He wished now he had not forced her confidence. It was easier to think of her as inadequate than as the victim of this tragic stroke of fate. Tom had been his friend. He knew Tom's qualities, and that he had been worth loving. Poor Laura. It was surprising, really, that he hadn't tumbled to it before. He remembered the odd way in which she had spoken the first time she told him of her visit to Hetty's—he had wondered that she persisted in giving him all that irrelevant wealth of detail. "I got a wire to say he was dead—of course I came straight home." Why wouldn't she come straight home? It had all seemed a little unnecessary. Mr. McAlister had said something about it too that afternoon while he and Miss Parks were waiting for Laura to come home from town, the day that George had given Laura lunch and then come up to the house afterwards to borrow the money to pay for it. Mr. McAlister had praised Mildred's prowess, first with her father ill, and then with Laura collapsing when she had returned home. So that was why she had been ill—a nervous breakdown. That was when Mildred had put the final seal on her supremacy. What was it that Mr. McAlister had said? The baby in the next house wailed again, and for a moment George could not remember. Then he did remember, and rolled over in the bed and gave a long low whistle of amazement. Mr. McAlister had said, "Your father lying unconscious for four days, and then Laura collapsing like that when she came home." His father had been unconscious for four days! George checked it up to make sure he was right. Yes, there was no mistake. Mildred had worked it. No-one but Mildred would have thought it up. In spite of everything he must hand it to her.

There was nothing he could do about it till the morning. He would go and see Mr. McAlister first thing, and make sure of his facts before he presented them to Laura. That would put an end to her scruples. When she knew how she'd been deceived—poor silly Laura—the gates of Marathon would be wide open for him and his family.

The father of the girl in the house opposite opened the window and shouted, and with a last giggle she went in, and the gate creaked behind her. The next-door baby was quiet at last. Mr. McGonigal switched off his wireless and knocked out his pipe. The road was asleep. George felt sleep further away from him than ever. He raised himself up on his elbow and kneaded at his pillow. Amy stirred, and half-awake, turned to him as she always did. George reached out an arm across her shoulders. Tomorrow would wait. First things first.

The youngsters in Mr. McAlister's outer office wore a chastened air when George arrived there next morning. There was trouble stirring. They looked at George uneasily, and when at last he persuaded them to take his name in to Mr. McAlister, he was told that Mr. McAlister could not see him. He called again in the afternoon and met the same reply. It was late in the evening, on his third visit, when at last he was given entrance, though not a welcome. The old man was looking tired and vexed, obviously not at all pleased to see him. " What have you come for ? " he barked over his papers.

" I just wanted to go on with that little chat we were having the other day," George told him.

" I can give you ten minutes."

George sat down and lit a cigarette. His youthful reaction to hostility—to aggravate it still further—had become a habit. He took time to settle himself while Mr. McAlister fidgeted about in his chair.

" Well, what is it ? Why have you come to see me ? "

" You were talking to me the other day about my father's illness."

" I remember."

" I would like to know a little more of the facts."

" If you had been at his bedside there would hardly be any need for telling."

George's pretence at casual ease wore thin. " Skip it, Mr. McAlister. I wasn't there, and you and I both know why. All right. What I want to know is—you said my father was unconscious for four days before he died ? "

" Yes, so he was."

" All that time ? "

" Yes. I've said so, haven't I ? "

" You're quite sure of that ? "

" Of course I'm sure. From the Friday to the Tuesday it

was ; I remember it well. I should have gone away that weekend, but I stayed in town in case he should ask for me. Of course his will was all in order—your father was methodical in everything—but had he had a lucid interval there was the chance that he might have wanted me."

" But he didn't have a lucid interval ? "

Mr. McAlister rose in his chair. " Are you suggesting that your father might, on his death-bed, have made some alteration in his will in your favour, and that I was not at hand to see that those alterations were carried out ? "

" I'm suggesting nothing. All I want to know is—did my father have a lucid interval ? "

" Certainly not. It was clearly understood that if he did I was to be informed immediately."

" You're quite sure of that ? "

" Quite sure."

" Thank you," said George, reaching a cordial hand across the desk, " that's all I wanted to know."

Chapter Fourteen

SHE had waited all day for him to come. Rising after a sleepless night spent in repeatedly discarding the ever-recurrent memory of her words to Mr. McAlister, she had faced the day knowing that only George's coming could help her. He must come. He had said he would come. She would suggest that he and the family move—not to Marathon, but to a larger house than their present one, where she could join them. This would mean drawing on Mildred's money, but in her extremity she was now fully prepared to do this.

He did not come in the morning. Hannah had wanted some errands from the shops, but Laura sent her out to do them, on the excuse of some household duty, and had gone about the unessential task in the certain knowledge that she would be interrupted by the telephone or the hall door bell. By lunch there was no word from him. Laura put in the early hours replying to letters at length which she could well have answered with the printed black-edged forms which she had directed Miss Parks to order for her. At four o'clock the door-bell rang. By an effort of will she remained in her chair while Hannah crossed the hall to answer it. It was Mrs. McClintock, the minister's wife, a comfortable friendly woman, come to offer Laura sympathy and an invitation to take tea at the Manse on the following Tuesday. Laura heard herself giving the appropriate answers. Hannah served afternoon tea and withdrew. Laura wondered if from the kitchen Hannah would be sure to hear the phone when it rang, for the minister's wife had a high-pitched voice which filled the room. She changed her position from one chair to another, where she could command a view of the drive. At last Mrs. McClintock rose to go ; still George had not come. Laura bade her visitor good-bye and thanked her for coming. It was a relief afterwards to sit alone and give her undivided attention to the waiting. But there was no sign from George. He will come after supper, she thought ; he has not been able to get away from his work today. She knew well that George was always able to get away from his work if it suited him, but the excuse was some help.

The long aching evening wore past. By ten o'clock Laura's nerves were ragged with expectation, her heart sick with disappointment. She went to bed in the hope of sleep, but was too tired to rest, and her fears increased as she heard the clock in the hall strike every hour. She drank her tea at breakfast, but could eat nothing, and when Hannah insisted that she needed air and should do the errands—it was Saturday— she agreed with the docility of desperation. By the time she returned to the house he would have come.

She met a neighbour in the greengrocer's, and lingered to talk to her. Time would slide past that way. The neighbour had always been a voluble woman, sympathetic to a degree bordering on inquisitiveness—how was her sister today ?—what kind of a night had she had ?—how tired Miss Laura was looking—what a strain it must all have been—these were the usual lines of her conversation. Now, robbed of her topic by Mildred's death she had little to say, and Laura realised she was no longer an object of interest or solicitude. Normally she resented the woman's questions, fretting at the loss of time for which she would have to render an account to

Mildred, but now she felt cheated of her due. The green-grocer too, she thought, showed a marked change of manner. Instead of selecting each orange individually—I know how particular Miss Percival is about the quality of her fruit—of course with an invalid fruit is so important—he shovelled them indiscriminately into the bag, took her money, and said "Next Please" in a tone of undeniable dismissal.

As she came up the drive again Laura scanned the windows eagerly for a sign that George had come. But there was none. Hannah was in the kitchen. No, no-one had called. No, there had been no-one on the telephone. Laura felt giddy and a little sick. She found it hard to swallow the good lunch Hannah had been at pains to provide for her.

During Mildred's illness the hour after lunch had always been treasured, an oasis, a withdrawal into herself, a renewal of courage while the invalid rested. Now the necessity of idleness confronted Laura and became a weight, a terror. What was there for her to do? What did people do? She glanced through the newspaper, reading the words, but under-standing little of what she read. At last, in an agony of lone-liness she went down the passageway into the kitchen.

Hannah was sitting at the side of the kitchen range, the room in shining order, her hands folded over her clean apron. There was no evidence of any occupation about her; her acceptance of the empty hours reassured Laura. She couldn't remember ever visiting the kitchen before except for the trans-action of domestic business. Now she cast about her for an excuse to stay.

"Hannah," she said stupidly, "I haven't anything to do."

Hannah wasn't surprised. "It's always the way," she said; "it's the week after you feel it. It was the same the time your mother died, and your father too."

Let her go on talking, Laura thought. No matter what she talks about, let her go on talking. The evening will come all the sooner if Hannah talks. If he doesn't come today there is always tomorrow. He must come tomorrow.

"You don't remember your mother, Miss Laura?"

"No," said Laura, "hardly at all."

"You wouldn't, all the size you were. Miss Mildred would be the only one who would remember her. And she did remember, remember her all her days."

" What do you mean, Hannah ? "

The old woman spoke slowly.   She had known them from
their cradles, but her acquaintance never trespassed beyond
the accepted conventions.   She had known her place and
had kept it.   " Your mother died three days after Master
George was born.   I mind it well.   They thought to the
last they could have saved her.   But she knew on the third
day she was going.   She sent for me to bring in Miss Mildred.
We went and stood at the bedside, and Miss Mildred never
let go of my hand the whole time.   ' I'm going,' your mother
says, ' see you look after them for me.   You'll do that,
won't you ? '   And the child said she would.   And she did,
Miss Laura, she did indeed."

Yes, thought Laura, Mildred had kept her word.   Had
that been the seed of so much that had gone wrong in the
house, the charge laid on a child of seven by her dying
mother ?   Be that as it might be, Mildred had kept her word.
Without Mildred Laura would not have pulled through the
long illness that followed her collapse after her father's
funeral.   She had not wanted to pull through.   At first her
life was a confusion of days and nights, none clearly defined,
of faces that came and went, of thoughts that were forgotten
before they could be comprehended, but little by little the
shadows cleared from the room, the faces became recognisable,
the succesion of night and day established itself, and it became, by an enormous effort, possible to remember and refer
one thing to another.   With this partial stability the recollection of her guilt returned.   Her father was dead.   The
shameful thing that she had done had killed him.   That was
the one certainty which emerged, and re-emerged with startling clarity each time the welcome shadows lifted a little
from her mind.   The horror did not become less acute as the
days wore on into weeks.   It became sharper, more vivid,
the only thing it was possible to think, the one thing it was
not permitted to say.   A hundred times in each hour the
knowledge would fade from her and a hundred times leap
back again.   Her father was dead ; she had killed him.
Earnestly she wished to die, so that this monster of recollection could be killed.

But she had not died.   It was possible, it seemed, to
live with this monster.   It was not only possible, but it

was necessary, there was no alternative. With her strength a little restored, she accepted the inevitable. Her father had died ; she had killed him ; she must go on living. Without a trace of hope or self-pity she saw that this was what she must do.

But there was more than this that she must do. It wasn't enough to lie in bed, week after week, passively accepting what had happened to her. The doctor said she was better ; Mildred said she was better. She must make an effort, she must get up, must learn to live and move for herself. She was not getting off so easy after all.

It was difficult at first to do things for herself, even the simplest things. To lift a cup of tea required a labour of thought, of concentration, and if anything happened to distract her while she did it, the whole train of thought must be rebuilt all over again. Magazines were put into her hands which she was to open and look at. The bright colours confused her. She lay with the pages open and studied the pictures, realising with a sweat of terror that her brain did not understand what they were. Only by deliberately shutting away her guilty obsession could she laboriously identify the images. Words at first were impossible. The letters became blurred as soon as she looked at them, or else a crowd of words leapt at her till her mind was spinning in panic. By taking each word in individual sequence, ignoring those that came before and followed after, it was at last possible to define a sentence. But always as she laid the book down the horror, refreshed by the brief oblivion, came back again.

Mildred said she must see visitors. They came, each armed with a quiver of light conversation. They talked and went on talking. Laura listened, until at last the words were only a noise battering at her ears, and she longed to shout at them to go away. Sometimes their eyes, as they talked, seemed to smile at her. We are talking of trivial things, the eyes of the visitors said, but we know what you know. Your father is dead. You killed him.

It was necessary also to go out. The street at first was a nightmare of noise and moving forms, each of which claimed attention till the eyes were confused and dazzled, and the brain, unable to ignore any sight or sound, or to absorb any, cried aloud for mercy. Mildred of course went with her. "Mrs. Parkinson is across the road, Laura. You must smile." Laura smiled. It was necessary to go into shops to buy clothes. "This hat will suit you, Laura. Put it on." Laura put it on. The mirrors in the shops reflected back a hundred giddy images, the ceiling weighted her down, the walls crowded in on each side, but she put on the hat.

It was necessary to attend Church. There was no comfort there for her, or any ultimate salvation, but Mildred said she must go. The solemnity terrified her, it was impossible to sit still, the air was stifling. "Sit still, Laura. People are looking at you." Laura sat still.

She never asked Mildred for any respite. How could she? Mildred knew what she was. Mildred had seen her shame. She could go nowhere, do nothing, without Mildred. If she did not know what to say, Mildred spoke for her. When she was able to reply for herself, Mildred's lips moved, directing her silently.

Mildred had promised her mother, Hannah said, to look after her. Certainly she had kept her promise. By the time Mildred herself was too ill to ignore her illness any longer Laura had attained a degree of independence which made it possible for her to turn round and look after Mildred.

The hall door bell rang. High up on the kitchen wall, one among the row of bells that hung there each with its wire, it jerked and jerked again. Hannah got up stiffly and went to answer it. The wire of the bell was still vibrating as she crossed the hall. Laura heard his voice. The period of waiting was over. George had come.

George, she saw, was looking pleased with himself. "I thought you said you would come yesterday," she accused him, vexed now at all the wasted suspense.

"Did I? More time on a Saturday. You look ill, Laura. Are you all right?"

"Of course I'm all right. Just tired a little. Hannah says that afterwards is always the worst time."

"Well, I've got news for you that will soon change all that."

"Oh, George," she leaned towards him, tears of relief in

her eyes, " you mean—you've changed your mind—I can come to live with you ? "

" Better than that," George said.

" Better ? "

" Great news, Laura.   Listen—when Father died Mildred told you it was a sudden attack."

" George—I don't want to talk about it."

" Well, you've got to talk.   Did Mildred say it was a sudden attack ? "

" Yes."

" When did she tell you that ?   Was it in the wire ? "

" I don't think so—no, it wasn't."

" Then it must have been after you came home ? "

" I suppose so.   We never talked about it ; it was better not to talk about it, Mildred said.   Why does it matter, anyway ? "

" I'll tell you why it matters—it wasn't a sudden attack. Father was unconscious for four days."

She heard the words, but at first they had no significance. She stared at him.   What was it he was telling her ?   Her head ached.   She wished George would not talk in riddles.

He took her elbows and spoke slowly, close to her face. " Father was unconscious for four days before he died. You didn't kill him."

" I didn't kill him."   Even though she said the words herself she did not understand them.   " I didn't kill him." Then she realised their significance.   " George, how do you know ? "

" From Mr. McAlister."

" You didn't ask Mr. McAlister about it, did you ? "

" No.   He just happened to mention it.   He was talking about it a few days ago, actually, but it didn't dawn on me at the time.   I've been to see the old man again, and he says it's quite true.   When Father took that last stroke Mr. McAlister cancelled a weekend engagement in case Father recovered consciousness and wanted to do any legal business."

Laura felt her way to a chair.   She clasped her hands between her knees to try to stop them shaking, but her knees were shaking too.   " He didn't recover consciousness ? "

" Mr. McAlister's sure he didn't.   He was to be sent for if Father had."

"Then—he didn't know that I was going away with Tom—he didn't get my letter?"

"No, Mildred got it."

"And I—didn't kill him."

Saying it over like that made it more possible. "I didn't kill him."

"That was Mildred's invention."

"But, George—why? Why did she do it?"

"Why do you think? Good heavens, Laura, can't you see it? Do you think Mildred fancied the idea of you running away with Tom?"

Mildred's face came back to her, Mildred standing in the bedroom, her face ugly and convulsed as she shouted at her over the ransacked suitcase. "No, of course she didn't."

"And have you thought *why* she didn't like it?"

George was looking at her oddly, a mixture of amusement and scorn. Laura felt the hot blood rise to her face. "You mean—she would be jealous?"

"Just that."

"Oh no, George. Mildred hated—anything like that."

"How do you know?"

"She never had any men friends."

"That's it. Not one. Not a single solitary one, Laura. But don't you suppose she knew what she was missing?" He spoke with deliberate cruel emphasis.

"Mildred was needed at home," Laura said, knowing how inadequate the words were.

"She was—she saw to that. Oh, she had a whale of a time organising our lives for us, hadn't she, and making herself indispensable to father? But what's the betting she'd have swapped the whole thing for any man that asked her? Only no man did ask her. There wasn't one that even looked at her. And once Father was dead and you in America—well, she hadn't much left, had she?"

The stark truth shocked Laura. It was the truth. Involuntarily she said, "Oh, poor Mildred."

George was angry. "Poor Mildred! Poor Mildred? Dear God, Laura, can't you see what she's done to you?" Laura wished George would not shout at her like that. She wished he would go away and leave her alone with all this until she had absorbed it. And why should he be angry with her ? "Have you any idea," he was saying, "how much these twenty years have changed you ? "

" I don't know what you mean."

" Don't you ? Maybe you don't want to know. Have you looked at yourself in the mirror for a start ? "

Laura remembered the first time she had looked at herself in the mirror after her illness ; studied herself, that was, not just glanced to see if her parting was straight or her collar flat. One day she had had the courage to examine herself, to find out what this person whose body she now painfully inhabited looked like. The small pale face, the dulled eyes, the drab hair unbecomingly caught back, the shoulders a little rounded as if perpetually apologising, they had all come to her as a positive relief. There was one enemy at least that she need no longer fear.

" I know I've changed, George," she said meekly, without shame. And then, " George, how can we be quite sure Father didn't recover consciousness ? "

" It's fairly obvious, isn't it ? Mr. McAlister was to be sent for if he did. And even if Father did come round, he wouldn't be well enough to read a letter or be told what was in one."

She couldn't accept anything but a certainty. " We can't be absolutely sure."

" If that's the way you feel we'll ask Hannah. She was here—she'll know. Or we'll talk to the doctor, or find out who was the nurse. We'll root it out, don't you worry. Look, I'll ring for Hannah to come and tell us about it right away."

" No. No, George, wait a minute."

" Why should we wait ? " He rang the bell. " Better to get it over and done with ; if you feel there's the slightest chance of a mistake it would be wiser to thrash it out and be satisfied in your own mind once and for all."

Hannah knocked and came in. " Did you ring, Miss Laura ? "

George seemed to have assumed a new position in the house.

" I rang, Hannah. Come along in."

" You wanted something, Master George ? "

" Yes. Look, Hannah. I wasn't here when my

father died. You were. You remember everything that happened ? "

Laura suddenly discovered she did not want to know. Even if it meant the ultimate release she did not want to know. But George was insisting. " You remember, Hannah ? "

" It wasn't my fault you weren't here, Master George. I said to Miss Mildred you should have been sent for. I said to her——"

" Never mind that. My father wasn't ill for very long, was he ? "

" He was ailing a few months, but he would never give in to it."

" He was at home those months ? In bed ? " The old woman backed a little from George's fire of questions.

" Often as not he was up. He fought every inch of it, Master George. It was shocking to watch him. He wouldn't let on he was ill at all. Sure, he allowed Miss Laura to go away on her holiday——"

George cut her short. " Did he look after his own affairs ? "

" Indeed he did. He was never off the telephone."

" And open his own letters ? "

" Up to the last."

" The very last, Hannah ? " George seemed to have grown taller, unfamiliar. Laura could bear it no longer.

" George—please——"

" The *very* last, Hannah ? "

" Up to the day he took the stroke."

" That was a Friday, wasn't it ? "

" It was. Friday at two o'clock in the afternoon. I was putting away the silver after lunch when I heard Miss Mildred calling for me to come——"

" Why didn't my sister send for Miss Laura to come home from England at once ? "

" The doctor said there was no knowing how long the master would last. Miss Laura was easy upset, Master George, she hadn't been well. The doctor said she would be better away."

" And my father lived for four days ? "

" Till midday on the Tuesday he lasted—as still as a rock."

"During those four days did he——?" But Laura's endurance snapped. A panic seized her. 'As still as a rock.' That was how he still looked when she had seen him. They must stop talking about it. She must make them stop.

"George—I can't bear it! Hannah, go away! I don't want to hear any more, George."

Hannah turned to her at once. "Miss Laura, don't take on. What are we doing, the pair of us, talking this way about what's past and gone? Sit down, Miss Laura. What did I tell you, sir, she was always easy upset." Hannah turned accusingly on George, but he ignored her, and said, "You don't want to hear then, Laura?"

"Of course she doesn't," the old woman went on. "We might have had more sense. He's gone these twenty years, and that's all there is to it."

George said, "Thank you then, Hannah. That's all."

"Very well, Master George." Hannah went unwillingly to the door and turned. "Miss Laura, can I get you anything? Are you all right?"

"Quite all right, thank you, Hannah."

"Then I'll—I'll just be going along."

George waited till the door was closed. Then he said, "Well, Laura, what was all that about?"

She had made him angry, she knew that. She was sorry to have done so, and she could not find any reason for her sudden change of heart. It wasn't only the repulsion she felt from being forced to recall those dreadful days, nor was it the pressure of quickly-moving events, which, as they had done during her illness, threatened to swamp and drown her. She was giddy through lack of sleep, through anxiety, and because she had not been able to eat properly. But it was more than any of these. The gates of her prison were open, but she lacked the courage to go through them to whatever new country was waiting for her on the other side.

"If you've any doubt at all, why didn't you let me get the whole story out of Hannah?"

"George—I'm sorry. I just—I just suddenly felt that I didn't want to know."

"You mean you were afraid to be told because you know it's true."

She put a weary hand to her head. "George, I don't want

to talk about it now. I can't explain to you; you wouldn't understand."

"Don't I?" His voice was rough and ugly. "I think I understand very well. You don't choose to learn the truth because you don't want your twenty years' sacrifice belittled by finding out it was all unnecessary. It *was* unnecessary, you know. She played it very cleverly, didn't she? Your—what was it—'twenty years' exemplary devotion'—you didn't owe her a day of it, not a single day."

He went and stood in the window with his back to her. In spite of her weariness his words stung her into unexpected anger. "George—why are you so anxious to make little of what I did for Mildred?"

"You know why," he said, without turning round, "so that you can get rid of her once and for all."

"To make room for you, you mean."

He spun round to face her. She had spoken quietly, but the words had gone home. It was years since she had spoken with anger, but she was glad to see his surprise. Her success excited her.

"Laura, what are you getting at?"

"You've been here almost every day since she died, haven't you?"

"Yes, I came when I could."

"But you never used to come."

"You know very well she wouldn't have me near the house."

"And you never tried to do anything."

"What was there I could do?"

"Why are you so anxious to do things for me now?"

"I want to help you of course." The words seemed lame and silly, coming from George. As if he knew this he repeated, "You know I want to help you, Laura."

"And to help yourself too."

"Laura!"

She had hurt him, she knew that. Knowledge of her power to hurt George exhilarated her. She leaned towards him, looking into his face. "Well, it's true, isn't it? Of course you wanted to help yourself. Her funeral hadn't turned the corner before you were on the doorstep in a shabby suit telling me how bad business was with you.

You took me out to lunch and then borrowed the money to pay for it. You don't want me in your house, but you want to bring your wife and your child to live in mine."

For a long time neither of them spoke. Laura was shaking with the graceless storm of spite that had swept her. The excitement, dying as quickly as it had come, left her sick and ashamed.

At last George said quietly, " You said that just the way Mildred would have said it."

" Yes," she answered, with a kind of weary hopelessness, " It *was* Mildred, wasn't it ? "

George took her trembling hands between his own and compelled her to look at him. " Laura," he said earnestly, " Mildred's dead."

" She's dead," Laura answered, meeting his eyes without emotion, " but the poison is living in us now."

" I don't believe it. Now that we know how shamefully she treated you, Laura, it sets us free—don't you see ?—it sets us free."

Laura said slowly, " I've never been sorry for Mildred before."

George laughed, throwing back his head, " Sorry ! Sorry for Mildred ? I thought you hated her."

" It was easier to hate her than to pity her."

" I don't understand."

" Try to understand, George."

" What good will your pity do her ? "

" Not her—*us*. If we could pity her, George, we would be free."

George turned away in irritation. " That's sentiment, Laura—sentiment, pure and simple. You know it is."

With her fingers on his sleeve she implored him. " I don't think so. If we could really pity her, George, for the empty unhappy life she led, we wouldn't be afraid of her any more."

" I'm not afraid of her."

" And she wouldn't—come back. You could live here in Marathon just as you wanted to, you and Amy and Kathie. I wouldn't mind. Once we could have pity for Mildred—and for ourselves—we could accept everything that has happened, and it wouldn't bind us any longer."

George looked at her. He saw that she meant what she said. She was asking him to have pity for Mildred. Pity! That was the rent he was to pay for residence in Marathon. It sounded easy enough but he knew what it would mean. To have pity implied willingness to accept pity. George wasn't going to allow anyone to pity him, any more than he would accept criticism. To accept pity needed humility. The independence he had been at such pains to create for himself since he left home was built, not on humility or on pity, but on the active intense dislike for his father and for Mildred. Every wrong they had done gave him fresh confidence, puffed up his own righteousness. Their treatment of him was the only way in which his own behaviour could be justified. His self-satisfaction throve on the memory of past insults.

Laura was waiting for his answer, standing at his elbow, her eyes never leaving his face. He knew he must decide now, and that the decision would be final. He turned again to the window, to hide his face from her scrutiny. She was asking him to be sorry for Mildred! He looked out into the spring garden. How near he had been to getting where he wanted! This was his house, his garden, as they had always been, if he would only be sorry for Mildred.

What would it be like, accepting residence under Laura's terms? He didn't have to puzzle that one out—he knew. Amy had an inbred veneration for wealth and position. She never lost an opportunity to improve herself. She would be out to copy Laura. Laura would tell her about Mildred. The two of them would set about the sanctification of Mildred's memory. What a kick Mildred would have got out of it! She wouldn't be dead any longer, she would smirk at him on every turn on the stairs. And Amy would learn that her husband was, after all, fallible, and Kathie would see her father as he really was. He couldn't do it.

" I won't pity Mildred," he said, " now or ever."

" But, George——"

He turned, angry that this ineffectual dowdy spineless woman who was his sister could have forced him to this position. " And I don't see what right you have to pity her. Haven't you enough to do, pitying yourself? Do you remember what she did for you? She lost you a

husband, didn't she ?   And children ?   And a mind of your
own ? "

She looked at him dumbly.   He was inflamed because his
words didn't even strike an answering spark from her.   She
accepted them.   " Did you ever think," he sneered, " what
Mildred made you do to Tom ?   You shuffled that off your
conscience pretty easily, didn't you ? "   That got home, he
heard her sharp intake of breath.

" And now you want me to pity her ? "

" Yes," Laura said, looking at him with entreaty.   She
was asking him to forget all the sly spites he had suffered
from Mildred, all the scorn, all the carefully cherished wrongs
he had chalked up against her.   " Well, I won't do it.   I
won't pity her.   I'm finished.   I'm going now, Laura, and
this time I'm not coming back.   If you want to be sorry
for Mildred, you are welcome to her.   You can have her,
all to yourself."

He felt the old familiar swagger on him before he reached
the door.   He was glad of it.   He knew it was the last time
he would go through the gates of Marathon, and it took all
of the swagger to see him through.

Laura was glad that he had gone, glad when the door
closed on him and she was alone in the drawing-room again.
It had suddenly become imperative for her to be alone.
The mounting weight of all that had happened over the last
weeks threatened to overcome her.   Mildred's illness and
death, her reunion with George and meeting with Tom's
son, the dismissal of Miss Parks, Mr. McAlister's extra-
ordinary behaviour and her own even more extraordinary
reaction to it—all these things happening so suddenly after
so many uneventful years bore down on her.   She knew she
must be alone.

It had happened like this several times after she had been
ill.   Sometimes visitors stayed too long or talked too much,
or church was hot and there was an extra interminable
anthem, or the bus was crowded and to reach the door she
must pass through a stifling tunnel that lurched under her
feet.   Then the increasing tension became intolerable, and
the mind refused to function and, discarding every stimulus,
spun in a giddy vacuum.   It was the ultimate horror of her
experience.   Mildred, of course had always been at hand.

Mildred would say "Sit down "—"Relax "—"It's all right ". Mildred was there to deal with events until by and by recollection returned to her and thought once more became possible.

She was alone in the drawing-room. Someone had been with her and had just left. Something had been said which mattered very much. Fighting back the panic she recalled with painful patience that it had been George who had been there. George had gone. Miss Parks had gone. Mr. McAlister had gone. She had sent them all away. Now she was alone.

George had been the last to go. He had come to tell her something, and then he had been angry and had gone away. He had come to tell her—that she had not killed her father. It was not her fault that her father had died. Mildred had told her it was, but Mildred was lying. Her father had not known—what was it her father had not known? She could not remember, but at least she was not guilty of her father's death.

Why was it that George had been angry? It was because of something she had done—" Did you ever think what Mildred made you do to Tom?—you shuffled that off your conscience pretty easily, didn't you ? " That was what he had said. It was true. She had wronged Tom, not her father. She had stopped thinking about Tom because Mildred told her she must. That was where her guilt lay. She owed her father nothing. She owed Mildred nothing. The debt was to Tom.

Chapter Fifteen

HE was busy packing up the last of his pictures when the doorkeeper came across and told him that there was someone asking to see him.

" Who is it, Fred ? "

" It's a lady, Mr. Richardson."

" I don't want to see anyone."

"What'll I tell her, sir? She was badly put about when she saw the notice was down. She thought the exhibition was closed. I said you were still here and maybe you would have a word with her."

"But there's all this stuff to pack yet."

"She says she wouldn't keep you a minute. She has important business, that's what she says."

He shrugged his shoulders. "Well, I guess that makes a change. There hasn't been much business, important or otherwise, in this place. All right, Fred. Tell her to come along, but shout at me that the van's come for the stuff if she hangs around yapping for more than ten minutes."

"I will, sir."

"Oh, Mr. Richardson, I'm so glad that you're still here."

It was the dowdy little dame that had fallen for his father's pictures. He'd nearly made a date with her to go into the country to see where some of them had been painted. He was glad now that he hadn't. He'd been feeling kind of low the day she'd been in, glad to talk to anyone. But now he was thankful he hadn't gone traipsing round with her. He didn't remember she'd looked as bad as this. She looked a mess. Her hat was crooked, her hair hung down from it in wisps. She was a proper mess.

"Look, won't you sit down?"

She sat down and dropped her gloves, and when he bent to pick them up dropped one of them again, and then her umbrella. At last he had her straightened out. She sat there looking at him, breathing quickly, saying, "Oh, Mr. Richardson, I'm so glad you hadn't gone."

"I'm due to move off any minute now."

"You do remember me, don't you?"

"Sure I remember you. We were going places, but you couldn't make it."

"I thought at first that you had gone and the exhibition was over." She smiled at him, as if it were all important that she should have found him. A nice old girl really, but he hoped she wouldn't stay long. "I expect I'm interrupting you."

"Maybe you are," he said, smiling back, "but it was kind of you to come. I went down to see that place at Ballinderry that you were telling me about. I'm glad I went. It gave me a new angle on my dad. He sure did enjoy himself when he painted those pictures. I wish I could figure out what happened to sour him."

"Where are you going after this?"

"Next stop Paris." He was talking big—why not?

"And after that?"

"As far as the money'll take me—not very far, at that." Somehow you couldn't keep up an act with her.

"That's what I came for. You can go anywhere you like—I'll give you the money."

He stared at her. Crackers, he thought, and wished he hadn't told Fred to let her in. "What do you mean, you'll give me the money?"

"But I want you to have it—you must have it. I'll buy those pictures of your father's—I'll give you anything you ask for them."

He said, "I'm sorry, I'm not selling my dad's pictures," and thought how his dad would have laughed to hear him refusing to take good money for any work of his.

"Your own pictures then."

"My pictures? What would you want my pictures for? Come clean; you know yourself you don't understand the first thing about my pictures."

"Perhaps I don't but I do want them—please."

She was leaning towards him, her hands clasped—she had dropped her gloves again—speaking with a kind of desperate urgency.

"I know you don't."

"If you won't sell the pictures to me then I want you to take the money. I have plenty of money. I can do what I like with it. It is my money now. I want you to take it."

She was becoming a nuisance. He felt hot under the collar, and wished Fred would give him a shout.

"See here—why should you want to give money to me? I just don't get it."

"So that you can travel, see the world. Every artist should travel. It would help you in your work, wouldn't it?"

"Sure thing it would help me. But you don't care about my kind of work; you don't even know what I'm after."

"You do need money, don't you?"

Nosy, but he knew she didn't mean it that way. "You bet I need money."

"Then you must let me give it to you."

The thing was getting out of hand, he wished she would go away. He wished he knew what to say to her. "You know as well as I do I couldn't possibly take money from you."

She thrust a wisp of hair back under her hat any way and pulled her chair nearer. "Why not?"

"See here," he said, "it isn't that I'm not grateful. I don't want you to get me wrong. I think you're—well, I think you're pretty wonderful—I don't know how to say it —but I just can't take money from you."

She wasn't going yet. Her face puckered up, as if she were going to cry. She dropped her gloves again, but he let them lie. She'd have to go soon. Poor old girl! He felt sorry for her. She looked real sick. If he'd had time he'd have taken her out and bought her a coffee. She needed it. But he hadn't time—or the money to spare for a coffee either.

"You must see how it is—I can't take your money."

But apparently she didn't see. "Listen, and I'll tell you why I want to help you. It's because of your father. Your father was a friend of mine."

Crazier and crazier. "He was? You didn't tell me that the other day."

"I know I didn't."

"Then why tell me now?" he said roughly. This was cruelty, she didn't know how badly he needed that money.

"I'm telling you so that you will let me do this for you. You'll be able to travel anywhere with the money I can give you—anywhere at all——"

"See here, I know you mean to be kind——"

"Oh, you mustn't say that. It would be kind of you to let me do it. Because of your father. I loved him. Do you hear?—I loved him."

Of course she was crazy. He should have spotted it at the beginning. She was just about the age. Probably she didn't have any money anyway.

"I loved him and he loved me."

He was filled with distaste and the need to get rid of her.

" I'm very sorry, but I think there must have been some mistake."

" You must take this money—please."

She had taken a thick wad of notes from her handbag and was thrusting them at him. " It's quite out of the question," he said.

" You don't believe me, do you ? You don't trust me ? "

She was so sincere he pitied her. " You see," she said again, sadly, " you don't trust me."

" I'm sorry," he said awkwardly, " it's a bad habit of mine —one I picked up from my dad."

He shouldn't have mentioned his dad. She was off again. " That was *my* fault. I taught him that. At least, it wasn't my fault altogether."

" I'm sure it wasn't," he said soothingly, and patted her hand ; " that's what I tell you, it's all a mistake." Let her talk, let her get it off her chest. She'd be better that way. Fred would shout in a minute.

" You see there was my sister. She wanted me to stay at home. But she told lies, you see, to make me stay. They were lies, I know that now."

" Well, what of it ? Don't we all tell lies ? The truth's a bit awkward sometimes, isn't it ? "

" But this is true, what I'm telling you now. That was why I stayed with my sister. And afterwards, you see, she was ill."

" She'd be glad you stayed with her, then. Now look, don't you think maybe you'd better be getting back to her ? "

She looked at him. It seemed as if the idea helped her. " Back to Mildred ? "

" You said she was ill."

" Yes." She rose at last and he collected her gloves and her umbrella again. " Yes—yes, perhaps I should be getting back. Oh dear, is it as late as that ? I'd no idea it was quite so late. Nearly twenty-five to four ! I hope I'll be in time ! "

" You will if you go right now. Good-bye then. And thanks a lot—for everything."

He didn't know what he meant by that. She smiled at him vaguely, but he knew she didn't hear him. " Good-bye, good-bye," she repeated, and without looking back, she was gone.

He breathed out a great sigh of relief and shouted at Fred. " Hi, Fred! Are you asleep out there? Any sign of that van? "

Hannah was in the hall when Laura let herself in at the front door. She hadn't heard Miss Laura go out. She thought she had gone to her room after Master George had left, and she was just on her way upstairs to ask if she would like her afternoon tea brought up to her. The tray was prepared and waiting.

" Miss Laura! I didn't know you were out."

" Oh, Hannah—I—I am in time, amn't I? "

" In time? Of course you're in time. What call is there to hurry? You shouldn't have hurried like that, Miss Laura. You look tired out."

" Oh, I'm so glad I am in time. I thought I was late. Is the tray ready? "

" It's all here in the pantry. Go you on and sit down— I'll bring it into the drawing-room to you as soon as I've wet the tea."

" No, no. I'll take it. Quickly, Hannah, make the tea at once."

" Miss Laura, what ails you? Are you not well? Away now and sit down——"

Laura followed her into the kitchen. " Hurry, Hannah, hurry. Hannah, you've only put out one cup."

" Isn't that all you'll need? You have no one coming in."

" Of course you must put two cups. What were you thinking of? There—that's right. Thank you, Hannah."

" Miss Laura—— "

" Now give me the teapot quickly."

" It'll take a minute to draw."

Laura had taken the teapot from her hand. " There. That's right."

Hannah laid a hand on her arm, and peered at her face with growing concern. " Miss Laura—Miss Laura dear— what ails you? "

" I'll be in time—I'll just be in time."

She crossed the hall quickly and reached the drawing-room door just as the clock was striking four. There she halted, waiting till the last of the strokes had died away. Carefully she knocked and opened the door. " Mildred ! Mildred dear ! It's four o'clock."

She went into the room and set the tray down on the little table near the sofa. She smiled towards the sofa. Then she poured out a cup of tea and brought it across. Suddenly she stopped, and with hands that trembled set the cup down again on the tray. She was on her knees beside the sofa, feeling up and down it with her hands. When she had felt and found nothing, a long shudder of recollection ran through her and she laid her head on the empty sofa and wept for the first time for Mildred, because she was dead.

THE END

VIRAGO MODERN CLASSICS

The first Virago Modern Classic was published in London in 1978, launching a list dedicated to the celebration of women writers and to the rediscovery and reprinting of their works. While the series is called "Modern Classics" it is not true that these works of fiction are universally and equally considered "great," although that is often the case. Published with new critical and biographical introductions, books appear in the series for different reasons: sometimes for their importance in literary history; sometimes because they illuminate particular aspects of women's lives, both personal and public. They may be classics of comedy or storytelling; their interest can be historical, feminist, political, or literary. In any case, in their variety and richness they promise to confuse forever the question of what women's fiction is about, while at the same time affirming a true female tradition in literature.

Initially, the Virago Modern Classics concentrated on English novels and short stories published in the early decades of the century. As the series has grown, it has broadened to include works of fiction from different centuries and from different countries, cultures, and literary traditions; there are books written by black women, by Protestant, Catholic, Muslim, and Jewish women, by women of almost every English-speaking country, and there are several relevant novels by men.

FOR THE BEST IN PAPERBACKS, LOOK FOR THE 🐧

In every corner of the world, on every subject under the sun, Penguin represents quality and variety—the very best in publishing today.

For complete information about books available from Penguin—including Pelicans, Puffins, Peregrines, and Penguin Classics—and how to order them, write to us at the appropriate address below. Please note that for copyright reasons the selection of books varies from country to country.

In the United Kingdom: For a complete list of books available from Penguin in the U.K., please write to *Dept E.P., Penguin Books Ltd, Harmondsworth, Middlesex, UB7 0DA.*

In the United States: For a complete list of books available from Penguin in the U.S., please write to *Dept BA, Penguin*, Box 120, Bergenfield, New Jersey 07621-0120.

In Canada: For a complete list of books available from Penguin in Canada, please write to *Penguin Books Ltd, 2801 John Street, Markham, Ontario L3R 1B4.*

In Australia: For a complete list of books available from Penguin in Australia, please write to the *Marketing Department, Penguin Books Ltd, P.O. Box 257, Ringwood, Victoria 3134.*

In New Zealand: For a complete list of books available from Penguin in New Zealand, please write to the *Marketing Department, Penguin Books (NZ) Ltd, Private Bag, Takapuna, Auckland 9.*

In India: For a complete list of books available from Penguin, please write to *Penguin Overseas Ltd, 706 Eros Apartments, 56 Nehru Place, New Delhi, 110019.*

In Holland: For a complete list of books available from Penguin in Holland, please write to *Penguin Books Nederland B.V., Postbus 195, NL-1380AD Weesp, Netherlands.*

In Germany: For a complete list of books available from Penguin, please write to *Penguin Books Ltd, Friedrichstrasse 10-12, D-6000 Frankfurt Main I, Federal Republic of Germany.*

In Spain: For a complete list of books available from Penguin in Spain, please write to *Longman, Penguin España, Calle San Nicolas 15, E-28013 Madrid, Spain.*

In Japan: For a complete list of books available from Penguin in Japan, please write to *Longman Penguin Japan Co Ltd, Yamaguchi Building, 2-12-9 Kanda Jimbocho, Chiyoda-Ku, Tokyo 101, Japan.*

FOR THE BEST IN PAPERBACKS, LOOK FOR THE (penguin logo)

☐ **MILLENIUM HALL**
Sarah Scott

First published in 1762, *Millenium Hall* was one of the first novels to show that marriage need not be the only ambition for a woman. In it, six women come to the mansion and establish a utopian community based on female friendship and support.   *224 pages*   *ISBN: 0-14-016135-X*   **$6.95**

☐ **THE RECTOR AND THE DOCTOR'S FAMILY**
Mrs. Oliphant

These two short novels will delight all who love Austen, Eliot, and Trollope's *Barsetshire Chronicles*. The setting is Carlingford, a small town not far from London in the mid-1800s. The cast ranges from tradesmen to aristocracy to clergy . . .   *212 pages*   *ISBN: 0-14-016151-1*   **$6.95**

☐ **HESTER**
Mrs. Oliphant

Catherine Vernon is seen as a none-too-benevolent despot by her dependent relatives living in the "Vernonry" near her home. Then fourteen-year-old Hester arrives, and as Hester grows up, Catherine finds she has met her match.
                528 pages   *ISBN: 0-14-016102-3*   **$7.95**

☐ **FAMILY HISTORY**
Vita Sackville-West

Since her husband's death in World War I, Evelyn Jarrold has behaved impeccably. Then she meets Miles Vane-Merrick, a rising Labor politician who is fifteen years her junior, and embarks on a love affair that will change her life forever.
                336 pages   *ISBN: 0-14-016156-2*   **$6.95**

FOR THE BEST IN PAPERBACKS, LOOK FOR THE 🐧

☐ **A STRICKEN FIELD**
Martha Gellhorn

Mary Douglas, a detached American journalist, arrives in Prague in October 1938 and finds the city transformed by fear. Through her friend Rita, a German refugee, Mary becomes irrevocably involved with the plight of the hunted victims of Nazi rule. *320 pages   ISBN: 0-14-016140-6*   **$6.95**

☐ **THE RISING TIDE**
M.J. Farrell (Molly Keane)

An absorbing tale of three generations of an Irish family in the first decades of the twentieth century, *The Rising Tide* centers around Garonlea, the huge gothic house which holds each family member in its grasp.
336 pages   ISBN: 0-14-016100-7   **$7.95**

☐ **DEVOTED LADIES**
M.J. Farrell (Molly Keane)

It is 1933. Jessica and Jane are devoted friends—or are they? Jessica is possessive, has a vicious way with words and a violent nature. Jane is rich and silly and drinks too much. And when Jane goes off to Ireland with George Playfair, the battle begins. *320 pages   ISBN: 0-14-016101-5*   **$6.95**

FOR THE BEST LITERATURE, LOOK FOR THE Ⓟ

☐ **THE BOOK AND THE BROTHERHOOD**
Iris Murdoch

Many years ago Gerard Hernshaw and his friends banded together to finance a political and philosophical book by a monomaniacal Marxist genius. Now opinions have changed, and support for the book comes at the price of moral indignation; the resulting disagreements lead to passion, hatred, a duel, murder, and a suicide pact.   *602 pages*   *ISBN: 0-14-010470-4*   **$8.95**

☐ **GRAVITY'S RAINBOW**
Thomas Pynchon

Thomas Pynchon's classic antihero is Tyrone Slothrop, an American lieutenant in London whose body anticipates German rocket launchings. Surely one of the most important works of fiction produced in the twentieth century, *Gravity's Rainbow* is a complex and awesome novel in the great tradition of James Joyce's *Ulysses*.   *768 pages*   *ISBN: 0-14-010661-8*   **$10.95**

☐ **FIFTH BUSINESS**
Robertson Davies

The first novel in the celebrated "Deptford Trilogy," which also includes *The Manticore* and *World of Wonders*, *Fifth Business* stands alone as the story of a rational man who discovers that the marvelous is only another aspect of the real.   *266 pages*   *ISBN: 0-14-004387-X*   **$4.95**

☐ **WHITE NOISE**
Don DeLillo

Jack Gladney, a professor of Hitler Studies in Middle America, and his fourth wife, Babette, navigate the usual rocky passages of family life in the television age. Then, their lives are threatened by an "airborne toxic event"—a more urgent and menacing version of the "white noise" of transmissions that typically engulfs them.   *326 pages*   *ISBN: 0-14-007702-2*   **$7.95**

FOR THE BEST LITERATURE, LOOK FOR THE 🐧

☐ **A SPORT OF NATURE**
Nadine Gordimer

Hillela, Nadine Gordimer's "sport of nature," is seductive and intuitively gifted at life. Casting herself adrift from her family at seventeen, she lives among political exiles on an East African beach, marries a black revolutionary, and ultimately plays a heroic role in the overthrow of apartheid.

354 pages   *ISBN: 0-14-008470-3*   **$7.95**

☐ **THE COUNTERLIFE**
Philip Roth

By far Philip Roth's most radical work of fiction, *The Counterlife* is a book of conflicting perspectives and points of view about people living out dreams of renewal and escape. Illuminating these lives is the skeptical, enveloping intelligence of the novelist Nathan Zuckerman, who calculates the price and examines the results of his characters' struggles for a change of personal fortune.

372 pages   *ISBN: 0-14-009769-4*   **$4.95**

☐ **THE MONKEY'S WRENCH**
Primo Levi

Through the mesmerizing tales told by two characters—one, a construction worker/philosopher who has built towers and bridges in India and Alaska; the other, a writer/chemist, rigger of words and molecules—Primo Levi celebrates the joys of work and the art of storytelling.

174 pages   *ISBN: 0-14-010357-0*   **$6.95**

☐ **IRONWEED**
William Kennedy

"Riding up the winding road of Saint Agnes Cemetery in the back of the rattling old truck, Francis Phelan became aware that the dead, even more than the living, settled down in neighborhoods." So begins William Kennedy's Pulitzer-Prize winning novel about an ex-ballplayer, part-time gravedigger, and full-time drunk, whose return to the haunts of his youth arouses the ghosts of his past and present.   *228 pages*   *ISBN: 0-14-007020-6*   **$6.95**

☐ **THE COMEDIANS**
Graham Greene

Set in Haiti under Duvalier's dictatorship, *The Comedians* is a story about the committed and the uncommitted. Actors with no control over their destiny, they play their parts in the foreground; experience love affairs rather than love; have enthusiasms but not faith; and if they die, they die like Mr. Jones, by accident.

288 pages   *ISBN: 0-14-002766-1*   **$4.95**